Prais

"Among the many pleasures of Sarah Elisabeth's writing are her attention to character, language, and period detail. In the *Choctaw Tribune*, a story grounded in history and the complexities of pre-statehood Oklahoma, she brings to life, with great heart, the compelling mix of cultures, faith, and political intrigue in the old Choctaw Nation. An intriguing read."—**Rilla Askew, author of *The Mercy Seat***

"Sarah Elisabeth Sawyer has become a distinguished voice for Native American stories. Once again, she has captured the essence of our nation's complex history while offering important lessons and renewed hope."—**Julie Cantrell, New York Times and USA TODAY bestselling author of *Into the Free* and *When Mountains Move***

"Outstanding research and superb writing that accurately depicts a tough and critical time of the Choctaw nation and its people. Author Sarah Elisabeth has an old soul in a young lady, a powerful combination that clearly displays her love and passion for the Choctaw ways. Cannot wait to read more of her writings!"—**Gary Batton, Chief of the Choctaw Nation of Oklahoma**

"Sarah Elisabeth is a young Tribal member with a deep passion and proven talent for conveying the spirit of Oklahoma Choctaw people through her writing. Her works of historical fiction are well researched. She successfully portrays in her characters and scenes the human elements that made those who came before us as vibrant and as alive as we are today."—**Dr. Ian Thompson, Director Historic Preservation Dept., Choctaw Nation of Oklahoma**

"Sarah spun a captivating plot that gave real insight into the lives of Choctaws, and contained engaging sensory details. I could see what Ruth Ann was seeing, and feel what she was feeling. It captured even my short attention span; I want to read the rest already."—**Josh McBride, Graphic Designer at Josh360.com**

THE EXECUTIONS

A Novel

SARAH ELISABETH SAWYER

To Rimmel —

God knows,

Sarah Elisabeth Sawyer

RockHaven Publishing

THE EXECUTIONS

The Executions © 2015 by Sarah Elisabeth Sawyer
All rights reserved.

RockHaven Publishing
P.O. Box 1103
Canton, Texas 75103

All rights reserved. No part of this publication may be reproduced, stored in a retrieval system, or transmitted in any form or by any means—for example, electronic, photocopy, recording—without the prior written permission of the publisher. The only exception is brief quotations in printed reviews.

Scriptures taken from the *Authorized King James Version*, Holy Bible. Used by permission. All rights reserved.

This is a work of fiction. Names, characters, places, and incidents are fictitious or used fictitiously. Any resemblance to real persons, living or dead, is coincidental and unintentional.

Editors: Lynda Kay Sawyer, James Masters, Kathi Macias

Interior Design: Sarah Elisabeth Sawyer

Cover Design: Josh McBride

Formatting: RikHall.com

Cover Photograph: Silon Lewis, The Choctaw That Was Executed At Wilburton, It. Nov. 5, 1894 [1982.072]. Courtesy of the Research Division of the Oklahoma Historical Society.

Author Photo by R. A. Whiteside. Courtesy of the National Museum of the American Indian, Smithsonian Institution

Print ISBN-10: 0-9910259-2-X
Print ISBN-13: 978-0-9910259-2-3
LCCN: 2015933987

To my mama, Lynda Kay
My mentor, my friend
Chi hullo li

♦♦♦

To my great-aunt Evelyn
Chi pisa la chike

Verily, verily, I say unto you, Except a corn of wheat fall into the ground and die, it abideth alone: but if it die, it bringeth forth much fruit.
John 12:24

CHAPTER ONE

Dickens, Indian Territory, 1892

ANOTHER SWING OF THE BROOM sent the last particles of evening dust through the open kitchen door. Eighteen-year-old Ruth Ann Teller squinted into the sunset and searched for signs of her brother Matthew. They expected him back any minute with news about Silas Sloan's execution.

Her mother, Della, sat by the fireplace, quietly stitching a shirt while mild flames danced. Ruth Ann didn't know who the shirt was for. Della maintained a strong sewing business from home, her exquisite needlework always in demand. This shirt was one she had started yesterday, not long after word came about the killings committed by Sloan and the men who rode with him that dark night. The Lighthorsemen killed the other men in a shootout. Of the riders, only Sloan had survived, and his fate was in the hands of the Choctaw law enforcement.

The sound of approaching hoofbeats sent Ruth Ann's heart to pounding with each one. She hadn't realized how frightened the killings had made her. Would her family be next? Was there enough animosity toward them from whites and Choctaws alike to bring violence against them? How much had her brother's newspaper infuriated those kinds of people?

Ruth Ann gathered her thoughts and committed them to her prayer time. She listened to the hoofbeats and recognized the gentle gait of Matthew's bay gelding, Little Chief. The Teller house was set at the edge of town and across from the railroad depot. It was from this direction the horse and rider appeared. The sunset outlined them like a halo as they loped to the small barn behind the house. In the barn, the family kept enough animals to raise eyebrows from the townsfolk.

She glanced back at her mother, knowing she had heard the hoofbeats as well, but Della continued stitching without looking up. Ruth Ann's mother was a beautiful mixed-blood Choctaw woman, with a soft but strong jawline and prominent cheekbones. Her black-brown hair with blue tones was folded up and tied with a ribbon in the old way. She generally said only what was necessary, when wisdom or instruction needed to be imparted at the right time. At the moment, she said nothing.

Ruth Ann leaned her broom by the kitchen door and slipped out into the coming night. They all knew what the results of the Lighthorsemen meeting would be, but Ruth Ann had other questions she wanted to ask without her mother hearing the fear in her voice.

The interior of the barn glowed with light from the lantern Matthew had hung on a nail by his gelding's stall. The barn was modest but functional with three stalls: one for the gelding, one for Ruth Ann's stout Choctaw pony, Skyline, and one for a buggy horse the family used for traveling short distances. The back of the barn held a milk cow and easy access to the chicken yard behind it. The smells of hay and grain blended into a calm scent, comforting. The inside of the barn, with the concern-free attitude of the animals, always felt peaceful to Ruth Ann. Animals didn't seem to know when trouble had come.

Matthew was pulling the saddle off his horse when Ruth

Ann approached. He said over his shoulder, "It's been decided."

Sweat moistened Ruth Ann's palms despite the feel in the air of the coming autumn. "I figured it had. But have you—decided, that is?" Ruth Ann dried her hands by smoothing the sides of her worn calico work dress. "Mr. Sloan and that bunch of Nationals went to killing those Progressive leaders who were negotiating with the U.S. government. Plenty others feel the same, but there are still more who don't. Every since both sides claimed they won the tribal elections for chief, the Choctaw Nation's been in an uproar. How are you going to put all that in the *Tribune*? It'll make one side or the other angry."

Curry comb in hand, Matthew brushed one side of his gelding, carefully detangling the mane with his fingers. Patiently. Matthew was very patient. Ruth Ann wasn't so gifted, though the Grandmother had done her best to develop that trait in her.

Ruth Ann twisted the folds of her dress before abandoning it for something useful. The pitchfork was still in the small haystack by the wall where she'd left it after feeding the stock. She grabbed it and hefted a forkful of hay into Little Chief's feed trough. "What are you going to do? What if they come after us?"

Matthew knocked the curry comb against the side of the stall. The sound echoed in the small barn, and Ruth Ann's skin prickled. Danger was coming, sure as anything.

With her brother's skin tone, he could pass for white man or Indian, depending on how he was dressed. He used it to his advantage, like when he went to the States for college. His classmates took him for being white. But in times of ferocious stickball games among their people, his tanned arms and bandana about his head gave him a definite Indian likeness.

This evening he had his newer look, one he'd adopted since starting the *Choctaw Tribune*. It was a mix of white and Choctaw, as he was. Not any one thing stood out as different, but to Ruth Ann, it was. Things had changed.

Matthew finally looked at her. "The execution is set for a week from tomorrow. Sloan wants to see his son when he comes back from Roanoke College in Virginia. He graduates then."

Ruth Ann dropped her chin, the pitchfork in her limp hands. "I'm sorry for them. Real sorry." She sighed. "But why? Why would he go killing our own people over all this talk?"

"It's not just talk any more, Annie." Matthew tossed the comb back into the bucket of grooming tools he kept by the tack wall. It clattered in protest before the barn fell to silence. Little Chief munched on the hay, a peaceful sound. Matthew put his hands on his hips, a sure sign he was thinking deep.

"Change is coming, and soon. Two nations—the United States and the Choctaw—are about to shake up like we haven't seen here since the War. We're in Indian Territory, but there are so many mixed-bloods—families like us—and whites that it's hard for folks to sort out. Those who can do something about it feel they have to, one way or another. That's what Sloan did. But he knew as well as any Choctaw that we keep to the old ways when it comes to taking a human life. You do it, and you must give yours. He just wasn't expecting to get caught. Or maybe it's like he said—he didn't do any of the actual killing, but he 'fessed up to taking part, making him guilty even in his own eyes. He has to face Choctaw justice."

Ruth Ann had seen an execution by the Lighthorsemen when she was a little girl. It had been a simple affair, but not the kind she looked forward to seeing again. From his downcast expression, she knew Matthew wasn't either.

Centuries of feelings and thoughts brushed by her, and an ache placed itself in her heart in a way she knew would last a long, long while. "Matt." She paused, trying to find words that meant something, something that compared to what she felt. "What are the old ways, and how long can we keep them?"

Matthew patted the rump of his gelding and shook his head. "I can't say for sure, Annie. I'm still figuring it out. But I have to make a decision soon. The newspaper is due out in two days."

◆◆◆

Quiet tension enveloped the town the next morning as Ruth Ann accompanied her mother to Bates General Store. The killings had shaken everyone—Choctaws, blacks, and whites. They didn't know if some Choctaws in the outlying areas were about to massacre the whole town despite decades of peaceful history. Things weren't like they were a hundred or so years ago, before the peace treaties started. Since then, the Choctaws had long been a peaceful nation, with educated lawyers and statesmen.

But all those facts faded when a band of Nationals went from farmhouse to farmhouse, killing Progressive statesmen who were advocating the newest U.S. government proposal. The proposal would divide the tribe by individual land allotments instead of communal tribal lands.

When Ruth Ann and her mother mounted the steps to the boardwalk that ran in front of the two-story mercantile, a young mother with two small children scurried off to the other side with nervous glances over their shoulders. They were dressed in rags and their faces were unfamiliar to Ruth Ann, but that wasn't surprising. The town was booming with new settlers weekly, one reason Matthew had convinced her and her mother to move in order to start his own newspaper less than four months ago.

This new family had probably heard of the killings and recognized Ruth Ann and her mother as Indians. Some of those coming from outside the Territory still wondered if the myths were true that redskins were scalp-hungry savages. In their simple red dresses with ruffles in old French style, flowing just at their ankles, the two women hardly looked threatening. But Ruth Ann understood the frightened woman and children's ignorance. She opened the door for her mother, enjoying the sound of the little bell that alerted the proprietor he had customers.

Mr. Bates greeted them with his jovial smile, relieving Ruth Ann that he wasn't angry at them. She simply didn't know what she would do if this good friend acted any differently toward her family.

In the store at least a dozen customers browsed, assisted by Mr. Bates' teenage son, Oscar. The inside of the only general store in town was large in anticipation of the continuing boom of the relatively new Dickens, Indian Territory. Set on the railroad route from Fort Smith, Arkansas, to Paris, Texas, this town had all the hopes and promises of dozens of families in its grasp.

Bates had come from three previously failed tries at making a success of storekeeping in various towns before landing with his last chance in Dickens. The building itself was owned by the mayor, Thaddeus Warren, who believed in getting a jump-start and thus built several large buildings to lease out to businessmen. Bates was one of the white men who operated legally in the Choctaw Nation. He had his permit, and his oldest son had even married a Choctaw girl last year.

On the other hand the self-appointed mayor, Warren, had married an older Choctaw woman in the northernmost part of the Nation, and had migrated south after she died of an unknown cause. No one had questioned his right to build on Choctaw land—yet.

The store had two long counters, one on each side. Shelving behind the counters went clear up to the top of the twelve-foot ceilings, all loaded with goods like a big-city store. Four displays filled the center between the counters, stacked high and impressive with stylish boots and high-button shoes, and even a mannequin displaying the latest fashion from the *Ladies' Home Journal.* Smells of fresh spices and homemade candles were enough to make one lightheaded with pleasure.

Mr. Bates had taken out a huge loan from a bank in Paris,

Texas, to build the sizable store. But the town's growth was paying off for those who invested early. They were counting heavily on Indian Territory becoming a state. Of course, Indians going on a murdering rampage could wreck any chance of that happening.

Coming from around the right-hand side of the counter, Mr. Bates took the egg basket from Ruth Ann and nodded to Della. "The usual staples, Mrs. Teller?"

Della nodded as she offered a large parcel pristinely wrapped in brown paper. Bates accepted it, his smile broadening. "My missus sure will be glad to have her Sunday best back before the picnic. That lace she wanted added to the cuffs give you any trouble?"

Without waiting for an answer, he laid the parcel on the counter, then not-so-carefully unloaded each egg into his bin of fresh ones as he rattled on. "Land sakes, if that woman don't try to keep up with the latest fashions even though she don't get to them until after everyone else it seems, and by then the latest is already old."

Ruth Ann moved away to admire a shipment of new bolts of fabric, prominently displayed in the center of the store with a mannequin sporting a factory-made dress out of the material. A cream satin caught her eye, and she laid it across her light cinnamon skin. It would compliment her deep brown eyes and dusty rose lips.

Bates went on in the background. "She's hoping to get it faster if'n this Territory joins up with the States like they say…" His words muffled as he bent under the counter to retrieve something, but Ruth Ann's spine straightened as she listened. Bates didn't say anything else about the statehood rumors. In fact, he seemed in a hurry to move on to another subject—a potato shipment fresh up from across the Red River in Texas.

Glad the controversial subject had been avoided, Ruth Ann turned back to the chatter and listened while Mr. Bates talked on and on about Texas and the summer drought that left the Red so low.

Other people drifted into the store, and polite but stiff nods were exchanged. Matthew was right. Things were changing. Lives were lost. Sides had to be taken. Truth had to be known. But whose truth? And what was the truth?

As they left the store, Ruth Ann held the basket with their weekly dry goods on her arm and glanced at her mother, noting the sad look in her eyes that had dwelt there since the killings. "Mama, what would Daddy say about all this?"

Her mother's look grew sadder. Ruth Ann wondered what had made her ask such a question. It had been only four years since Daddy's death and the death of her oldest brother, Philip. Coping with the loss still seemed foreign, with waves of shock striking her at the oddest times. Now grief washed fiercely through her, and she might have cried except for the smile that touched Della's lips.

"He would say, 'God knows.'"

Ruth Ann couldn't help but let a smile lighten her heart. Daddy had always said "God knows" when warning his children they had better not get into trouble.

"God knows, and He will tell me," he often said, especially to the boys.

"God knows," he said to Ruth Ann when she asked why her favorite puppy had died.

"God knows," he said to his wife when they stood as a family and looked over a field of crops destroyed by drought. That was why they moved from their farm to his brother-in-law's larger one. It was why Daddy had taken a job with the Choctaw Nation as an annuity distributor. And it was why, ultimately, he and Philip had been killed in a robbery on a lonely road west of Arkansas State in the Winding Stair Mountains.

God knows.

Ruth Ann clung to this truth in her heart, dulling some of the ache within.

CHAPTER TWO

THE PRINT SHOP WAS SET up in a storage shed with a wood floor and gaps in the board walls wide enough to poke two fingers through. Ruth Ann had tried it, as had curious boys often enough. Matthew papered over it when he could get damaged brown wrapping paper at a discount from Mr. Bates. It held well for a while, until storm winds and hail pecked it full of holes that gradually expanded day by day until it was a shredded mess and had to be done again. It was mostly at that point now, at least to Ruth Ann's eye.

Still she kept the inside tidy and swept, and Matthew kept the press cleaned and oiled, always ready for the next weekly edition of the *Choctaw Tribune*. It was one of two newspapers in Dickens, a town that had sprung up in three years with its population doubling each year. It had gained its name thanks to the mayor's new wife, who adored that particular English author. Mayor Warren apparently had special reason for wanting to please his wife, so Dickens it became.

With the railroad and proximity to the Texas border, it seemed a solid, smart place to start a business. But the Teller family wanted more than to build a money-making enterprise. Matthew had started the Choctaw Tribune in a not-so-subtle protest of the one-sided reporting he witnessed when he worked part-time as a typesetter at the *Dickens Herald*. The larger newspaper, with its five employees, boasted special editions and flyers in addition to its weekly circulation, while the *Tribune* could only do a weekly, no extras. But writing stories from a different perspective was Matthew's passion, and it drove him to diligently gather all the facts, not just the information the town founders wanted to see in print.

It had been a difficult transition to leave the safety and close family at Uncle Preston's farm to move into the town made up of mostly whites, but Ruth Ann admired her brother's dedication and was pleased by his success, thanks to the support of readers and other leading men like Bates and Choctaw business owners. That support was bolstered by Pastor Rand of the First Baptist Church—the first and only church so far in town, built nine months prior.

The congregation, with its white pastor, had started long before, meeting in rotating places until a building location was chosen on the outskirts of Dickens. The primarily Choctaw and black congregation grew to include the town's founding men and their families. It soon boasted an average attendance of 156, a blend of whites, Choctaws, and blacks.

From the pulpit Pastor Rand had endorsed the *Choctaw Tribune's* story about the town's garbage situation and what prominent business owners should do about it. The article had caused a ruckus among those who thought ankle-deep garbage along the boardwalks was less of a priority than pushing for a saloon, illegal in Indian Territory.

There were always conflicts and arguments over typical growth issues of a new town. But the recent killings dwarfed all those things, reducing former headline stories to sideline columns. Now it was turning into a matter of survival. Life and death. It was time for Matthew to choose what side the newspaper was on.

Ruth Ann knew all these things without asking her brother. She'd come straight from putting away the dry goods at home to the newspaper office to begin work, determined to help.

She kept her head down, carefully placing the tiny type pieces in the proper little compartments in their respective cases after they'd dried from the last cleaning. They would be ready for Matthew's article about the recent events. When it was time, she would take the article and set the type with fingers she'd trained to be nimble and fast.

To keep up with the *Dickens Herald*, they had to be efficient since it was only the two of them. Daddy had sometimes joked that two Tellers were worth eight workers. Matthew and Ruth Ann managed all the advertisement sales, story coverage, writing, typesetting, printing in two languages on the letterpress, and distribution throughout town and to the outlying farm and ranch subscribers.

Often they hired young boys to help with the final task, and occasionally Della stepped in during a deadline. They worked their fingers raw to finally stand back in the end and admire their production: a stack of neatly creased newspapers called the *Choctaw Tribune*. Daddy would have been proud.

But nothing was at work this morning. The press stood still and silent. The type pieces were almost arranged in the proper drawers in the cubby-compartment cabinet Matthew had built. Blank papers stacked on the production table looked bored as they waited to be filled.

Ruth Ann stretched her neck and flexed her ink-stained fingers. It was an excuse to glance over to Matthew's desk and observe his intense look as he stared out the only window in the shop. A naked white sheet of paper lay before him, ignored, and a sharpened pencil twirled between his fingers. He had to get the story about the killings written this morning, then start the type-setting process in preparation for printing come morning.

Already it looked to be a late night. He'd interviewed the Lighthorsemen, local townspeople, farmers, anyone who might have an influence on the story. All the facts were gathered and it was time. But still he sat, staring at the occasional wagon rolling by. One brought yet another new white family to settle in the Choctaw Nation.

Around lunchtime Della came to the office with a basket of food, knowing her offspring were under too much pressure to take the time to eat at home. Ruth Ann thanked her, yet felt guilty that she and Matthew were sitting around the newspaper office doing nothing at all.

Della took a seat in an armchair Matthew had bought last month from a peddler. He wanted something he could offer potential advertisers when they stopped by his humble print shop. Someday they might be able to take in other print jobs like flyers and handbills for more income, but currently all such requests went to the *Dickens Herald*.

The spread of pulled pork and grape dumplings sat neglected on the desk. Della finally broke the silence. "What does Silas Sloan say about what happened?"

Matthew's head came up, and Ruth Ann recognized the comprehension in his eyes. "I haven't spoken with him. But I will now."

A bolt of fear shot up Ruth Ann's spine. "You can't. I mean, he's a...he might..." She faltered at the determined look on Matthew's face, and her mother was no help. Della simply nodded to him. "Do what you must."

"But, Mama—"

"She's right, Annie." Matthew wadded the blank paper and tossed it into the cold cast-iron stove near his desk. "This is the most important story I've ever done. It's not just about Progressives or Nationals or white politics. I can't base my report on secondary sources when there's a primary one still alive. Sloan is waiting in his own home for his execution date. He's done what he set out to do. Now it's time to hear his story."

Della stood and gathered the remnants of their uneaten lunch. "I will pray for you." Then she glanced at Ruth Ann with a familiar look that said she should support her brother.

Ruth Ann opened her mouth to offer a prayer, but instead she whispered, "I want to go with you."

There was no way to tell who was more surprised—

Matthew, Della, or Ruth Ann. But Ruth Ann pushed on, her voice stronger. "What he did was wrong, but I want to hear his story too. I need to know why our people are killing each other."

Matthew looked to Della, who had raised one eyebrow but made no protest. He stood and reached for his hat hanging on a nail behind his desk. "Then let's go. We'll get what we need for the story."

"And make sure the townsfolk know the whole story before they make up their minds one way or another." Ruth Ann removed her apron and hung it by the cabinet.

Behind her, Matthew pounded a fist on his desk, making her and Della jump. "There's nothing more powerful than the press except God Almighty!"

Fear still tingled in Ruth Ann's spine, but an unfamiliar strength mixed with it. Maybe it was true, the power of the press. There was only one way to find out. The next edition of the *Choctaw Tribune* had to be published tomorrow. But first they were off to talk with a condemned murderer.

CHAPTER THREE

THE ROAD LEADING TO SILAS Sloan's cabin was little more than a dirt path. It wound through the northeast side of the foothills near Dickens, the trail marked with rocks that had tumbled into it years prior. Dirt cut between the larger rocks, signs of running streams when the rains came heavy.

Ruth Ann followed Matthew on his gelding, carefully guiding her surefooted pony, Skyline, up a steep bend in the path. Her sidesaddle was secure, her skirt arranged modestly in spite of the briars that snatched at it in the narrow places between trees. When they went on family visits to the farm, Ruth Ann often rode astride, doing things she wouldn't dare near town. But this visit called for formality. They were going to see a condemned man.

When the cabin came into view after nearly an hour of riding, Ruth Ann was only slightly surprised to see it wasn't a cabin. It was a *chukka*, a traditional house like her great-grandparents might have had in the homelands of Mississippi. It was circular in shape with a thatched roof and undoubtedly a single room inside. Made from clay, dried grass, and tree posts, this was an old-style winter dwelling.

A hoe rested in the hands of a young Choctaw woman

who watched them warily. Evidence of modern living showed in the front area with a worn plow half-cocked in the large garden.

Matthew nudged his horse up to her. "I'd like to speak with Silas Sloan." When the woman frowned at him, he switched to Choctaw and repeated the request. She still frowned but turned toward the chukka. A man came around from behind it with a Winchester pointed straight at Matthew.

Ruth Ann gripped her reins, and Skyline danced from the tension. She forced herself to a calm state, translating that to her pony. The mare settled, and Ruth Ann prayed as Matthew slowly looked down the barrel of the rifle and continued to speak in Choctaw.

"I am unarmed because I'm not looking for a fight. You know who I am. Matthew Teller, son of Jim and Della Teller. I own the Choctaw newspaper in town, and I want to talk to you about what you did. Someone's going to write this story. It should be one of our own, shouldn't it?"

Sloan spat a stream of brown juice to the ground and adjusted his rifle to rest in the crook of his arm. "You speak with the tongue of your grandmother but have the look of a white man."

Matthew didn't back down. He shook the reins of his gelding and stepped closer to Sloan. "If the white intruders are your enemy, why did you kill your Choctaw brothers?"

At this, Sloan's expression changed. Something in his shell loosened. "Get down." He looked toward the garden and spoke to the woman. "We have water?"

The woman, who looked considerably younger than Sloan, put aside her hoe and picked up a wooden bucket before going off into the woods. That was when Sloan targeted Ruth Ann with his eyes for the first time. He pointed with his chin at her and asked Matthew, "Is this your *ohoyo?*"

Ruth Ann trembled but kept her hands loose and relaxed on the reins. She wanted nothing more than to pull her pony's head around and charge away from the place, but something held her where she was. Curiosity, perhaps? She slid down from her sidesaddle.

Matthew glanced back at her. "This is my sister, Ruth Ann Teller."

She came forward to Matthew's side. Close to Sloan now, she could smell the tobacco on his breath and the scent of blood on his cotton shirt. She tried not to shiver, tried to convince herself the bloody knife in his belt indicated he'd been behind the chukka skinning freshly killed game when they'd arrived.

Sloan nodded to a rickety bench long enough for three to sit. Ruth Ann feigned interest in the chukka, stepping close to run her fingers over the dried clay-and-grass mixture covering the vertical poles that rounded the chukka. Any excuse to avoid being offered a place on the bench. Sloan and Matthew sat on each end, facing one another with understood caution, yet a trust known only to them.

Sloan propped his rifle in the slight space between the bench and the chukka and offered Matthew a plug of tobacco, which he declined. Sloan drew his hunting knife and wiped the blood off with a rag from his pocket. He sliced a piece of the plug and slipped it from the blade to his mouth. There was a time of silence before he began.

"Long ago, our ancestors lived together in peace and war."

At the first two words, Ruth Ann shifted her feet on the soft sand as she stood behind Matthew and listened. This would be a long conversation.

"We fought the Creeks and others; we didn't all get along always. But we did it our way. The Indian way. Then the whites came. We had to fight their way. We fought with the Americans against the Creeks. We fought with the Americans against other whites. Then the Americans decided they wanted our land even after Chief Pushmataha and his warriors fought by Andrew Jackson's side in the Battle of New Orleans. Andrew Jackson was a bad man. Bad white father of the Americans. He forced our leaders to sign the treaty to leave our homeland—our hearts—and come west to this place.

Families broken. Friends. Clans. Our once mighty nation. And still the whites were not satisfied. They fought a war with each other. We fought with the South, the ones who promised to not harm us after the American government left the Territory. But Dixie lost. Then the American government said we had broken faith with them by joining the South."

Sloan chuckled. It was such a peaceful sound, as if he'd been created to do just that. Ruth Ann smiled and she was sure Matthew did too, though she couldn't see his face. His shoulders relaxed.

Sloan quieted and rolled the tobacco around in his mouth. Trees rustled and the woman appeared from them, sloshing along with a bucket of water. The day was warming now despite the coming change of seasons, and Ruth Ann looked forward to a cool drink from the spring where the woman must have gone.

Once they'd all had their fill from the dipper, Silas Sloan nodded and said *yakoke* to the woman, who tossed the remaining water over her corn stalks. She went back to work with the hoe.

After a time of listening to the scrape of dirt and the cheerful flutter of a flock of birds flying south, Sloan picked up where he'd left off. "We broke faith, maybe. If there had been faith to break. They abandoned their forts here. We could not trust the American government then. We cannot trust them now. Yet they are here. They are all around us. They are within our tribe." He looked hard at Matthew, then Ruth Ann. With a shake of his head, he turned away and sent a long stream of juice to fly with the breeze that came up. "You are mixed. Not Choctaw. Not white. Not anything."

Never before had Ruth Ann heard anyone speak so blatantly against her heritage. She stood in quiet shock. The mother of her mother was a full-blood. The father of her mother was half. The mother and father of her father were mixed. It was acceptable in the tribe—had been since before the Removal in the 1830s. Sure, she knew there were some full-bloods who didn't like mixed, as there had always been.

But the prejudice coming from Sloan was oppressive, filled with subtle hate. Deadly.

She unconsciously took a step back, but Matthew put a hand on his leg and sat straight and tall. "Is that why you rode with the men who killed leaders of the Progressive party? Because they were mixed-bloods? Or because they were in favor of continuing to cooperate with the American government's interference in our ways?"

Sloan picked up his rifle and laid it across his lap, idly cocking the hammer and releasing it. "Those mixed-bloods do not do what is best for our people. They are bad and should not lead our tribe. I rode with my friends who promised a better way, a way to stop the change from coming. Only one way to have done it."

"Will you go to your execution?"

Sloan stiffened, and Ruth Ann recognized the first signs of real anger in the man. He lifted his chin. "When a Choctaw is found guilty of taking another life and sentenced to die, it is acceptable to finish the task at hand and then go to where one needs to go. The Lighthorsemen have passed sentence and set the date. *Chahta sia hoke.* I am Choctaw! I will be there."

Somewhere deep inside her, Ruth Ann believed him. Then she remembered something—the final task Sloan had requested a stay of the execution for. "Your son, George. He comes home from college next week…"

Realizing she'd spoken aloud and that Matthew and Sloan had turned to look at her, Ruth Ann froze, feeling her cheeks flame. "I mean, um, does he know?" It was such a ridiculous question, such a horrible thing to bring into the conversation it didn't deserve an answer. It didn't get one. Sloan went back to talking to Matthew.

"Even in the old days, we knew we had to get education to keep the white man from taking everything. We got so educated we knew how to get money from them to pay for it." Sloan started chuckling again, and Matthew joined in.

It was a good time to make an escape, and Matthew must have realized it. He stood and stepped on Ruth Ann's foot as he backed up.

Swallowing her yelp of complaint, she scrambled backward. Matthew never looked at her, understanding the delicate situation. "Thank you for speaking with us. You have my word I will write nothing in my newspaper that is not true of what you have spoken."

Sloan grew somber then, standing with his rifle gripped in both hands. Ruth Ann recognized the stance as defensive, an easy position to turn and shoot from. "You will write nothing of what I have told you, or I will kill you and burn up your newspaper. What I have said is not for white intruders to read in their language."

Matthew stopped his retreat, but Ruth Ann did not. She scrambled onto her pony's sidesaddle, hearing him say behind her, "I'm a newspaper reporter. It's my job to report what happens as truthfully as I can for anyone who wants to read it."

Slinging her loose hair back from her eyes, Ruth Ann straightened in her saddle in time to see the rifle barrel level on Matthew. She gasped, unable to scream.

Matthew finished calmly, "And my newspaper prints in English and Choctaw."

Sloan hesitated, finger poised on the trigger. Matthew turned, stepped easily into the stirrup and pulled himself into his saddle. He nodded at Sloan. "*Chi pisa la chike.*"

Matthew used his chin to point back down the trail, indicating he wanted Ruth Ann to go first. She didn't need urging. Once near the trees, she shook the reins and leaned forward, letting Skyline take the fastest route down the hill and away from the Sloan chukka. The familiar hoofbeats behind assured her Matthew was safe. Alive. This time.

◆◆◆

An intense night of preparing to publish the newspaper lay ahead. Ruth Ann stabled the horses for Matthew while he went straight to the print shop. She informed their mother of the conversation at Sloan's and his threat, all the while gathering a supply of dinner and coffee. Della was no doubt worried about them, but she said nothing except a quiet prayer before Ruth Ann left in the approaching twilight.

The outline of the makeshift print shop lay just down the main street of Dickens. It seemed to waver and shiver next to the closed freight office, like a meek soul trying to contain greatness. Would it be a coffin next?

As she walked, Ruth Ann practiced her speech to Matthew, ways to tell him not to push Sloan too far. A condemned killer had little to lose, Choctaw honor or not. The threat was as clear and present as the alley Ruth Ann passed that ran between the freight office and print shop.

A hand reached out and grabbed her shoulder. She yelped before another hand covered her mouth. The basket of supplies fell to the ground. Then the hands freed her and a familiar face came into view. It was Christopher Maxwell, owner of the *Dickens Herald*.

CHAPTER FOUR

"GOOD EVENING, MISS TELLER. I didn't mean to frighten you." Maxwell smiled in a way that said he meant the opposite of his words. He picked up her basket and handed it to her, but didn't retrieve the tin cups and jar of cold beans that had rolled out into the dirt. "You really shouldn't be out alone this time of evening."

Maxwell continued to smile, folding his hands together in front of him. He was dressed in a gray coat with cloth-covered buttons, matching vest, and floppy bowtie, which set him apart from most of the men in town who wore less fashionable suits. His generous mustache and pointed beard did not hide his enjoyment of the moment. "Town's growing every day with all sorts of characters passing through. We're right on the Texas border, and you never know when some *desperado* might slip across the Red and hide out around these buildings."

Ruth Ann trembled, trying to decide if she was afraid of Maxwell. He'd been in Dickens from the beginning, operating his newspaper with a permit from the Choctaw Nation. He hadn't liked Matthew leaving his job as a typesetter four months ago, but Maxwell had remained polite in public, especially at church. But now that he'd grabbed her so roughly, she watched him closely and noted something lying behind his smooth smile.

Ruth Ann lifted her chin, hoping it didn't quiver. "Thank you, Mr. Maxwell, but the only one lurking around here is a businessman who should be home with his family." She had no idea where the blunt words came from, but she might as well take advantage of them.

Shoulders squared, she tried to move past him, but he stepped in front of her. Not missing a beat, she sidestepped, only to land her foot on one of the tin cups and nearly roll her ankle beneath her skirt and petticoat. Ruth Ann gasped, more from Maxwell grabbing her arm than from the stumble. She jerked back but he held on. In the darkness cloaking them now, she could hardly see his face except the white teeth of his grin.

"As I said, Miss Teller, you really should be more careful."

The print shop door opened and a beam of light fell across the dark street behind Maxwell. The man released his hold on her, and she stumbled back. He turned to face Matthew, who kept one hand on the door as he leaned out and glanced around before seeing them. As soon as he did, he came out fully and strode over to Ruth Ann. "What happened?"

"*Hal-a-to*, Matthew." Maxwell butchered the Choctaw greeting. "I was passing by and saw your lovely sister. But I was really coming to see you."

Matthew never took his eyes off Ruth Ann, but she quickly bent to scoop the rest of her things into the basket so her brother wouldn't see how upset she was. She shivered at the tingle in her arm from where Maxwell had grabbed her, and tried not to think about the layered meaning behind the things he'd said. She rose and stood as still as possible.

Matthew drilled Maxwell with his gaze, the light from the print shop full on his face. "Why is it you want to see me?"

The grin dropped off Maxwell's face as he tugged his vest

back into place where it had rumpled under his coat. "I came with a friendly word of advice. Seems someone saw you and your sister out near Silas Sloan's place. Not a bright idea for a once-bright lad. Aside from the obvious danger of conversing with a murderer who should be behind bars, there are those who won't take kindly to you siding with him in your little paper. In fact, they'd just as soon nothing about the little incident ever went into print in any paper. Bad publicity, you know."

Matthew crossed his arms. "I appreciate your *little* word of advice, Mr. Maxwell. Good evening."

Maxwell leaned forward as if about to share a secret. "Nothing will be in the *Dickens Herald* about the killings. If you want to keep your *little* paper in operation, I suggest you follow suit."

"Good evening," Matthew repeated, signaling an end to the conversation.

Maxwell bowed to Ruth Ann. "Good evening, Miss Teller. I do hope at least you will take my advice." She was sure he winked at her.

Ruth Ann moved slightly behind Matthew's shoulder as Maxwell passed by, heading down the street toward the opposite end of where the Teller home was located.

Matthew turned to her. "What happened?"

Ruth Ann bit her lip and hurried toward the safety of the lighted print shop.

"Annie!" Matthew followed her in and closed the door. "Out with it."

"Nothing," she mumbled, keeping her back to him as she emptied their partially spoiled dinner on the prep table. When Matthew reached out to still her movements by barring her way with his arm, she realized she still trembled. "He…he came out of nowhere is all. Spooked me."

"He said something to you."

"It wasn't important."

"Annie…"

"Please, Matt." Cheeks flushed, she lifted her eyes to beg

her brother not to press. He frowned and turned away. Seconds later clanging sounds told her he'd gone back to work on oiling the printing press. He worked in silence for a time while Ruth Ann wiped dirt out of their tin cups. She was absently going over them a fourth time when Matthew spoke.

"Don't come back to the print shop until after the execution."

Ruth Ann dropped the cup at the sudden sound of his voice. It clanged on top of the other one before rolling to the floor. "But...I don't think anything would really happen..." She trailed off and faced Matthew to see the determined set of his jaw. Just like their daddy, so there was no use arguing. Matthew was one stubborn Choctaw. Ruth Ann bowed her head. "I can at least help get this edition out."

"I'm walking you home right now. I'll get Carl and James to come and help in the morning."

Ruth Ann suddenly felt smaller than a fawn. If Matthew could replace her with two young boys, she must not have been much use to him ever. Still, she knew he was protecting her. Inwardly she felt relief but wouldn't sleep a wink not knowing if Matthew was being attacked in the shop or not. "You'll put the lock on the door?"

Matthew moved around to his desk. "The pen may be mightier than the sword..." He opened one drawer and withdrew a six-shooter and holster. "...but a bullet is deadlier than threats."

While Ruth Ann watched, he strapped it around his waist and even tied it down on his leg like a gunfighter. "Matthew! You...you going to shoot someone?"

"Only if they try to harm me or mine." He grabbed his hat and headed for the door. "Let's get you home. Then I have a newspaper to get out."

"But the article. What did you write about Mr. Sloan and the killings?"

"You can read all about it come tomorrow. Now let's go."

♦♦♦

Della had witnessed a great deal of injustice in her life. She lived it when she suffered the death of a husband and son. She did not want such again. But it was life. Many lost all before they finally saw their own death. Her brother, Preston, had laid three infant children to rest before burying his wife, who died of grief. As a youth her own mama had buried both parents on the long walk from the homeland in Mississippi.

None of these thoughts brought her a thimbleful of comfort as Della sat in her rocking chair by the dying fire, slowly withdrawing her needle from another careful stitch in the blue shirt. Ruth Ann had hurried off into the darkness of town, off to help her brother with an object of passion that could get them both killed. They were her grown children, the two who remained after Philip's death.

That loss had devastated her. To successfully rear a son all the way to manhood should have ensured him a long and happy life. But Della would never see his happiness of taking a bride, never hold his children, never hope to live to watch him grow old.

Nor could she grow old with her own love, Jim. He had been a good husband, a faithful one, a rare man filled with tenderness yet stubborn enough to make good in this country. How she missed scolding him! At times he had been as mischievous as the boys, though he often used that to dote on her. Like the time he spent too much money on the fine sofa he knew she would love. She spent a week not speaking after he'd brought it in. She stewed a sufficient amount of time to warn him against such foolishness in the future.

But it was her way of letting him know how deeply the action touched her, how it moved her heart in a good way to know the kind of man she'd married. And he knew this without her having to explain with words. He loved her. She loved him.

All that remained of that love was Matthew and Ruth Ann, their strong and wise children. They had the potential of carrying on their father's legacy, if a bullet didn't stop them first.

Slowly Della lowered the shirt and needle to her lap.
God knows.

◆◆◆

Ruth Ann jolted awake in the pre-dawn and pre-chore hours after a restless night of sleep. She rubbed her gritty eyes and let them adjust to the upstairs room she shared with her mama and brother, where she and Della slept on twin-sized beds. Back on the farm, Ruth Ann had shared a room with her brothers that sported a wooden partition between them. Her parents had a bedroom off the kitchen in the three-room house.

Now the room's wood partition gave the womenfolk privacy from Matthew's side, which housed her parent's larger bed. This plain box-house Matthew had erected with the help of some cousins had a sizable attic. The Tellers had converted that attic into the bedroom they all used in order to save the one downstairs for Della's sewing and work room. This spared visitors from being assaulted by the constant supply of new material and needles in the front room.

Ruth Ann slipped quietly from her bed into the chill morning air. Her teeth chattered as she fumbled in the darkness for her clothes and shoes. If Matthew wasn't home, she'd light a fire in the kitchen stove and dress by its warmth.

As she tiptoed past her mother's bed, she saw it empty, neatly made as though it had never been slept in. Perhaps it hadn't. Della had still been by the fire, sewing on that shirt, when Ruth Ann bid her goodnight.

Ruth Ann crept down the stairs, each cold board making her bare feet ache. As soon as she hit the last step, the warmth from the kitchen stove touched her bare hands and ankles. She peeked around the kitchen, but her mother's voice found her first. "Dress in there. Your brother isn't home."

Though Ruth Ann was grateful for the chance, it didn't

offset the sick feeling that washed over her. Matthew wasn't home. Where was he? Was he well? Hurt? Dead? She hadn't worried over her father and Philip when they left for the annuities distribution. She'd asked her father to bring her fancy writing paper when he passed through a city. She'd asked Philip to take note of what the townswomen wore. He'd winked and assured her he would. She hadn't asked if they thought they might not come home at all.

The Teller family had to adjust—another new home and two less stacks of laundry to fold and put away. If anything happened to Matthew, it would leave just her and her mother. Ruth Ann couldn't bear the thought.

God knows.

Warm clothes on in place of her nightgown, Ruth Ann stepped into the front room where her mother was wrapping the blue shirt in brown paper. Ruth Ann wondered who had ordered the shirt her mother had worked on diligently each evening.

This wasn't the time for questions. All Ruth Ann wanted was to rush out and check on Matthew at the print shop. But she halted beside her mother, remembering Matthew's admonishment that she was not to go near there until after Silas Sloan's execution in six days. Yet surely it would be all right to go once the sun rose…wouldn't it?

Della motioned with her chin to the center of where the string crisscrossed on the brown paper she'd folded over the shirt. Ruth Ann put her finger down to hold the knot while her mother finished the bow. Della picked up the package and laid it sideways on the mantel that held a framed photograph of the family, including Daddy and Philip.

"Your brother is a brave man. Leave him be." Saying nothing more, Della moved to the kitchen where Ruth Ann heard the rattle of the skillet in breakfast preparation.

When the sun finally peeked out, she hurried to the barn for chores, her heart fluttering in uncertainty. Every little sound made her jump, and she continually looked over her shoulder. She wished they had a dog again like back on the farm when they had four good hunters and protectors—at least one that would bark if anyone approached.

But no one did. Ruth Ann safely tended to the morning chores in the mist that had burned off by the time she finished. Instead of following the alluring scent of bacon and eggs, she slipped around the side of the house and stayed behind the white picket fence that secured their small yard. She squatted and looked through the boards, squinting to see the print shop. Main Street was already bustling with activity. Wagons rolled up and down the street, and the freight office door slid open in preparation to receive a delivery. The large wagon in front of the dock blocked her view of the *Choctaw Tribune* newspaper office.

A cramp started in Ruth Ann's leg and she stood up when no one was looking her way, embarrassed that she had been hiding like a child. One last glance toward the newspaper office revealed young James and his cousin Carl running toward it. When they didn't reappear minutes later, Ruth Ann breathed a sigh of relief and scolded herself. She shouldn't be so frightened. The execution would be over soon. She only had to stay calm and brave like Matthew.

That resolve lasted as long as it took for her to realize someone was watching her. While observing the unloading of farm equipment, Mr. Maxwell had his thumbs hooked in his vest as he smiled across and down the street at her. Ruth Ann turned, lifted her skirt above her ankles and fled for the front door. She slammed it behind her.

♦♦♦

When the *Choctaw Tribune* finished delivery late that afternoon, Matthew came home, clomping through the front door. He plopped hard on the sofa with its rich, buttery yellow silk fabric highlighted by the dark wood trim that ran down to its curved feet.

Though they had cared for the treasure well, it showed its age and use. Della swooped down on Matthew from the kitchen, shaking a doughy spoon at him as he tried to shove one boot off with the toe of the other. Ruth Ann sat on the edge of her mother's rocker, anxious to see the newspaper Matthew clutched in his hand.

Della stood in front of him, ready to whack him with the wooden spoon. "That sofa leg will not hold another repair if you break—" She stopped. Ruth Ann knew why. Della had spotted the six-shooter still strapped to Matthew's waist.

The stubborn boot finally popped off and landed with a thump on the hardwood floor. Matthew's head fell to the low back of the couch, his eyes closed. "I'm sorry, Mama. I'll fix it if…" A soft snore rose through his words.

Della sank onto the old flat-top chest they used as a small table. She laid the spoon aside and folded her hands in her lap, dinner forgotten. "You cannot fix a bullet hole."

Slowly, Matthew's head came up. "I know, Mama. I know we've wondered that if Daddy hadn't pulled his rifle on those outlaws like it looked like he did, he might still be alive. But he did something more than live. He did what he thought was right. Sometimes that's what a man has to do."

Ruth Ann leaned forward and shook her head behind her mother's back. Matthew saw her and sighed, starting on the other boot with his sock-covered toe. Della watched him for several seconds. Finally she bent over to grab Matthew's muddy boot. She yanked and jerked until he howled and the boot released. With a chuckle Della set it and the other one neatly by the sofa. "Stubborn, stubborn Choctaw." She took herself and her spoon back to the kitchen.

It was Ruth Ann's turn to slip over to her exhausted brother. She tugged the newspaper from his grip. The paper was crumpled, making it hard to read. Ruth Ann jumped up and hurried over to the lamp on the mantle. She scanned the front-page headline.

CHOCTAW SILAS SLOAN FOUND
GUILTY OF MURDER

Her heart sank lower as she read the article. It was fine writing for sure, some of the best Matthew had ever done. But there was no regard to the wishes of the town founders, or Maxwell, or Sloan, none of whom wanted any of the story printed. Matthew didn't quote Sloan, but he did put in the facts and reasons behind the shootings. All things no one would like.

Ruth Ann dropped onto the couch, the paper held close to her face as she finished the article. "Oh, Matt, are you sure you should have done this?"

A snore was her only answer.

Dinner passed quietly, with Matthew hardly awake enough to spoon his stew and munch on a biscuit. He finally pushed away from the table. "Excuse me, but I best go to bed before I make a mess."

Della clicked her tongue and shook her head. Ruth Ann smiled sadly as her brother pulled himself up the stairs from the kitchen. "He worked hard on that issue. I wish I could have helped."

"You can help me with the dishes." Della stood and gathered her own.

♦♦♦

Later that evening the two women sat in the front room, Ruth Ann darning one of Matthew's socks and Della reading her son's paper in the Choctaw language. A faint thump caught Ruth Ann's attention. Della lifted her head before a harsh rap sounded at the front door.

Ruth Ann stabbed herself with the needle. She pulled it out and sucked on the injured finger, staring at her mother, who went to the door and opened it. Darkness silhouetted three men standing on the porch. Ruth Ann rose, dropping the sock back into the mending basket by her chair. She recognized the voice before the face. It was Mayor Warren. "We want to talk with Matthew Teller. Now."

Before Della could respond, the man stepped inside. With a grunt, Della put her hand on his chest and shoved him back out where he stumbled and fell into the two men behind him. She calmly closed the door and waited a moment. Then she reopened it and looked at the stunned men.

"You want to come in?" She opened the door wide and pointed toward the sofa with her chin. "Sit. I will call my son."

CHAPTER FIVE

RUTH ANN SCURRIED TO THE kitchen and put on a kettle of water for tea. The three men moved with caution into the front room and looked around as if they'd never been inside. Now that Ruth Ann knew who they were, she realized it was, in fact, their first time to grace the Teller home. Accompanying Mayor Warren was freight-office owner, Mr. Carter, who helped found Dickens and had leased the old shed to Matthew for a print shop. The third man was Jake Banny, another Dickens founder. He owned the hotel and was behind the push for a saloon inside his building.

It was obvious to all why they were there.

Ruth Ann was thankful she could busy herself in the kitchen, preparing teacups and saucers after Della went upstairs to get her son. Ruth Ann added more wood to the stove to the beat of Matthew's padded footsteps coming down the stairs. His boots were still by the sofa, and he looked as if he had indeed just rolled out of bed. He paused in the kitchen, combing his hair with his fingers, out of sight of their guests.

After licking his fingers and patting his hair one more time, he looked to Ruth Ann for approval. She frowned and shook her head. His shirt collar was half flapped up. She straightened it and buttoned his top button. He was still rumpled, but that wasn't why Ruth Ann watched him with concern as he entered the front room. Della came down behind him and took over the tea-making while she nudged Ruth Ann away.

"Good evening, gentlemen," she heard Matthew say. "Is it customary among whites to call so late without notice?"

Ruth Ann went to stand beside her brother. There was no sense in leaving it three to one.

Mayor Warren stood from his spot on the sofa, and the other two men popped up like comical jack-in-the-boxes. "It's more customary than what you printed today. You should have known better."

Matthew raised an eyebrow. "I printed the news. That's why I call it a newspaper."

The mayor's Adam's apple protruded suddenly, like he'd swallowed a chicken leg whole. His face turned red. "Look here, young man, you can't come into our town and set up shop like you own the place. You don't have a stake in it like we do. You haven't bet your whole life, your whole savings, your whole family on this town's success. You don't know what it's all about."

Matthew crossed his arms over his chest and said nothing. Della came into the room with tea, which all three men refused with a semblance of politeness.

Mr. Carter spoke next. "Look, Matthew Teller, I did you a favor leasing that building to you. You can't break faith like this. This news spreading around to our locals is one thing; it's bound to happen. But you put it in print, and there's no counting how far it will go now. Could even end up back East. Stop dozens or even hundreds of settlers from coming to Dickens. You want that to happen?"

Matthew remained silent, and Ruth Ann considered telling the men they might as well leave. Or at least interject that it wouldn't bother most Choctaws if whites stopped invading their nation. White intruders already outnumbered them.

Mr. Banny stepped forward. He was the only one of the men wearing a six-shooter, his thumb resting in the crook of the hammer as he leaned to that side. He wore a long black coat that was flipped back behind the handle of the Colt. The youngest of the men, he was mid-thirties with the look of an ill life already lived, yet hard and smart. Ruth Ann kept her hands folded in front of her, afraid to look at Matthew to see the challenge she knew was in his eyes.

Banny spoke quieter but surer than the other men. "Boy, if you know what's good for you, you'll stop harassing honest folks who just want to make a decent living here in this town. We aren't leaving. So you'd best do things right, or you will be. One way or another."

Back stiff, arms still crossed, stocking feet planted slightly apart, Matthew's quiet confidence left nothing more to be said.

Mayor Warren let out a grunt of frustration and donned his derby hat. He turned and marched to the door, Carter following behind like a needy puppy. Banny lingered a moment longer, looking over the family before he moved toward the exit. He glanced back before stepping outside. "Guess I got one more reason not to like your kind," he growled. He slammed the door behind him with a force that rattled Ruth Ann's ears.

"Matt, what are we going to do?"

Matthew sighed and relaxed, rubbing his bloodshot eyes. "I'm going back to bed." And he did, leaving her to stare at her mother, who merely poured them both a cup of tea before settling back in her rocking chair with the newspaper.

♦♦♦

For the next two days Matthew insisted Ruth Ann not come to the newspaper office or work her usual route, gathering advertisers and bits of local news. That left her with little to do other than work on the religious column she wrote after each Sunday service, which wouldn't be until the next day. This was Saturday, a day the town bustled with activity. Farmers coming in for their weekly supplies, cowboys getting baths, haircuts, and shaves at the barbershop, and families treating themselves to a formal meal at the hotel restaurant.

Ruth Ann watched all this activity from the front window. She'd moved her mother's rocking chair and the mending basket to it so she could see the goings on and still be useful.

She hated to admit it, but she was glad for the confinement. Matthew was right; folks were mad at him right now and would probably take it out on his family until things cooled down. She could avoid everything from snide remarks to rude looks simply by staying home. There was no telling what kind of things the mayor, Mr. Carter, or Mr. Maxwell would say to her if she happened to pass them in the street.

Before they moved into Dickens, Ruth Ann had asked Matthew why no one challenged the mayor's claim to the town he boasted of establishing. Dickens wasn't the only town potentially formed illegally in the Choctaw Nation. But someday, Matthew said. Someday he would be ready to challenge Mayor Warren's claim.

Besides the upset leading men, there would be reactions from farmers and ranchers, white and Choctaw alike. They wouldn't be happy with the news of the killings spreading. Folks were on edge and betting their investments on the town growing and on shipping staying strong on the railroad, which was becoming more heavily used every day.

Twice daily the train passed the Teller home and stopped at the depot across from them. It ran from Fort Smith in the north down to Paris with several stops between, including Dickens, before making the same run from the south up to Fort Smith once again.

A railroad meant civilization from a white man's standpoint, and more civilization meant land prices shooting sky-high. That was, if the Choctaw Nation lost its foothold with more settlers coming in after the land rush of '89 north of them up in Oklahoma Territory.

More intruders moving into Indian Territory and onto land that was promised to the Choctaws by Andrew Jackson, Ruth Ann thought, *land he said would be ours forever as long as the grass grew and the water flowed.* As far as Ruth Ann could tell, nature had held up its end of the bargain.

Shouts in the street drew her attention from the petticoat she was re-hemming. Ruth Ann pulled back the lace curtain, already knowing what the sounds meant. The train came through twice a day, and the southbound was right on schedule, rattling the window panes. It rolled into the station, bits of paper and debris swirling through the air in its wake. After shipments were unloaded or loaded, it would be on its way again.

Usually a few people got off the train at Dickens, though new settlers mostly came in wagons with all their worldly goods. Locals sometimes rode the train down to Paris or up to Fort Smith. The arrival of the train was always an affair to see, with folks gathered around the depot for any taste of excitement or social activity they might get.

Ruth Ann's thoughts were jolted back to the present when the passenger car yielded someone slightly familiar, though unexpected. She could barely see through the bustle of those loitering on the platform across the street as a man in city dress stood high on the train steps and looked around before descending. But she did recognize one thing about him, and it made her gasp.

Suddenly tired of being afraid and holed up and not being a help to Matthew, Ruth Ann shot out of the rocker and fumbled through the mess on the old chest table. Under piles of clothing material that had migrated from Della's sewing room, Ruth Ann found the small tablet she used on her advertisement and news-gathering rounds. Her mother was in the backyard hanging laundry and likely wouldn't be inside in time to miss her, so Ruth Ann flew out the front door without hesitation.

CHAPTER SIX

IGNORING HER ILLUSIONS OF PEOPLE staring angry holes through her, Ruth Ann hurried as fast as a respectable woman could when dealing with petticoats and a full, floor-length skirt. In seconds, she was on the depot platform and in the midst of the gathering that mingled around the train.

Most waited for the mail to be offloaded and taken to the post office. Others simply had nothing better to do, like the two cowboys lounging in the chairs reserved for waiting passengers. A third cowboy, with a freshly washed red bandana tied around his neck, leaned against a stack of crates. He was harassing the only passenger who had gotten off, the young man Ruth Ann had seen.

"Looky, looky at this fine fellow, boys." The cowboy whistled under his breath.

"Ain't he pretty?" one of the others hooted, tipping his chair back on two legs. Ruth Ann wished he would fall.

In truth, the young man was handsome and finely dressed in a dark three-piece suit and string tie. But it was his prominent cheekbones, ruddy brown skin, and unmistakable resemblance to Silas Sloan that had brought Ruth Ann running. She stood back, watching the exchange. A decent woman couldn't get in the middle of something like this. Her eyes darted around, hoping to see that Matthew had come to meet the train for some reason, but he was probably behind in his work or busy making his usual Saturday rounds.

The young man, George Sloan, ignored the harassing cowboys as he retrieved a small trunk from the porter. The cowboy who had been the most vocal slipped up behind him and snatched the trunk from his hands. "What you got in here, city dude? Doilies and chocolates?"

The other cowboy dropped his chair back onto all four legs. "I want the doilies!"

The third cowboy, an older man, stood and strode over to the one with the red bandana. With a swipe of his open palm, he hit him across the back of the head, knocking his hat clean off the platform and under a team of horses hitched to a wagon. The horse skittered and stomped, crushing the worn felt hat.

The cowboy yelped and looked at his partner, but said nothing. He dropped the trunk and hopped off the platform to retrieve his ruined hat. The older man hissed, "Stop making a scene. Act like the civilized human being you're supposed to be." He nodded to George Sloan, who didn't return the gesture, his lips pinned as he continued to watch the three.

The older cowboy took off his hat and whacked at the other two, driving them away from the platform. "Go on, git!" When they stumbled off, he resumed his seat and continued eyeing the people milling around who had paid little attention to the exchange.

Ruth Ann released her breath and moved up to George Sloan before he entered the train depot. "Excuse me, Mr. Sloan. May I have a word with you?"

George Sloan turned to her, and Ruth Ann stepped back. He appeared more menacing up close, and she wondered how much of his daddy's hot blood boiled in him. "Who are you?"

"I...I'm Ruth Ann Teller," she faltered. "My brother Matthew owns the *Choctaw Tribune*, and he spoke with your father..."

George Sloan's expression darkened. "If your brother wants something from me, tell him to come and get it." Trunk slung over his shoulder, young Sloan strode into the train depot.

Ruth Ann stood on the platform, the thin tablet hanging loosely in her hands. Most people had moved on about their business. The train blew its whistle, preparing to depart.

Hoping no one had noticed her, Ruth Ann started toward home. She'd only taken a couple of steps when the sound of a throat clearing drew her attention to the old cowboy still sitting in the chair. In one hand he held a stick, and in the other a pocketknife, which he was using to shape the stick into a penny whistle.

He nodded to her. "Name's G.W., ma'am. I read your newspaper yesterday. My Choctaw boss subscribes to it and passes it on to me when he's done. Tough thing, those killings. But I was glad to read about it from someone who actually studied up on what happened. Your brother must be a brave man."

Any encouragement was welcome, even from an old-time cowboy. Ruth Ann smiled at him. "Thank you, sir. I'll tell him." As she headed home, Ruth Ann muttered her mother's words with her own. "Brave, maybe. Or just one stubborn, stubborn Choctaw."

♦♦♦

When Matthew came home for dinner, Ruth Ann met him at the front door. "Guess who got off the train today?"

"George Sloan."

Ruth Ann frowned, not happy her bone-weary brother had stolen her moment. "How did you know?"

Matthew took his hat off and hung it by the door before slamming it shut and heading for the sofa. He wasn't wearing a gun belt.

Probably not the friendliest thing to wear when calling on clients.

"I'm a newspaper reporter, that's how." He plopped down, not gently. "Lost four advertisers today."

"Oh." Ruth Ann moved to sit by him but hesitated when she saw the look on his face. It was obvious he didn't care to talk, so she went back to the kitchen where she continued preparing dinner. Their mother was putting fresh sheets on the beds upstairs.

Minutes later, Matthew came to lean against the wall near the stove. He put his hands in his back pockets and sighed. "I'm sorry, Annie. It hasn't been a good day. There are plenty of people who secretly appreciated my covering the story, but they don't want to say so in front of anyone. Then there are those downright mad about it. Mr. Carter's freight office won't be advertising; I expected that. Banny with the hotel, too. But I didn't think I'd lose the blacksmith shop. Charlie Simms is Choctaw, and he's been a friend since we moved here." He shook his head. "And I sure didn't expect Mr. Bates to back down like he did."

Ruth Ann halted in mid-bend of putting apples in the oven to bake. "Mr. Bates? He won't be advertising specials about the mercantile anymore?"

"No. Mayor Warren owns the building he's in, and they must have had a talk."

Ruth Ann was glad she could keep her face turned away from Matthew as she adjusted the pan of sliced apples on the rack. She didn't want him to feel worse when he saw the disappointment in her expression.

Mr. Bates was one of the nicest men in town. She always looked forward to talking over his advertising needs each week. He often ran specials on bolts of fabric he needed to sell to make room for new ones. If a farmer brought in an abundant harvest of beets, Mr. Bates announced it through the *Choctaw Tribune*. He'd even stopped most of his advertising in the *Dickens Herald*. It wasn't right for the mayor to pressure him into backing off using the *Choctaw Tribune*. Wasn't right at all.

Hands still deep in his pockets, Matthew continued. "You asked about George Sloan. He didn't want to talk much, but I did find out why he came today instead of Tuesday, the day of the execution."

Ruth Ann tried to remain casual as she sliced potatoes on the cutting board. Hopefully George Sloan hadn't mentioned she'd tried to talk with him earlier. "Why's that?"

"He wants more than to tell his father goodbye. I found out he studied law back at Roanoke College in Virginia. A lot of the young men I went to college with studied law because of all the legal dealings we've had with the U.S. government. But George Sloan has something more in mind. He went to the judge in Fort Smith and got a stay of execution for his father. Says a new law passed banning our old way of trying and executing someone."

Surprised, Ruth Ann paused before dropping the potato slices into a pan of boiling water. "Fort Smith has no jurisdiction in Indian Territory. We have our own justice system for our people."

Matthew snagged a potato slice from her tray. She swatted at him and dumped the rest into the pot. He shoved the whole slice into his mouth and said around it, "I told you, Annie. Things are changing. They're changing."

Ruth Ann moved the large cast-iron skillet to the front of the stove. She lifted slices of ham from a nearby plate and laid them into the skillet. As they sizzled and began filling the kitchen with an enticing aroma, a mixture of sweet and meaty, she asked, "Anything going to be left the same?"

Matthew looked down at the frying ham, one hand on his hip. "Well, I'll always be your stubborn brother."

Ruth Ann tried to smile, but her stomach knotted. *If I don't lose you like I did Philip.*

CHAPTER SEVEN

SUNDAY MORNING WAS QUIET AND tense as the family prepared for church and the afternoon picnic social. On Saturday Choctaws had started gathering in from farms as far as twenty miles away, some camping, some staying with family or friends. Most gathered around the church during the afternoon for singing and eating well into Saturday evening. Della and Ruth Ann had worked into the night on food preparations for the Sunday lunch. Grape dumplings were always a favorite and shared liberally, so the women made a triple batch.

At the same time, uncertainty of how their supposed friends would treat them shadowed every word that morning, though not much was to be said. It only had to be done.

One thing they looked forward to was that most their whole family was coming as always. Uncle Preston's farm lay nine miles south of town, joining the Red River that separated Indian Territory from Texas. His impressive spread contained over 500 head of cattle, a 100-acre cornfield, hogs, and a gristmill. The large natural lake and woods on the property provided plenty of opportunity for hunting and fishing.

The Tellers had moved there when their smaller farm

failed to survive the drought six years earlier. After Jim and Philip were killed four years past, Matthew returned short of finishing his education at college in order to care for his grieving mother and sister. When Dickens sprang up a year later, Matthew went to work part-time in town for the *Dickens Herald*.

It was only four short months ago that Matthew convinced them to build the box-house in town and start their own newspaper. Living in town required adjustments on a daily basis, especially dealing with the dynamics they had avoided before on the farm. But there were still regular events like church and social picnics to remind them that some things stayed the same.

Arms loaded with the picnic basket, blankets, and their Bibles, the Tellers set off down Main Street for the church at the other end. The church sat on its own little knoll adjacent to a grassy field layered with wildflowers smashed down under the many wagons and pony strings every Sunday.

On their way they exchanged greetings with other families going toward the same destination. Mrs. Bates smiled gleefully at Della, while her husband averted his gaze as though ashamed. His wife looked mighty fine with her newly redone lace cuffs fresh out of a catalogue.

It wasn't until the churchyard that Ruth Ann spotted her uncle's wagon with his crew milling around. It was an assorted lot that included cousins, in-laws, and former slaves who had stayed on at the farm after the war.

Fifteen-year-old Peter, Uncle Preston's youngest, lounged in the back of the wagon, already wearing the grin that won hearts and made him Ruth Ann's favorite cousin to scold. But he had learned to restrain himself on Sundays after more trips to cut a switch in his childhood days than he'd ever admit to his own children in the future.

Uncle Preston saw the Tellers and nodded solemnly as they approached. His expression was all Ruth Ann needed to see. Her uncle had been hesitant about the whole business of the *Choctaw Tribune*, and he didn't seem pleased now. But there was no time for discussion or scolding by anyone as Pastor Rand rang the hand-bell on the front porch of the little white church, summoning them all inside. Peter helped the Tellers stow their picnic goods in the back of Uncle Preston's wagon before joining the crowd.

The inside of the one-room church echoed with peace in the midst of Ruth Ann's fear. She could snuggle safely in the middle of their pew, which was on the right-hand side, three rows back from the altar. Surrounded by family and friendly folk, Ruth Ann was happier than ever it was Sunday.

But not all smiles were genuinely kind that morning. Plenty looked freshly plastered on for appearance only, as wooden as the pews. Ruth Ann was especially careful to avoid the gazes of the mayor and Mr. Carter, though they made no attempt to gain her attention.

Sounds from the pump organ, bought and paid for by Mr. Carter and shipped from St. Louis, filled the frame church, rattling the rafters. The congregation stood and the singing began. And what singing it was! Most of the Choctaws sang in their native tongue, blending in sweet harmony with the soulful strains of the blacks. The whites chorused with strong, steady rhythm. It was enough to make the spirit fly or the flesh faint, depending on the state of one's soul.

Wealth and honor I disdain,
Earthly comforts, Lord, are vain;
These can never satisfy:
Give me Christ, or else I die.

All unholy and unclean,
I am weighted by my sin;
On thy mercy I rely;
Give me Christ, or else I die.

The singing went on for a long half-hour as the temperature rose on the unusually warm autumn day. One elder swayed and had to be helped, though objecting, to a seat near a back window.

Finally the organ slowed, and a respectful hush filtered through the congregation as the pastor took his place behind the pulpit. He raised his arms high. "Forgive us, Lord!" he shouted.

A murmuring of agreement rippled through the room, and someone on the front pew sang out, "Lawd, save my soul!"

The pastor, a white man with a hearty soul, bright lips, and a red face, pulled his string tie loose. Most in the congregation took their seats, knowing a long sermon was forthcoming. Ruth Ann took the moment to dab moisture from her upper lip as she glanced around before sitting. Her eyes met a stern look on the face of a man standing by the back wall, arms folded. George Sloan.

She dropped into her seat next to her mother. Matthew sat on Della's other side, and Ruth Ann was sure from the tight pull of his lips that he had seen Sloan.

Pastor Rand raised his arms again and shouted, "Thou shalt not kill!"

Yes, this would be a long and painful sermon.

◆◆◆

The pastor's sermon left Ruth Ann questioning what he was preaching against—the killings Silas Sloan committed or the upcoming killing *of* Silas Sloan. Maybe both or neither. It seemed he was against the whole sad situation.

When the service finally came to a close after more singing, everyone mingled while they made their way out the door to shake the pastor's hand. The womenfolk started spreading the banquet of food on makeshift tables of scrap boards placed on sawhorses. Whole hams, turkeys, brisket, and hand-rolled sausage were the meats of choice, signs of a profitable harvest and hunting season. Prosperity and hope marked the town of Dickens and the outlying areas.

But the pastor's sermon had put them in remembrance of

THE EXECUTIONS

the dangers still surrounding them: danger from those who opposed their ways; danger from the spread of bad news that could be deadly for the town—as deadly as a bullet; danger for every choice any of them made. That was why Ruth Ann was not surprised when Uncle Preston approached Matthew after the meal. The two of them walked off a ways into the meadow behind the church, talking.

Preston had helped rear his sister's children, especially the boys, Philip and Matthew. He and their father took them hunting, taught them the ways of their people, and together, announced the day the boys had become men. He was a mentor to them and one they'd been accountable to. It was doubly so now for Matthew, who no longer had his father.

Matthew had always taken everything his uncle said into careful consideration, and Ruth Ann recognized that attitude as she observed their distant conversation. If anyone could talk Matthew down from his determined stance to report the news—all of it—it was Uncle Preston.

To take her mind off the conversation she couldn't hear, Ruth Ann helped her mother salvage scraps to send home to her uncle's hogs. As she worked, she glanced around and noticed George Sloan standing off to himself near the collection of wagons, arms still crossed as he watched everyone.

He was no longer dressed in his fancy eastern clothes, opting instead for a simple blue cotton shirt. Most people politely ignored him, and Ruth Ann hadn't seen him get a plate of food. She hesitated, her heart thumping even as a kind and sensitive spirit moved her. How could she shovel good food into a canister for hogs while a man went without eating? Ruth Ann found a clean plate and dished up a healthy serving onto it, including the last remnants of their grape dumplings.

George Sloan watched as she approached, making her conscious of each patch of dirt and grass she stepped on before finally reaching him. Her intention was simply to hand him the plate and run, though not literally. Just fast enough to get away from his grim aura. She brought her eyes up.

"I thought...didn't know if you wanted...well, here," she mumbled as she offered the plate. Surprising her yet again, he took it, though she wondered if he intended to dump it in front of her. He didn't. Instead, he spoke.

"Yakoke. I have news for you." The way he said *news* made her figure he was going to make fun of her attempt to interview him before. "My father will not come to his execution Tuesday. I told him about the new law and how the Lighthorsemen have no right to sentence him to death. He killed in self-defense. So there is your news. Tell your brother to put that in his paper." George Sloan jabbed at the dumplings with the fork, never taking his eyes off Ruth Ann, seeming to challenge her for a response.

She had none and merely said, "The next edition won't come out until Thursday."

George Sloan snorted—or maybe chuckled. Ruth Ann didn't wait around to figure it out. It was time to clean up the rest of the vittles for hog slop.

♦♦♦

The sunshine was brilliant and welcome. Matthew walked alongside his uncle Preston to a spot among the wild sunflowers by the church, away from the main group cleaning up after the picnic lunch. Gloom had coated him all week, and this was translating to those around him. Now his uncle would set him straight, and Matthew was glad for the warm sunlight helping to offset the apprehension he felt.

Disappointing people he respected was not something he liked to do—or be rebuked for; that made the offense real. But it had to be done, so Matthew waited in silence with his hands resting in his back pockets, staring off at the line of trees that hemmed in the meadow.

It was a few minutes before Uncle Preston spoke. Arms folded, he stared at Matthew thoughtfully. "You've done good work."

Surprised, Matthew glanced into his uncle's eyes. He

accepted the approval with a short nod.

Uncle Preston continued. "We need people to stand up and speak truth. We need people to look after our tribal rights. We need warriors."

When the pause lasted longer than a minute, Matthew knew a big *but* was coming.

It did. "But maybe it's time for you to come home. Fight from there by becoming a successful and old Choctaw. Build a future for yourself, not a moment of glory here that history will never remember. It may be your newspaper changes nothing. It may be it changes great things. But what will be left for you? What of your mother? Can she stand to put another son in the grave of her heart?"

Matthew lowered his eyes to the wild sunflowers struggling to finish their work and drop seeds before the grip of winter snuffed out their short lives. But they would bloom again. Like the words Jesus spoke: "*Verily, verily, I say unto you, Except a corn of wheat fall into the ground and die, it abideth alone: but if it die, it bringeth forth much fruit.*"

But Matthew did not say this aloud. He remained silent, listening to the wisdom and meaning of his uncle's words as he had since boyhood.

"There's a cabin by the lake on the farm I rented to white farmers. They stayed there a time, but moved on to Texas. The cabin has sat empty a year now. Coons and possums are finding ways to make it home." Uncle Preston chuckled, and Matthew smiled.

"Think on it. Think if it would not be better to start a family there, care for your mother and sister. But if you decide you are doing good here, if you want to spend your life on this work, you do so with my blessing."

It was the blessing Matthew had barely hoped to gain. Letting out a day's worth of worried breath, he looked up again to his uncle's eyes. "I'll consider both, and I'll speak with Mama and Ruth Ann. I want to do what's right."

Uncle Preston kept his arms folded, though he dipped his head in approval. "That is what I want you to do."

They talked awhile more about the upcoming hog-butchering Matthew was to help with the next day, and the conversation drifted to the troubles and disagreements the tribe faced.

In his heart Matthew wished he knew what his decision was to be, what the right thing was. It was hard to tell in this shifting world that threatened to drop everything he knew and loved through the fissures it created. But the decision had to be made, and soon. He had to trust God to give him wisdom when the time came.

...except a corn of wheat fall into the ground and die...

♦♦♦

"There was a shooting up at Silas Sloan's place."

Ruth Ann heard the news while delivering crocheted doilies to Dr. Anderson's wife. Mrs. Anderson had invited her for tea in their modest parlor, and the two sat primly on the edge of her velveteen sofa the doctor had received from a client in exchange for his services. The client and his family had pulled up stakes after two of their children died of snakebites the doctor couldn't treat in time, so they gave him some of the fine furnishings they'd brought with them from the East. Much of the Anderson household was filled with such payments in lieu of cash. Even the small basket of doilies Ruth Ann brought was for services when Dr. Anderson treated Matthew's sprained wrist that summer.

Mrs. Anderson was a pleasant woman who also served as her husband's nurse. They had met in medical school and were an ideally suited couple, at least in the opinion of the town gossips. But it was Mrs. Anderson's announcement of a shooting that brought Ruth Ann up straight in her seat.

"What happened?"

Mrs. Anderson sipped her tea. "I'm not sure. Outlaws, perhaps. Someone did claim to have seen the Abernathy gang ride up that way last night. A man from one of the farms near there came into town this morning and said Silas Sloan had walked to his place and asked for a horse. Said he had the look of murderous vengeance in his eyes and a gun in his hands. The farmer thought maybe his wife had been shot."

The teacup in Ruth Ann's hand clattered in the saucer, so she set it carefully on the low, round table in front of the sofa. "Did Dr. Anderson go up there?"

Mrs. Anderson put a hand to her throat. "Heavens, no! That man Sloan is a murderer. No telling what he may do. Besides, Dr. Anderson is on a call to a farm down by the Red. Won't be home 'til evening I expect." She picked through the basket and lifted a small round doily. She turned it over in her hands, admiring the work. "But I'm sure *someone* went up there…"

Disturbed by the news and wanting to know more, Ruth Ann stood. "I best be going home. Mama will need me to help make bread."

"Oh." Mrs. Anderson sighed as if disappointed the visit was so short. "Of course. Give my regards to her, please, and thank her for the lovely job on the doilies. They will look exquisite on the arms of the sofa and chairs."

"Yes, ma'am," Ruth Ann muttered as she hurried to make her exit.

Matthew had gone out to Uncle Preston's farm early that morning to help with hog-butchering. He would bring home salted pork in return, more than worth his trip, but that wouldn't be until evening.

At a fast yet modest walk, Ruth Ann was home in a minute and skittered through the open kitchen door.

"Mama, there was a shooting at Silas Sloan's place!" Ruth Ann shouted the news.

Della halted from kneading dough on the table and looked up at her. Then she used her chin to point at the flour bin. Ruth Ann hurried to wash her hands in the basin on the counter. She carefully dried them before adding more flour to the dough so Della could go back to kneading. Only then did Ruth Ann relate what little she knew about the incident.

Della slapped the dough into the bread pan and covered

it with a dish towel. She washed her hands and removed her apron. "Saddle your pony for me."

Ruth Ann stared at her mother several moments, somehow knowing all along she would say that and yet shocked when she did. As she observed her mother, she thought of all the nice people that went to their church. Friendly, kind, good people. Then she thought of Jesus. He wasn't just friendly, kind, and good. He went to places others wouldn't. But surely that didn't hold true for two defenseless women, did it?

From the look in Della's eyes, Ruth Ann had her answer.

Ten minutes later, Ruth Ann helped her mother mount the sturdy pony before handing up her basket of herbal remedies. Hoping no one would see them, Ruth Ann swung herself up and astride behind her mother, who sat in her husband's old saddle, not the sidesaddle. They took off at a trot, with Della guiding Skyline toward the foothill trail. Silas Sloan's place lay at the end of it.

CHAPTER EIGHT

WHEN THEY RODE INTO THE Sloan yard, Ruth Ann peeked around her mother's shoulder. The sight made her cry aloud. A man lay on his back near the chukka door, blood turning his blue shirt red. Ruth Ann wanted to beg her mother to turn back but instead slid off the pony and rushed forward.

George Sloan stared up at the sky as it darkened with coming storm clouds, his arms spread out to both sides. Flies accumulated around his open mouth, and blood soaked the ground around his body from the hole in his chest. Ruth Ann halted by him. Della joined her and bent to close George Sloan's eyes.

Moaning sounds came from inside the chukka. The women stepped over the young lawyer's body and went inside. It was dark and cool in the one room hut-like structure. The thatched roof and clay chinking gave it a natural smell, though it mixed with the scent of freshly tanned deer hide. Clay cooking pots and eating bowls sat around a hearth in the middle of the room. Finely woven cane mats covered much of the hard-packed ground.

But it was a cane stool to the right of the burned-out fire that caught Ruth Ann's attention. On it lay a copy of the

Choctaw Tribune with a hunting knife pinning it down.

Della spotted the source of the moan before Ruth Ann, who followed her mother to a shelf built on the far wall. It was mounded with hides for cushion and warmth. In the midst of it lay Silas Sloan's wife. Blood trickled from her left side, and her ashen face begged the question of how much blood was left in her body.

Della frowned and tore away the cloth from the wound, then began washing it with water from a canteen she'd brought. Straightening from her patient, she glanced to Ruth Ann, and said quietly, "She will not live."

Approaching hoofbeats pounded from the opposite direction of the trail. They were not the comforting sound of Matthew's gelding, nor the sound of a peaceful acquaintance. They were the sound of someone on a mission. A mission of vengeance?

Through the open chukka door, Ruth Ann watched the rider come into view. He was easy to recognize as thunder rolled in with him. Praying for courage and protection, Ruth Ann stepped out to meet him, stopping by George Sloan's body.

Silas Sloan slowed his horse to a trot and then a stop a few feet from her. As the dust calmed, it became clear he hadn't come back alone. A half-dozen riders waited back near the trail. Rifles in their scabbards, six-shooters on one or even two hips, and scars on every face told their whole story. This was the Abernathy gang—or what was left of it.

Silas Sloan dismounted, rifle in hand.

"Does my wife live?" He had a murderous look in his eyes, just as the farmer had said.

Ruth Ann barely looked at him, didn't dare look at the riders who waited on the road, appearing none too patient.

We are going to die. The thought came unbidden, but sure.

"She...she is not well," Ruth Ann managed to answer. "Why did you leave her?" The only excuse Ruth Ann knew for her sharp words was the fact she no longer held her life to much value. The image of the *Choctaw Tribune* virtually slaughtered on the cane stool haunted her.

To her surprise, Silas Sloan answered in English, which she had spoken. "I had to go shoot the two who shot mine. They are dead. Those men there..." He jutted his chin toward the riders. "They want me to take their place. I told 'em no already. They say they didn't mean for those two to shoot mine while I was gone. Argued with my son. Wife tried to stop the shooting. Those two kill mine. I find them and kill those two. Gang still wants me to ride with them."

Ruth Ann had heard of outlaws coming to try and force a Choctaw who was already under a death sentence to join their gang. This was a case when it had gone too far with men who saw other peoples' lives of little consequence—including hers and her mother's.

Before she could answer, Silas Sloan hefted his son's body and carried it to a spot near the garden. A hoe and shovel lay there, as if the family had been in the middle of work when the riders came.

Silas Sloan began to dig a grave in the soft dirt. One of the gang members joined him, as if wanting to hurry the process. He swung the hoe dangerously close to Silas Sloan's head. The latter pulled back and gave the outlaw a look that caused him to move to the other end of the grave.

The outlaws paid little attention to Ruth Ann, who tried to make herself as small as possible as she eased back toward the chukka. In the process she bumped into Della, who had come out to join her. "Better tell him to dig two graves. We need to go now."

Ruth Ann stifled a gasp and answered in a whisper. "Mama, that's the Abernathy gang out there. Won't they kill us for seeing them?"

Before Della could respond, the shadow of Silas Sloan fell over them as he blocked the last remnants of sunshine before the storm. He moved past them and into the chukka where he pulled the hunting knife out of the stool, the action sending the *Choctaw Tribune* floating to the floor. He stared at the women a few seconds before glancing at his dead wife.

67

Suddenly, Ruth Ann wasn't ready to die. *What will Matthew do? How will Uncle Preston take it? I'm only eighteen...*
God knows.

Ruth Ann closed her eyes and let the voices of her fathers, both heavenly, comfort and soothe her heart.

But Silas Sloan's rough voice snapped her back to earth. "Go. No one will harm you."

Della led the way to their pony, where she had tied her to some brush. Skyline waited calmly despite the claps of thunder shaking the air and the nearby snorts and stomps of the horses north on the trail. The Teller women mounted and turned south toward home. All the while Silas Sloan watched as though he were guarding them. As they neared the path at a soft lope, Ruth Ann glanced back to see him lay the hunting knife on his son's chest. In that moment, she realized the knife hadn't been Silas Sloan's. It was his son's, and he was to be buried with it along with whatever disapproval he'd had of the *Tribune*.

Before the scene faded from sight, Ruth Ann watched Silas Sloan and the outlaw lift George Sloan's body and lower it into the shallow grave.

◆◆◆

Dry thunder followed Della and Ruth Ann as they trotted up to the barn at a cloudy dusk in time to see Matthew watering his saddled gelding at the well. From the look of both man and beast, they'd just returned from Uncle Preston's farm, worn out but not ready to stop. Matthew jerked his head up and dropped the water bucket he'd held to Little Chief's muzzle. "What's going on?"

He strode up to meet them, quickly helping the haggard Ruth Ann and their mother down. "As soon as I got home and found you gone, I asked around and heard about the shooting at Silas Sloan's. Do not tell me you went up there."

Ruth Ann knew he was trying hard not to disrespect their mother, but he was furious. Probably Uncle Preston had warned him against putting his family in danger over the newspaper, and then something like this happened. Ruth Ann tried a diversion. "Silas Sloan's wife was hurt, Matt. Mama tried to help her, but she died."

"And Silas and George Sloan? Where were they?"

"George Sloan is dead." Della heaved her basket of remedies away from her son when he offered to take it from her. "The woman is dead, and Silas Sloan is with the outlaws. But he will come tomorrow."

"George Sloan is dead? Outlaws? Mother..."

Della headed for the house. Matthew growled after her, loud enough for Ruth Ann to hear, "And you call me a stubborn Choctaw."

Not able to scold his mother, Matthew turned on Ruth Ann. She ducked away and led Skyline toward the barn. Matthew followed with his gelding, ranting.

Ruth Ann said nothing as they unsaddled. She waited until he quieted to ask what was foremost on her mind. "Will he come?"

With all the uncertainties and wrongs around them, Ruth Ann wanted something she could be sure of, something that hadn't changed for her people, for right to be right again.

But Matthew snapped, "Does it matter?" He halted with the saddle midway on the saddle tree. "I'm sorry. But you shouldn't have taken Mama up there." He shoved the saddle into place with a thud, then grabbed the curry comb from the bucket. "And you shouldn't be so concerned over whether Silas Sloan shows up for his execution. What does it matter? Nothing is good and right with our people any more. Our homeland, our traditions, our ways. The Choctaw way. That way means nothing. I wonder if the newspaper means nothing. It makes no difference, changes nothing."

The image of the *Choctaw Tribune* with the hunting knife cut through it burned bright in Ruth Ann's memory. What had angered George Sloan when reading it? Matthew talked about the Choctaw way in the article. About honor and the old ways. Maybe George Sloan had simply lashed out in pain, knowing if the old ways were kept, they would take his father's life.

Matthew wrote things that evoked real emotion, real truths, things the *Dickens Herald* would never dream of printing. Surely that amounted to something, but Ruth Ann couldn't say what.

After brushing down the mare, Ruth Ann stood by her neck, rubbing her long face. "It does matter, Matthew. You'll see. It matters."

Pitchfork in hand, Matthew heaved a generous portion of hay for the animals. He plunged the fork back into the hay stack and stood still a moment, staring at the fork, still gripping the handle. "Uncle Preston questions if it's wise to continue the newspaper. He offered the cabin on the south side of his lake that's sat empty of tenants over a year now." Matthew shrugged. "Farming, ranching—it's a good way of life, and profitable. Town living is expensive, and the newspaper may lose all its advertisers after this week with the poison spread by Mayor Warren. What's left?" He looked at Ruth Ann as if expecting a worthy answer.

She dropped her eyes. "Truth. Maybe. I don't know."

The hay rustled as Matthew moved away from the stack and past her. He stopped at her shoulder and put an arm around her, squeezing tight. In their growing-up years they rarely hugged or consoled one another. That had changed with the death of their father and Philip. Ruth Ann felt the need for those reassuring arms but feared losing Matthew too. She leaned her head against his shoulder.

They said nothing else, understanding without words. As the clouds broke open, the siblings parted and raced for the house, dodging the raindrops on their way to wait for tomorrow and the supposed Choctaw execution of Silas Sloan.

CHAPTER NINE

MORNING CAME, BUT THE SUN did not. The furious after-wind from the storm continued to rip through the turning leaves on the old oak tree that stood guard by the freshly built town hall building set in the center of Dickens. The oak had grown for more than a hundred years and suddenly found itself surrounded by machine-cut timber hammered into submission by foreign hands. Ruth Ann stared up through the colorful but dying leaves and into the gray sky, able to understand the frustration of mixing man with nature. But it had to be. God gave man dominion over His creation. But did He give one race of man dominion over other races?

She rubbed her hands on the shawl she wore around her arms, seeking warmth amidst the sudden change in weather brought by last night's storm. Many years ago the Grandmother had taught her how to sew these Choctaw shawls with fringe, as she'd also taught Ruth Ann's mother. Della had sat in on Ruth Ann's sessions, but the importance of the Grandmother teaching was clear. In the end, when the Grandmother declared her accomplished, Ruth Ann knew she wasn't just speaking of her sewing skills. Patience and perseverance had developed in Ruth Ann's character, traits meant to carry her through and profit her in life. If only she could remember to exhibit those traits when she needed them most!

Right now was one of those times. She was impatient for the day to end. The sweet thought of moving back to Uncle Preston's farm and being close to the Grandmother on a daily basis melted her determination to see the newspaper business through. Ruth Ann desperately felt the need for another lesson right about now.

Shame taunted her over her wish for the day to hurry and be over, for when it was over at last, Silas Sloan would likely be dead. The newspaper would print its sixteenth and last edition tomorrow. The town would say goodbye and good riddance to the *Choctaw Tribune*.

Though it was still morning, an hour before noon, people had begun to gather in front of the town hall. They occasionally peered up toward the end of the street that twisted out of sight, the road where Silas Sloan would appear—assuming he really did show up. Truth be told, few believed he would, and most came to joke about how silly it was to expect a man to show up for his own execution.

Only the Choctaws didn't joke and soon migrated to their own group under the shelter of the oak tree where Ruth Ann stood with her mother and brother. She didn't know why they'd come early. It just seemed right, and it felt good to do what was right this morning, even if right was also hard.

A familiar wagon rolled up to the back of the town hall building and pulled in among the others. Uncle Preston and the Grandmother, along with Peter and other cousins, joined the Choctaws under the tree.

At exactly eleven o'clock, shouts and clatter rose at the opposite end of Main Street as the train rolled into the depot. It was the train George Sloan was supposed to have been on, returning after his college graduation to say a final goodbye to his father. But his coming early might still save his father's life. Silas Sloan now knew he was not legally obligated to come to his own execution. The U.S. government said so.

On the other hand, if George Sloan had waited to ride on this train, he would be alive and disembarking right now. Instead, two finely dressed gentlemen got off with armloads of baggage and headed for the hotel across and down from the depot. No one paid the gentlemen much mind, and they did the same toward the townsfolk as they went inside.

A door opened from the town hall building and Jake Banny, gun belt in place, stepped onto the porch. He looked down on the crowd before descending the steps and making a wide circle around the people to the street.

Ruth Ann wanted to shrink from sight, but she watched with curiosity as Banny bent and tied down his holster to his leg. She shivered as he started up the street toward them. Straight toward them.

Coldness claimed her when Matthew stiffened and took note of the approaching man, and it became clear they were destined to face each other.

Why? Ruth Ann's heart cried. *Oh, why do you have that gun on, Mr. Banny? Why did Matthew wear his? Why?*

God knows.

Before coming within civil-talking range, Banny spoke for everyone gathered to hear. "Well, Indian boy, you still plan on making trouble?" He halted in the street, several feet from them. "Are you going to keep reporting about garbage and such in our nice little town?"

While the man spoke, Matthew separated himself from the group who watched silently. In her mind Ruth Ann grasped Matthew's arm, stepped in front of him, shouted at Mr. Banny to leave them alone. Outwardly, she stood silent, frozen.

Movement from behind Banny diverted Ruth Ann's attention long enough for her to breathe. The two gentlemen from the train were coming toward them, arms full of...what? Maybe poles of some kind, wrapped in a black tarp. One of them carried most everything, his arms full of the poles and hands clenching two black cases as the men strode along the boardwalk, up toward the town hall building. They were behind Banny, and no one paid them much mind.

Matthew remained silent, exactly as he'd done when the three leading men visited their home that night. When he was clear from the crowd, he faced Banny, arms resting to his sides, his right hand hanging just below the holstered gun on his belt.

Banny continued in a mocking tone. "You think you can face me, huh? Facing a man ain't like shooting tin cans. That's all you've ever shot, ain't it? You think you're a man, Indian boy?" Banny braced his legs, set shoulder-width apart, and flexed his fingers over the handle of his gun as if expecting Matthew to draw so it would be clear and simple self-defense. Matthew didn't flinch.

Ruth Ann tried to pray but couldn't. She could think of nothing but the truth of Banny's words. Matthew had practiced with a six-gun only on tin cans in a meadow south of town. He'd shot plenty of deer, coyotes, and even bears with a rifle, but facing another man with a pistol wasn't something their uncle or father had raised the Teller boys to do. The only time Matthew had shot a living thing with a six-gun was one day in the meadow when he'd been practicing with Ruth Ann, teaching her to shoot the new Winchester he'd bought after their father was killed.

While Ruth Ann fumbled with loading it, she dropped several cartridges in the dirt. Squatting to retrieve them, the sickening hiss of rattles threatened death. With her fingers outstretched toward the worthless bullets, four feet away she saw the snake's cold, black eyes before it struck.

Only it never did. A shot deafened her ears and hot lead nearly singed her bare fingers. The black eyes disappeared, the hissing stopped.

Without moving from her position, she had lifted her eyes to see Matthew standing as shocked as she was, holding the smoking six-gun where he'd drawn and fired it from the hip. He'd done what he had to do when he needed to do it.

But saving someone you love was different from facing an arrogant man who wanted you dead. And Banny wouldn't stop talking. "You Indians are all the same. Think you can get educated like a white man and that makes you as good. It ain't even half as good. You're lucky to be roaming free at all instead of caged up like your animal brothers."

Legs still braced, Banny waved at Della and Ruth Ann. "Those squaws are mighty fine-looking. I guess you plan on getting one of your own and making more half-breeds. Be better for all if I…"

He didn't finish. His hand flashed down and gripped the butt of his gun, expecting Matthew to draw. Matthew flinched and grabbed for his gun in defense.

Shouts from behind Banny broke the moment.

"Hold on! Hold on!"

"Let us get the camera set up!"

"Wait!"

Banny whipped around. The pudgy man carrying his armload of poles and black cases had lost his derby hat while running toward them, his fancy black boots slinging flakes of mud through the air. The other, taller man waved a tablet like a white flag.

From the town hall building, out popped Mayor Warren, Mr. Carter, and Mr. Maxwell. It appeared the leading men had been hiding out and watching from behind the curtains of the mayor's office, waiting for the shoot-out and any other danger to pass. Whether Silas Sloan showed or not, they no doubt saw this as an opportunity to silence their antagonist, the *Choctaw Tribune*.

Ruth Ann clenched her hands into fists, trying to keep from crying in anger. They had it all planned, planned to kill her last living brother through Banny.

Mayor Warren mopped his brow with a large white handkerchief despite the cold wind that hit him as he hurried up to the gentlemen who had already gone to work setting their poles on the ground off to the side of Banny. Now that the tarp was off, Ruth Ann realized the poles were actually a tripod like surveyors used.

Despite his excess pounds, the man who had carried the

equipment quickly opened one of the black cases and removed a complex looking device. Instantly she realized it was a camera, something typically used to take portraits of people as they sat very, very still, like one done of her own family. But cameras were also used at large and important events back East. She decided that must be where these men were from. And Mayor Warren knew it.

"Gentlemen, may I introduce myself? I'm the mayor of Dickens, Thaddeus Warren at your service. Won't you come into my office and have a cup of coffee?" He took the taller man by the arm, the one who held the tablet and was already scribbling notes. The rough grip caused his pencil to slide across the paper, and he frowned before jerking his arm away from the mayor's desperate clasp.

"Pardon me, sir, but I'm John McMillian from the *Tennessee Gazette*, and I do not appreciate being accosted when I'm covering a story."

Mayor Warren patted his dry brow as Mr. Maxwell stepped forward with a glance at Banny, who stood looking like a fool in the midst of a suddenly cordial exchange. Matthew relaxed his position and moved toward the group, but Maxwell stuck his hand out to the reporter to gain his full attention. "Pleased to make your acquaintance. I'm Christopher Maxwell, editor of the *Dickens Herald*. I've subscribed to the *Tennessee Gazette* for years. Excellent paper, one I use as a model in my humble shop."

Mr. McMillian wiggled his pencil to show his hand was too full to shake and looked Maxwell over with an experienced eye. "A pleasure. I reported for *The New York Times* over twenty years before moving to Nashville and starting the *Gazette* six months ago. But I'm pleased to know you've received it for years."

Without waiting for Maxwell to stammer an excuse, McMillian pocketed his pencil and offered his hand to Matthew, who introduced himself. Recognition showed in McMillian's eyes. "I understand you started your own venture in this nice little town. The *Choctaw Tribune*, isn't it? I picked up your last edition when we arrived at Fort Smith on our way to Texas. My friend and I haven't been West in some time, and were due for a trip. We were heading to Paris, but after reading your fascinating stories about the thriving progress here, we determined to stop and see if Dickens is striving to become as civilized and advanced as you made it out to be. Seemed to be the case until we witnessed a shoot-out about to take place right in front of the town hall."

McMillian let silence fall as he turned to the mayor and raised his eyebrows, waiting for an explanation. Mayor Warren had none, and Mr. Carter, the freight office owner, tried to fill in. "He, um, that is, we have indeed made progress in the short time of our history. Did you, um, notice the church? We have high attendance rates—"

Recovered at last, Banny cut in—literally. He stepped in front of the other town leaders to face McMillian as if he might challenge *him* to a duel. "I'm Jake Banny, and I've got as much if not more stake in this town than anyone, and if you want to report the real story around here, it's those savage, murdering Choctaws who can't get civilized no matter how much religion, education, or white blood they claim to have."

He waved his hand at Matthew as he spoke. McMillian turned to Matthew and asked, "Are you Choctaw?"

Though it was obvious from his ruddy skin tone and facial features that he was, Matthew nodded, still stiff. "I'm the son of Jim Teller and Della Frazier Teller, both mixed-bloods with ancestry running back to great chiefs and statesmen in our nation."

McMillian nodded. "Since your people have been here longer than these men's, you are well-qualified to report on the current events and condition of this territory. I hope you have the full support of the mayor and businessmen." He turned back to Mayor Warren who had finally wadded his white handkerchief into a ball and calmed himself enough to nod.

"Of course. Young Teller is one of our model citizens. We're quite pleased with the work he does."

Banny opened his mouth, but Mayor Warren cleared his throat like a bear growling, stopping Banny before he could say a word.

McMillian smiled, a dry expression as he pulled out his pencil and looked to Matthew. "Now then, I suppose you're here to cover the execution you wrote about in the *Tribune*. It's set for..." He turned to the pudgy man with the camera, who pulled a gold watch from his vest pocket. He spoke for the first time. "At noon, twenty-four minutes from now, according to my time." He nodded to Matthew. "Angus Rice, editor-in-chief of *The New York Times*."

Mr. Maxwell coughed and turned away, striding back toward the town hall building. Carter followed, leaving Banny to snort, "You wasted a trip. That sorry Indian will never show." He yanked the string of his holster loose and followed the others inside. Mayor Warren chuckled, bowed awkwardly to the newsmen, and scurried off to his office—to watch from the window again, Ruth Ann imagined.

Now that things had settled down, Matthew looked at Ruth Ann with a mature expression, yet his eyes twinkled with a boyish thrill that said, "By George, I almost died, but look what happened!"

Ruth Ann wanted to slap him silly and thought she might before the day ended, if her mother didn't do it first. But he waved Della and Ruth Ann over with a smile as the rest of the crowd broke out with whispers. Matthew introduced them to the Eastern reporters, adding, "I don't know how I'd manage the paper without Annie."

The gentlemen smiled and nodded to the women, and Mr. Rice said, "Miss Teller, I read your religious commentary and the side column you have for children. Well done. I'm sure you are indeed a valuable asset to the *Choctaw Tribune*."

Ruth Ann blushed and stepped closer to her mother. She murmured, "Matthew does most of it."

As if overcome with a sudden burst of relief and emotion, Matthew slapped his leg. "There's nothing short of God Almighty more powerful than the press!"

THE EXECUTIONS

Mr. McMillian chuckled and nodded, then let his smile fade as he glanced up the road. "Will he come?"

Silence answered his question. Before, there could be no doubt. Silas Sloan, like any condemned Choctaw, would arrive at the appointed time and face his execution. His family would bury him, and the ordeal would end.

But that was in the old way. Silas Sloan might hold to it, yet his son had said he didn't have to. The U.S. government would try him and maybe put him in prison for the killings, or even let him go if they deemed it was self-defense. The outlaws might have compelled him to ride to freedom with them. Besides, they wanted him to replace the two of them he'd killed.

What honor or purpose was left for Silas Sloan anyway? He had no family to represent. The Choctaw way was fading fast. He'd tried in his own way to stop it, but he hadn't stemmed the change one bit.

Ruth Ann couldn't answer the reporter who asked if the condemned man would come. Like Matthew said, things change. Everything changed. A part of their past was given up and they had adopted white ways. Their present was lost in the past. Did that leave a future to hope for her people?

Minutes ticked by. District Choctaw councilmen arrived quietly with the Lighthorsemen, who would carry out the deed. Della pulled a brown package from beneath her shawl, and suddenly Ruth Ann knew who her mother had made the blue shirt for. Blue, the Sloan clan's color.

Mr. Rice pulled out his pocket watch and frowned. "Three minutes."

Ruth Ann felt her heart deflate. Silas Sloan wouldn't come. Why did she even want him to? For what purpose? To prove the Choctaw way was still a good one? For these whites to understand something only a dramatic act would cause? She didn't want to watch a man die, yet it was just. It was their way. And that way was lost.

God knows.

A loud whistle ripped through the crowd and all eyes

turned at the sound, looking north toward the road leading into town. In the brief moment before Ruth Ann turned in that direction, time seemed to stand still.

She glanced at Matthew, who had his eyes locked ahead on the twist in the road. She looked to her mother, who began unwrapping the brown package, one sleeve of the blue shirt flapping out, catching the wind. She glanced at the district councilmen and the Lighthorsemen, who shifted in their positions, all peering up the road. She saw Uncle Preston, the Grandmother, and Peter had joined in. She watched the town hall door open, and the mayor, Maxwell, Carter, and Banny stepped onto the porch, craning their necks to see. She spotted a newly familiar face in the crowd. It was the old cowboy, G.W., the one who had saved George Sloan from being mocked when he first arrived on the train. G.W. was a white man. A good man.

In that moment race didn't matter. All were looking the same direction, feeling mostly the same thing, though no one could have put it into words. Ruth Ann sure couldn't, not right then, as she finally turned her face in the same direction as everyone else.

There, riding down that twisting road, was Choctaw Silas Sloan.

CHAPTER TEN

THE BREEZE STILLED AND WAS forgotten as Silas Sloan rode slowly up to the crowd gathered to watch his execution. Ruth Ann tucked herself by her mother's side and helped unwrap the brown paper to reveal the blue shirt Della had made for this occasion. Matthew removed a tablet and pencil from his pant pocket and scribbled a headline across the top Ruth Ann couldn't see. The Eastern reporters focused on positioning their camera to take a shot of the crowd gathered, leaned forward on their toes.

The brown paper crunched in Ruth Ann's hands as she watched Silas Sloan come to a stop before the Choctaw tribal councilmen and dismount. One of them took the reins of Sloan's horse and led it away to join the string of horses tied to the town hall hitching rail.

Della approached and silently offered him the shirt. He took it with a quiet yakoke. He changed and went as directed to the other side of the hundred-year-old oak most of the people stood under. One by one, the Choctaws went by him, shaking his hand or taking a moment to say a word to him, though nothing of malice, not even the ones who were friends of the men he'd helped kill. Now was not the time for bitterness and anger. What was done was done, and the time for justice had arrived.

The only white person who spoke with Silas Sloan in his final moments was Pastor Rand. He gripped the Choctaw's hand and said several things to him, quietly where no one heard. Not much changed on Silas Sloan's face. It was impossible to tell if there was any change in his heart.

Ruth Ann went behind Matthew and her mother in line to see Silas Sloan in his last moments. When Matthew reached to shake his hand, the condemned man stared at him a moment before saying, "You're a good Choctaw. Your newspaper, it's good. Keep telling of our ways. They are good ways." With that, he shook Matthew's hand. Again, he thanked Della as she went by. Ruth Ann could only offer him a quick nod before moving along.

When the last of the Choctaws had taken their turn, they all stood off to the side as the Lighthorsemen moved into position, one standing ready with a loaded Winchester, another with a small jar of red paint. That man was in the midst of painting a circle over Silas Sloan's heart when a loud voice disrupted the sacred moment.

It was Mayor Warren, coming off the town hall porch where the rest of the town's leading men stood. He hurried through the crowd which parted for him as they watched the whole thing with curiosity. The Eastern reporters, Mr. McMillian and Mr. Rice, had finished resetting their camera in a new position, and they were the ones the mayor approached.

Mayor Warren held his head higher than he had before and seemed to force confidence into his expression. "Gentlemen, I want you to know I did everything within my power to stop this uncivilized event. These Choctaws have their laws and we don't have full authority over them—yet. If you are going to write a story about this, I do hope you will keep in mind this is a rare event and one that will not repeat in the future of Dickens."

When the Eastern reporters merely frowned and gave him a look of irritation, Mayor Warren wiped his brow with his white handkerchief and stepped out from in front of their camera lens.

The Lighthorsemen had not stopped their proceedings for the mayor. The circle painted, they had Silas Sloan kneel on the dirt twenty paces from the oak. Ruth Ann twisted the paper in her hands. The crackle sounded loud in the quiet moment. Matthew stood between her and Della, his pencil still as he watched the proceedings without taking notes for the article he had to produce about this execution.

For all the care and time leading up to this moment, things happened quickly. A man tied a bandana around Sloan's eyes and stepped back. The Lighthorseman with his Winchester shouldered it, took aim from twenty paces away, and fired. A few women gasped when the bullet hit its mark, center of the red circle. The redness spread before Silas Sloan's body jerked and pitched forward. He fell face-first in the dirt.

Ruth Ann bowed her head and said a prayer. Silas Sloan never went to church. He had ridden with other Choctaw Nationals to the homes of men who belonged to the Progressive party of Choctaws and shot them dead. But the thief on the cross next to Jesus had been saved. Ruth Ann couldn't know what Silas Sloan believed in those last moments.

Mr. McMillian scribbled away on his tablet, though he paused and watched closely when the Lighthorsemen moved to Silas Sloan's body and rolled him onto his back. After examining his wound, they made the official announcement: Silas Sloan was dead. The camera clicked as Angus Rice, editor-in-chief of *The New York Times,* froze the moment in time.

Condemned and executed in the old Choctaw way. This, despite the piece of paper from Fort Smith George Sloan had brought, saying the Choctaws had no legal right to execute his father. But Silas Sloan had made his decision. Maybe he'd had a direct hand in the killings and maybe not. Still, he'd been convicted and chose to follow the custom of taking care of a final task—seeing his son again—then arrived for his own execution as expected. Ruth Ann wondered how she ever questioned whether he would come.

The Lighthorsemen carried Silas Sloan off to a grave they'd already dug in the church cemetery, where only three others had been buried in the town's short history. The Eastern reporters moved among the Choctaws and asked questions. They continued to ignore the mayor's attempts to intervene.

Matthew stood still, making no notes of his own. Ruth Ann looked up into his face and hugged her shawl closer. He was thinking deep again, probably on how this might be the last execution in the old way. She turned her attention to where the reporters had moved their camera near the town hall steps, preparing to take a photograph of the dispersing crowd.

Banny trotted down the steps and bumped into Angus Rice, causing the pudgy man to pitch forward into the camera. He fumbled with the tripod, but couldn't prevent it from toppling to the ground. The camera hit the packed dirt with a painful thud, wood splintering on its delicate frame, and the lens cracked.

McMillian glared at the arrogant hotel owner, but Banny shrugged. "Guess it was in my way. Not good when things get in my way." He glanced at the Tellers, and Ruth Ann held her breath, hoping he wasn't about to lure Matthew into another standoff.

But Rice drew up in front of Banny, shoulders squared. "That is an expensive piece of equipment, young man."

Again, Banny shrugged and strode off toward his hotel. For a moment, it looked as if Matthew was going after him, but Della put a cooling hand on his arm. Matthew changed directions and helped Rice and McMillian pick up the pieces of the camera and examine it. Rice declared it ruined and sighed. "We'll have to get another one in Paris. I hope they have a suitable selection."

"May I take a look?"

From the thinning crowd, a man came slowly, hesitantly forward. Ruth Ann didn't recognize him, but that wasn't unusual with all the new settlers coming into town. Still, this man was different. He was white—had to be even though his features didn't quite match the typical white man. He wasn't a mixed-blood—black or Indian. He was just...different. Even his speech was odd, though so low she could scarcely make out his words.

He came up to them, carefully withdrawing tiny spectacles from his vest pocket. Their smallness matched the equally small man, both thin as a whisper. He even bent slightly at the waist like an old man, making him that much shorter than the other men in the group. Ruth Ann almost expected him to tremble, but when Mr. Rice nodded, the small man reached out with perfectly steady hands. He took the damaged camera and turned it this way and that, while *hmms* came through his pressed lips.

"Mm, hmm," he murmured, taking the section from Matthew that had broken off. Finally, he gazed at the broken lens. The small man spoke slowly, as if he had been born patient and quiet and had never changed. "I can repair this. Find a new piece to replace this one. The lens—I have one I can use from another camera."

Ruth Ann detected a thick accent, though she couldn't say what it was. It was something even more foreign than the Eastern reporters' New York jargon.

Mr. McMillian raised his eyebrows. "I take it you are a traveling repairman—clocks, watches, cameras. How soon could you have it done?"

Again, the man turned the large boxlike camera over in his small hands. "Three days. Yes, I can do it in three days' time."

Mr. Rice shook his head. "We will need another one before then. We'll simply have to buy one in Paris." He looked suddenly to Matthew. "I like what you're doing, son. I like that you aren't afraid to buck the big boys. Keep it up and you can soon go head-to-head with the *Dickens Herald*.

Nothing wrong with a good fight." He grinned, and Ruth Ann was sure he was being mischievous. It was as though his many years in New York had taught him an appreciation for competition and well, *fighting*, that she would never understand.

"Son, how would you like to be the proud owner of a broken camera to be repaired in three days' time?"

Matthew's jaw went slack, but he quickly recovered and tried to be professional. Ruth Ann wasn't that quick. She stared in amazement at the Eastern reporters who suddenly seemed glad they had made a stop in Dickens, as if they had won some sort of prize.

If only they knew not even the *Dickens Herald* had a camera yet! Maxwell had ordered one from St. Louis, but it was damaged in the freight and they were still arguing over whose fault it was and who should pay. He hadn't gotten around to ordering another one.

Without hesitation, Matthew nodded and shook Mr. Rice's hand. "You have a deal. I mean, I certainly appreciate this."

Rice motioned toward his tripod. "This goes with it. Looks like a leg was bent. But I don't believe in giving something away for nothing. You have to do something for me."

A worried look crossed Matthew's face, and Ruth Ann wondered what in the world they could offer a big city newspaper editor. But Rice grinned. "You knock that *Herald* to its knees so they're on your level. That way it'll be a fair fight."

Matthew smiled. "I report what really happens and not what a select few want that's best for them."

Rice nodded and turned to the repairman, who was practically taking the camera apart while they talked. Amazingly, his short fingers dropped nothing as he kept the large camera perfectly balanced in one hand. Rice said, "One more thing. You'll have to settle up with the repairman on your own. I'm sure you'll find a way."

While Matthew agreed to the terms, a Choctaw boy shyly approached the group, holding a muddied derby hat. Rice laughed and took it. "Thank you, son. I do believe this came flying off when we rushed to see the shoot-out." He winked at Matthew. "Never look back when you have a story in front of you."

"Yes, sir." Again, Matthew shook their hands, and they said their goodbyes to Della and Ruth Ann before heading back to the hotel. They would catch the morning train to Paris after more looking around Dickens.

Only after they had disappeared inside the hotel did Ruth Ann realize those men had likely saved her brother's life. Banny would have killed him sure as anything, if the reporters hadn't intervened. She had a feeling that was what they had intended all along, rather than making an attempt to document the shoot-out.

As that realization sank in, Ruth Ann started trembling, enormous terror and anger overcoming her at the thought of how she'd very nearly lost her brother. Without warning, she spun on Matthew, swinging her balled fist into his stomach.

He gasped and doubled over in mid-speech while talking with the repairman. The man stepped back, eyes wide as he clutched the camera case with alarm. Matthew coughed and snapped in Choctaw, "What are you doing, crazy woman?"

Della watched her children silently. Ruth Ann straightened her shawl and lifted her chin. She replied in English, "I'm not so crazy as you are, trying to get yourself killed. What would we do then?"

"So you try to kill me yourself?" Matthew, still bent, shook his head and looked to the repairman. "I'm sorry. My sister is crazy sometimes."

Ruth Ann drew back her fist again, but Della cleared her throat and Ruth Ann dropped her hand with a sigh. She looked at the small man. "I'm Ruth Ann Teller, and if I'm crazy, it's crazy with worry that my brother seems bent on getting himself killed."

With an agitated sigh, Matthew said, "I'm Matthew Teller

and this is my mother, Della. You're a traveling peddler?" He made it a question, looking at the man who relaxed slightly at the change in demeanor among the family.

"No. Well, yes, of sorts. I hope to not continue traveling. I purchased a permit to open a business in the Choctaw Nation. I wish to settle here with my daughter and open a timepiece repair shop." He lifted the case with a smile. "And cameras as there is need. My name is Henry…um, Henry Smith."

Ruth Ann noted the way the man's eyes darted to the side. If her brother thought anything of it, it didn't show. He nodded. "Mr. Smith, I'll pay you for the camera repair but I don't know when."

Henry Smith met Matthew's eyes and smiled. "Perhaps we might come to a reasonable agreement. I will need advertisement for my new shop. You have a newspaper. I see no reason we cannot make a deal, as you westerners like to say."

Matthew offered his hand then laughed when Mr. Smith tried to shake it while still protectively holding the camera case. "Come to the print shop tomorrow and I'll take care of whatever you need. Or if she behaves, I may let Annie look after it." He managed to dodge Ruth Ann's swat at his shoulder. Della shook her head and walked to where Uncle Preston was loading his family into the wagon.

Ruth Ann suddenly felt shy about seeing her relatives. She didn't know what Matthew had decided about moving to the cabin on Uncle Preston's farm, or even what her mother thought of the whole thing. They had agreed to the move into town with Matthew when he said he would not leave them behind and strike out on his own. He felt keenly the responsibility of looking after them and knew they respected his decisions.

The three would have to make the choice together, and Ruth Ann didn't know where her heart's desire lay. Going back to the ranch where there was safety and more family was most appealing, yet there was purpose here in Dickens. The

Choctaw Tribune would do well. She knew it and so did Matthew. They were both educated and hard-working, an ideal combination for the undertaking. They had proven they could do it. But it was hard, and with bullets starting to fly Ruth Ann would just as soon get out of their path.

Matthew and Mr. Smith conversed a few more minutes before the man left with the pieces of his project. Ruth Ann watched him, noting the covered wagon the man placed the camera and tripod in. The side of the wagon was loaded with wood chairs, crates, and a barrel tied securely with rope. He appeared to speak with someone inside the wagon before climbing onto the seat and clucking at his tired-looking mules. They rattled off and soon disappeared down the crossroad. It would be interesting to speak with him again when he came to talk about advertising.

But the first visitor in the print shop the next morning was not whom Matthew or Ruth Ann expected. Not at all.

CHAPTER ELEVEN

THE NEXT MORNING, BEULAH LEVITT did nothing for several seconds but stare at the piece of paper her father had handed her before turning away to continue inspecting the broken camera. He sat on a wood crate left over in the backroom of the barbershop, a room no more than a dirty space, nothing important. Nor would it ever be if Beulah accepted what her father had written.

Henry Smith. Smith... No, she mustn't accept that at all, the way she had before. What would her mother have said? Once she recovered from mortification at the very idea, she would set her husband straight and instill a pride he couldn't back down from. But her mother was dead and gone, and Beulah wasn't in a position to set her father straight on anything.

But this had to be done. Beulah lifted her chin and moved next to her father at the makeshift workstation he'd created with the scattering of wood crates in the storeroom. She lifted a pencil from her jacket pocket and boldly laid the paper near him as she bent over and drew two slow, harsh lines through *Smith*.

Her father looked at the paper through his spectacles,

never shifting his hold on the large camera. He then lifted his eyes to look at Beulah over the rim of his glasses. She steadily met his gaze, then over the top of the false name, she wrote "Levitt" in bold letters.

When her father frowned, she let a knowing smile play on her lips, a tactic that had worked often enough for her mother. "Thou shalt not lie." Another of her mother's tactics; from the agitated look on her patient father's face, he remembered it.

Without a word, he shook his head and turned back to his work, sanding off the splintered corners of the wood camera frame.

With this victory, Beulah turned and took up a shawl and her reticule for departure. She hesitated, then smoothed the piece of paper against the rough wall and swiftly added another advertisement below her father's.

Beulah sighed in contentment. It was time to embrace the woman her mother raised her to be, in every way. It was time to stand up to her own responsibilities.

Yet not in the rebellious spirit of her youth.

That last thought in mind, Beulah halted her hasty flight, paper tucked in her reticule. She spun back to the makeshift workshop, this forlorn place they found themselves in, and put both hands on her father's shoulders. She bent and pecked him on the cheek before hurrying for the door once again. Her father's gentle voice followed her out. "Do not be gone long, daughter."

♦♦♦

The print shop was quiet early that morning as Ruth Ann set the type for the front-page story—the execution of Choctaw Silas Sloan. It was a hard story to read, so she paid attention to only one word at a time, not the sentences they formed. This slowed her, but there was time. Matthew was out drumming up new advertisers, or at least trying to, and Ruth Ann felt at peace that he thought it safe enough for her to return to her work at the print shop.

Last night at dinner, the family hadn't discussed Uncle Preston's offer. In fact, they hadn't discussed anything. Respectful silence seemed appropriate after the day's events. Though Matthew was excited about meeting the Eastern reporters and getting the first camera in Dickens, he sat somberly at the table after writing the front page article. They contemplated the Choctaw way and what was changing around them, but no words were needed. They were a part of something no one could fully understand, not even them. They could only live in that moment of time.

These thoughts occupied Ruth Ann's mind as her neck began its familiar ache. She sat on a high stool that boosted her up to just above the angled desktop of the cabinet that housed the type pieces. It would take an hour to complete setting type for the article, but she always managed. They would print the edition in Choctaw and English that afternoon and evening, then deliver them tomorrow.

Behind her, the door opened with a gust of wind that warned the mild fall was quickly shifting to winter. Expecting Mr. Smith, Ruth Ann rotated on her high stool with a smile that faded in an instant as the door closed.

Jake Banny stood there with a smile as he looked around the room. There wasn't much to see—the large letterpress printing press in the middle of the wood floor, a long prep table with blank paper along the left wall, Matthew's handmade oak desk and swivel chair near the right wall with a single armchair in front of it for visitors, the cast iron stove ablaze, and the tall typesetting cabinet Ruth Ann sat by near the back.

She froze in place.

As usual, Banny wore a Colt six-shooter on his hip, thumb resting casually in the crook of the hammer as he moved further into the room. Ruth Ann's mind snapped to the gun Matthew had stowed in his desk drawer. She hadn't often handled the pistol, but it wouldn't be any use now. Banny was between her and the desk as he eyed her up and down. "You look scared, girl. Something wrong?"

Ruth Ann cleared her throat. "May I help you with something?" Her voice was a mere squeak and she prayed for Matthew to walk through the door. Or Mr. Smith. Anyone.

They didn't.

Instead, Banny leaned against the printing press, looking it over as if interested in the machine. "Fine press you have here. Turns out a first-rate newspaper according to some no-account Easterners. They don't know much about your kind, do they?" Again, Banny brought his eyes over her as she tried to slowly but calmly get to her feet, hands folded in front of her.

He grinned, though no hint of humor showed on his face. "But you're mighty fine, girl. Mighty fine for an Indian." He pushed off the press and stepped toward her.

A spare iron handle lay on the prep table, and without thinking Ruth Ann lunged for it, grasped it firmly, and turned to Banny. "If you want to place an advertisement in the paper, you may speak to my brother. And now, you may leave."

Banny straightened in surprise and then laughed. "Feisty, aren't you? Like your pretty mama when she up and shoved the mayor right off her porch. 'Course, the mayor's a pushover." The false humor left his face. "Don't ever make the mistake of thinking I am."

His demeanor shifted suddenly and he acted like a business owner instead of a rank gunslinger. "You got me off track. I came with a bit of news for the *Choctaw Tribune*, something the *Dickens Herald* doesn't know about yet. News hasn't gotten around town. Your brother can be the first to break it in tomorrow's edition."

Caught off guard by his change in attitude, Ruth Ann lowered the handle slightly but stayed ready to use it. "What happened?"

"Seems a white man by the name of Crandall Murphy went to Paris on the train yesterday and found some whiskey at a warehouse near the depot. Came back roaring drunk and got in a fight with his brother-in-law seven miles north of here. Shot him dead with a shotgun. Ranch hand saw the whole thing. Knocked him out and hogtied him in the barn. Came here to see if the U.S. marshal might be around with all the killings lately, but I told him it was all Choctaw business, no marshal came. So the ranch hand went on over to Spencerville for help."

Banny hooked his thumb over the hammer of his Colt again and shrugged. "Thought you could use a juicy bit of news to spruce up your paper."

Still leery, Ruth Ann gave a cautious nod. "Thank you."

When she made no effort at further conversation, Banny tipped his hat and left as quietly as he'd come.

Ruth Ann let the handle of the press clatter back onto the table, unsure if she had overreacted to the visit and confused about what kind of person Banny was. She tried to connect him to the angry man who had called her brother out for a gunfight, but his parting words blurred the memory. Why would he want to help the *Choctaw Tribune*? Yesterday, he tried to make certain it never published another word. If this was to be their last issue, such a story as the one he'd brought would be a valuable addition.

Whatever his reasons, she was glad he was gone.

No sooner had this thought entered her mind than the door burst open again. With a gasp, Ruth Ann reached for the iron handle but halted when she saw the billowing skirt caught by a wind gust before the young woman could close the door behind her. Coughing from the dust, she used both hands to swish her long blonde hair back from where it had escaped from under her lace-trimmed bonnet.

When she looked up, Ruth Ann was lost in the depth of her blue eyes that stood out so clearly next to her fair complexion. Her constrained but fashionable navy-blue dress gave her the look of a serious and proper school teacher. There was an undeniable elegance there too, in the white collared shirt with dark trim on the cuffed sleeves she wore beneath the dress.

The taller woman smiled, chin high and strong but

friendly. "Hello," she said, accent thick but understandable. "I believe you met my father yesterday. He's doing work in exchange for advertisement in your newspaper. I have come to see about that."

Relieved, Ruth Ann wiped her soiled hands on her ink-stained apron and strode forward. "Pleased to meet you. I'm Ruth Ann Teller. My brother, Matthew, owns the newspaper, but I help handle the advertising. I'd shake your hand, but you'd get more than you bargained for."

The woman laughed, a genteel little bell sound. She wasn't small like her father, and had the presence and strength of a lioness, perhaps inherited from a strong mother. Not that Ruth Ann thought anything ill of Mr. Smith, but she wondered how such a slight and gentle man might survive in the near wilderness of Dickens.

"I am certain a little ink would not make me melt. I have helped my father often enough in his work to fear neither oil nor grease nor ink." The daughter opened her reticule and withdrew a neatly folded piece of paper. Instead of handing it over, she stood a moment, studying Ruth Ann. She still smiled, but signs of hesitation showed in her eyes for the first time. "Perhaps your brother might not want to run the advertisement after all. There could be…problems."

The idea almost caused Ruth Ann to laugh aloud. Matthew had already proven he had no intention of avoiding trouble with the things he printed. Now that he was getting a camera and new advertisers, it looked like the *Choctaw Tribune* might stay in trouble awhile. "As long as my brother is the publisher, he will good and well print what he pleases."

The smile faltered a bit but remained brave as the woman handed over the slip of paper. Ruth Ann took it and read not one, but two advertisements. The first said:

LEVITT REPAIR SHOP. Clocks and watches, and cameras. Reasonable rates. Henry Levitt, Proprietor. Main Street in the Barbershop.

Two things stood out from the advertisement. One, the "and" between clocks and watches had been scratched out and "cameras" was written above "Reasonable rates." The next thing that stood out, more importantly, was the name "Smith" had been crossed out with two bold pencil marks and "Levitt" written above it in both places.

The second advertisement was even bolder.

Violin and singing lessons. Mathematics Tutoring. See Beulah Levitt in the Levitt Repair Shop.

Ruth Ann looked up at the now pensive young woman. "Are you Beulah?"

"Yes."

"Your father is Henry Smith Levitt?"

Beulah Levitt tightened her lips. "You may leave any reference to 'Smith' off the advertisement. My father was…concerned his real name might not be well received, even in obtaining that nasty back room at the barbershop to work from temporarily."

Everything fell into place for Ruth Ann. Now that she looked passed Beulah's blonde hair and blue eyes, she saw the distinct nose. The accent, the names, the fear…

"You're Jewish? From…" She couldn't venture a right guess, but when Beulah offered nothing, she persisted, "Romania? Poland? Germany—"

"Russia," Beulah finished. "We have been in America for ten years, living first in New York, then Kansas. Drought destroyed our farms, and our colony dispersed. Without the strength of a community, things have been difficult. And then my mother died…" Beulah hesitated, her eyes glistening. "…two years ago. My father—it has been difficult for him, especially when something triggers memories of the old days in Russia when the state police harassed him. Once, they came to our home in the middle of the night and rousted him from bed. They took him outside and…"

Her exterior strength faltered and she drowned Ruth Ann in the deep well of her blue eyes. "He still has nightmares at times. But why am I telling you this? We speak of our past to no one. They do not need to know of our struggles. Who are you to understand?"

Ruth Ann ran her fingers over the printing press, thinking of the trouble it had already caused and what it may bring in the future. It could get Matthew killed. It could even get her killed. But maybe, just maybe, if it was more powerful than anything except God Almighty, like Matthew said, maybe it was worth dying for. If they could do good for folks like the Levitts. And Silas Sloan. And the untold number of people who would live for generations to come on her tribe's land.

Once more, she unfolded the slip of paper with its pristine writing and scratched-out words. "Oh, I don't know why, but I think you somehow know that I *do* understand. Maybe we can understand each other more in the days to come."

She reached her inky hand out. Beulah gave it a firm shake with her confident smile back in place. "I think that may be possible, Ruth Ann Teller. And now, let's talk business."

A strange excitement came over Ruth Ann as she had Beulah sit in the visitor's chair while she perched on the edge of Matthew's desk chair. It was the first time the visitor's chair had been used properly by a real customer. Maybe the *Choctaw Tribune* was in business after all.

A business-minded woman, Beulah Levitt was. Sharp and savvy, she bargained for not one or two advertisements in exchange for her father's work and supplies, but a whole three months. Ruth Ann agreed, hoping Matthew wouldn't be upset with her. But she had a feeling he would forget any such things once he developed his first photograph.

CHAPTER TWELVE

"THAT'S AN INTERESTING STORY." THE way Matthew said it meant he was thinking something else, in a different context.

Beulah Levitt had left before he arrived back at the print shop after regaining two of his advertisers who had quit over the Silas Sloan story. Mr. Bates said he didn't care what others thought and that he still believed advertising in the *Choctaw Tribune* was a good investment. The blacksmith owner, Charlie Simms, agreed to reinstate his former block about his shop. As a Choctaw, he viewed the execution differently, and something about pride and heritage had won out over threats made toward his business by the mayor or anyone else.

Of course, they all knew the driving factor was the Eastern reporters who had taken a shine to the *Tribune*, giving Matthew an edge. At least for now. Once the freshness of their visit wore off and their prestige forgotten, the Tellers would be back where they started. Which was all the more reason to bolster their work now, become established to the point no one or no story could run them out of business.

Which was why Ruth Ann skipped telling Matthew the story about the Levitts and shared Banny's tidbit of news before Matthew could even sit at his desk. He looked tired, worn out from the events and impending shutdown of the paper. He only half-listened to the rest of her retelling Banny's story before he repeated, "Interesting."

Ruth Ann had left out any mention of the other things Banny said, and if Matthew had paid attention, he would have noticed her nervousness when speaking about the man. But instead, Matthew rocked back in his swivel chair and interlaced his fingers behind his neck. He stared at the press a long moment. "I'm thinking on selling the equipment and moving back to Uncle Preston's."

Shocked, Ruth Ann sank into the visitor's chair, which less than an hour before had held its first official visitor to the makeshift newspaper office. "But...but how can you think that? Why would you...?"

With an explosion of frustration, Ruth Ann struck the desk with her balled fist, surprising both of them as it caused a pencil to roll off and onto the floor. "Matthew! Here you near get yourself killed over *one* story, determined nothing will stop you from printing the real news. Now when things are going good, you want to up and quit? Are you addled in the head?"

Matthew dropped his hands and rocked forward, eyebrows raised at her outburst. "Since when are you so set on keeping the newspaper going? I thought you'd be glad to move back to the farm, get away from this town living." He cocked his head with a frown, as if noticing something about her for the first time. "I know you've had your own problems here, being a...a..."

"Woman?" Ruth Ann straightened her spine, thinking of Beulah and how strong and sure she was while still being feminine. "Well, I can still set type faster than you, and I want to see truth told, not fabricated stories of how glorious and civilized this town is."

Matthew smiled and looked out the window. "I was trying to find the right adjective. Maybe beautiful. But you summed it up. A woman. When did that happen?" He murmured the last part and shook his head. "If you want truth told, best remember the rules of reporting. Check the source. Banny isn't what I'd call a reliable one, and what I heard from Charlie Simms lines up with that."

Settling down, Ruth Ann ignored the jab at her reporting skills. She knew as well as any not to trust Banny. Maybe more than any. She leaned forward. "What did you hear?"

"I heard that Crandall Murphy, the man accused of shooting his brother-in-law, didn't make a trip to Paris. He got his whiskey right here. In Dickens."

Ruth Ann gasped and scooted to the edge of her seat. It was clear, but she still asked, "From whom?"

"Can't prove anything, but Charlie said Murphy came stumbling to the blacksmith shop in the middle of the night and woke him up trying to saddle his mule. Instead, he was saddling Charlie's gelding. Charlie got him straightened out, saw he was stone drunk, but didn't ask questions. Just pointed the mule toward the man's home. Charlie didn't say where he thought the whiskey came from, but he did say Murphy stabled his mule around suppertime, which was after the train left for Paris. Meaning he likely bought his whiskey right around here."

Agitated, Ruth Ann repeated, "From whom? It's Jake Banny, isn't it? He's been after the mayor about letting him put a saloon in the hotel. He knows it's illegal, but he figures to get away with it if the *Dickens Herald*, or the mayor, or no one else gets word out to the Indian agent."

"Except the *Choctaw Tribune*."

Ruth Ann leaned back with a shaky breath. No wonder Banny had so kindly surrendered the information. "That's why he wants you dead or at least running false news."

She hugged herself, thinking of the peacefulness on Uncle Preston's farm. Northern geese would be settling on the lake about now, on their way further south. Or they might take to the milder climate of Indian Territory and stay on—if too many of them didn't end up prey to Uncle Preston's sharpshooting. A roasted goose for dinner sounded more than tasty, especially when Ruth Ann realized they had once again forgotten to go home for lunch.

Matthew shuffled through the handwritten notes scattered among Eastern newspapers on his jumbled desk he insisted Ruth Ann not organize. "What's this?" He read the note written by Beulah Levitt's hand.

"Henry Levitt's daughter came by and wants to run those advertisements in exchange for his work."

"Levitt?" Matthew raised his eyebrows again, this time with a reporter's curiosity.

Remembering the excitement she'd felt when sitting behind the desk and working like a real newswoman, Ruth Ann summoned a measure of enthusiasm as she told the Levitts' story from Russia to Indian Territory, and how she didn't think Beulah would want any of that in the newspaper. Her openness with Ruth Ann appeared to be an exception.

Matthew nodded. "I'll see if I can get a story out of Mr. Smith…Mr. Levitt sometime." Looking at Ruth Ann's notes on the advertisement, he mumbled, "He'll end up owing me at the end of three months."

♦♦♦

The *Tribune's* next edition featured the execution of Silas Sloan. But also front page was the killing of Lewis Webb, a farmer shot dead by his brother-in-law, Crandall Murphy. After investigation by the Spencerville sheriff, Matthew reported, there was little doubt as to Murphy's guilt. Mr. Webb's wife confirmed it was her brother, stone drunk and mean, who killed her husband in a late-night rampage. She didn't say where he might have gotten the whiskey, and the sheriff didn't ask. At least that was what he told Matthew. The Spencerville sheriff was known to run his own whiskey still in slack times.

But, the news report said, it was also known Crandall Murphy had come to Dickens sober and left drunk. Nothing about the Paris train as Banny had said.

Soon, the whole town whispered about where Murphy

had gotten his whiskey, though most of them likely knew it was from Banny. Plenty of men in town probably bought secretly from him, and it was sure to be known by Mayor Warren and Mr. Maxwell, editor of the *Dickens Herald*, who put out a very different story from Matthew's.

Maxwell reported that Crandall Murphy was a mean man to begin with, always bound to end up on the short end of a rope. There was bad blood between the men, the *Herald* said, and things were destined for one to kill the other some day. Also, the *Herald* suggested it could have been self-defense. The story left off the fact that no one, including the sheriff, speculated this, nor had Crandall Murphy claimed it.

But there it all was, in black-and-white print as if it were the pure gospel itself. Ruth Ann wasn't surprised when Matthew slapped a copy of the *Dickens Herald* down on the chest table in front of their sofa. "That's why the *Choctaw Tribune* exists!"

He fumed and fussed while Della sat quietly in her rocker, crocheting. She had a little smile on her face, as though recalling fond memories. If Ruth Ann ventured a guess, she'd say her mother was thinking of Daddy and how passionate he used to get over politics and such. The older Matthew got, the more he acted just like their father.

Soft footsteps approaching the door distracted Ruth Ann from Matthew's diatribe. She had laid aside her Bible to reach for the *Herald*. Now she froze at the sound of boots on their porch. Matthew heard it too and stood as a knock began. It was hesitant and unsure, making Ruth Ann wonder if it was Mr. Levitt, come to talk about not running the advertisement with his real name as his daughter had insisted.

But it wasn't Mr. Levitt.

Matthew opened the door to reveal Mr. Carter. The freight office owner held his hat in hand, running his fingers anxiously around the brim. Matthew invited him in and Carter stepped inside, clearing his throat and nodding to the women. When Della rose to fetch refreshments, he waved his hand. "Please, ma'am, I can't stay. Just need to speak with Matthew a minute." Glancing at him but not quite meeting Matthew's gaze, he asked, "Can we step out on the porch?"

Matthew crossed his arms, bringing to Ruth Ann's mind the last time Carter had visited. Carter had had an advantage then, with Mayor Warren and Banny. Now he fidgeted so, she wondered how he'd ever had the backbone to launch a successful freight business. But people changed. She knew from rumors of before they came to live in town how Mr. Carter used to be a cheerful, nice man. Then his Choctaw wife and son died of a fever. Seemed he was a shell of what he once was, and that didn't leave much.

But those thoughts must not have come to Matthew, because he stood as if to show no mercy to the nervous man. "My mother and sister are involved in all my doings. Anything you want to say to me you may say in front of them, but I warn you not to abuse that."

With an agitated sigh, Carter finally brought his head up with a frown. "You need to vacate my storeroom. Town's growing and I need the building for what it's meant for—storage."

Ruth Ann came to her feet, unsure how she felt. Without a building for the newspaper office and print shop, they could not continue the *Tribune*. With all the controversies, it was highly unlikely they could get another building.

No question or decision remained about moving to Uncle Preston's. They had to. Ruth Ann couldn't decide if it was immense relief or a fighting anger that filled the pit of her stomach. Maybe both. She had nothing to say, but she couldn't sit either. She moved to Matthew's side where he stood near the door, staring hard at Carter.

When the man showed no sign of backing down, Matthew turned and strode to the chest table. With one swipe of his long arm, he cleared it off, sending newspapers, tablets, and two balls of yarn to the hardwood floor. Della shrieked and scolded him in Choctaw. Matthew said something quietly to her as he lifted the lid of the chest and heaved out a large wooden box. Plopping it on the floor, he flipped the lid up and rummaged through bits of paper. He grabbed a folded piece of brown parchment, the kind Mr. Bates used to wrap meat.

Carter froze at the sight of it, and Ruth Ann let out a long breath as she realized what it was and what Matthew had decided about the *Choctaw Tribune*.

Coming back to them, Matthew thrust the folded paper toward the man, but Carter ignored it, narrowing his eyes as if his backbone was being replenished. "I know what that is. That unofficial lease thing you wanted drawn up about the building. I don't care that it says you get eight more months. I want you out. Now." Carter backed to the door and fumbled it open. He stepped onto the porch and glanced back with a polite nod to Della before slamming the door behind him.

Ruth Ann sighed, her feelings mixed with disappointment that they really were going to stay in town—in ridicule and in danger. At the same time, she couldn't hide her excitement over the prospect. She looked at Matthew. He winked at her.

Della grunted and pointed with her chin at the mess on the floor. "Every last scrap. Clean it up. Every last scrap. And while you're down there, wipe the chest with a rag and polish the wood. Every square inch." She laid her crochet project in her sewing basket and headed toward the stairs off the kitchen. She glanced back. "Every last scrap. Every square inch. Do not come up until it's done."

Her footsteps sounded loud as she thumped up the stairs. Ruth Ann laughed softly, and Matthew punched his hand. "You'll see, Annie. The pen is mightier than the sword, and there is nothing short of God Almighty more powerful than the press!"

Maybe. Maybe it was true after all. Their paper had enough influence to scare men like Banny, who knew it was only a matter of time until the *Choctaw Tribune* forced his illegal operations into the open. He was scared enough to pressure Carter to try to get his building back.

But that hadn't stopped the *Tribune* from seeking the

truth about the whiskey runner. Nothing would now.

CHAPTER THIRTEEN

NIGHT-WALKING BROUGHT A STRANGE comfort Henry Levitt's dear wife had never understood. His daughter didn't understand it either. Truth told, Henry himself didn't understand. He only knew he had to do it, even on this, his second night in a new and strange town.

It wasn't like walking through the peaceful colony they'd enjoyed in Kansas. It didn't compare to the sounds of an alive but content forest they camped in on their travels to Indian Territory. This was a town, one filled with men who viewed each other as enemies, yet one with the semblance of faith and courage he sought every night.

Staying in the shadows, Henry passed Bates General Store, long closed after a productive day. One thing Henry had observed in his short time in town was that the rumors of prosperity in Dickens had proved true. It was an ideal place to start over once again.

Except he had wanted to start over as Henry Smith, not Henry Levitt. But what was he to do with such a strong-willed daughter? So much like her mother, the reason he found himself tolerating her behavior since her mother's death.

Ah, sweet Beulah. He'd chosen the name to represent

hopes to be realized, a promised land where they could find peace and solitude. Some day. It had been true for some of the time, and not for others. What kind of times did they face with the truth of who they were?

A growl sounded from under the porch of Bates' store, causing Henry to jump. Then, with a smile, he squatted and gazed under the porch until his eyes detected the furry form, hovered protectively over her whelps. "There, there, now little ones. It's only Henry Levitt, a poor Jewish man far from home. But as you have found seclusion under this porch, may we find seclusion and peace in this place."

He straightened and continued his walk and thoughts. From Beulah's report, the Tellers would be accepting of them. Ruth Ann, the lovely child, seemed to have established a bond with his daughter. But as Henry had witnessed, the Tellers had problems of their own as mixed-bloods with a foot in two worlds. He was anxious to know more about them.

Henry looked up the street toward where he knew the makeshift print shop was. Humble beginnings were never shameful, even if they never blossomed.

"Abba, You have brought us to this place. May we do something good for these people..." Henry's voice trailed off as a poignant smell, carried along the breeze, halted him. He squinted, thankful he still had vision for far range. He was not thankful for what he saw. A golden flame shot from the side of the newspaper office before retreating once again.

Frozen with visions of his village burning when he was a boy, Henry dug his fingernails into the palms of his hands, willing himself to move, to flee, to forget.

Fire, fire, fire!

Burn it down! the men had shouted. *They have innocent blood on their heads!*

"Papa...Mother..." Henry whispered. *Fire, fire!* his mind screamed. It was several seconds before he realized he had screamed the words aloud.

◆◆◆

"Fire!" A voice roared somewhere in the recesses of Ruth Ann's mind in her semiconscious state. Perhaps it was only a dream. With all the frightening things happening, the next horrible thing would be—

"Fire?" She sat up in her bed to hear the thump of boots on the other side of the partition in their upstairs bedroom.

"There's a fire, Annie." Matthew's voice sounded groggy but coherent from the other side of the partition. A light blazed in her vision, causing her to rub her eyes as Della lit their oil lamp.

By the time Ruth Ann realized she wasn't in a dream but a real-life nightmare, Matthew was already thundering down the stairs and Della had pulled her dress right over her nightgown and yanked her boots on.

Ruth Ann struggled to do the same, but her stubborn boot refused her foot entrance. When her mother trotted for the stairs, Ruth Ann abandoned her efforts and followed after Della in her bare feet.

It wasn't their house on fire. That much she comprehended. No smoke or flames in sight until Ruth Ann hit the last step and stumbled through the kitchen into the front room. Through the drawn lace curtain, she saw angry flames leaping over a small structure down and across the street from them. A very familiar place.

"No!" Ruth Ann's voice was raw, like it had been the day they told her that her father and brother were never coming home.

Della bumped past her with soggy wet blankets she had doused at the pump in the kitchen. She shoved them into Ruth Ann's numb arms and threw open the door before charging toward the crowd gathering around the burning structure. Ruth Ann couldn't move until she saw the door of the engulfed newspaper office fly open and Matthew run inside.

"No." This time it was a whisper, but enough to get her bare feet moving in that direction. Then she was running with the heavy blankets clutched close.

"Stand back!" someone shouted, and most did. But not Della. She shoved her way to the front with Ruth Ann behind her. Ruth Ann felt the intense heat on her face despite the cold air. Della grabbed one of the blankets and rushed forward to meet Matthew as he staggered through the door, trying to drag the print press. Everyone stayed frozen, but shouted that they needed to douse the other buildings before they caught fire too.

Della slung the wet blanket around Matthew's singed shoulders before trying to grab a solid part to pull on the press that stood nearly as tall as she. Ruth Ann draped the remaining blanket over her own head as she squeezed onto the other side. The press wouldn't budge through the door. It had been assembled inside; it was simply too big to come through.

But they refused to give up, even as the flames reached the doorframe and snaked out at Ruth Ann's arms. She bent and grabbed the back end of the press still inside. She screamed and cried.

Strong hands grabbed her from behind and pulled her aside. She was vaguely aware of soft arms going around her and pulling her further away as she coughed and stumbled.

"No," Ruth Ann whimpered and turned back to see a small man in her place by the press. Fire shot all around it. With heroic strength, he tipped the press sideways and yanked it through the disintegrating doorway. With a final effort, Matthew and Mr. Levitt hauled the heavy machine free of danger.

Matthew shouted at Mr. Levitt, "Do you smell it?"

Ruth Ann had no idea what he meant as her sobs softened and trembling overtook her body. Instead of standing back to watch the flames devour the building, Matthew ran inside once again, blanket wrapped around his head and mouth.

Della screamed. Ruth Ann pulled from the comforting arms of Beulah Levitt and tripped to her knees. Before she could get up, Matthew emerged, coughing violently and dragging the blanket in the dirt.

But he stayed on his feet and walked in a zigzag line straight toward someone. It took a moment for Ruth Ann to see in the darkness lit by the roaring flames, but she made out Jake Banny's smug expression as Matthew came to stand in front of him.

Suddenly, Ruth Ann smelled it. Close. She sniffed her sleeve. Mingled with the heavy scent of smoke was a disgusting odor she'd gotten from rubbing against the printing press. It struck her with such force she choked on the realization.

Whiskey. The press had been doused with rotgut whiskey.

Throwing aside his smoldering blanket, Matthew whipped his Colt from his holster. He placed the end of the barrel to Banny's forehead. Banny dropped his folded arms and smug look, eyes wide with shock as he stared into the grim and soot-streaked face of one angry, stubborn Choctaw.

Calmly, Matthew asked for all to hear, "You do this?"

Banny said nothing, his face drawn but unafraid.

Ruth Ann whimpered, not daring to look at her mother who she knew was praying.

It was Mr. Levitt who made the next move by coming to Matthew's side and placing a hand on his gun arm. "Son, you do not want to do this. It is a bad thing to take a man's life. Let him live, and you will live in greater peace."

Matthew didn't move for a minute. Then, keeping his body perfectly still, he lifted the gun barrel slightly and uncocked the hammer. Banny still said nothing aloud, but his eyes said he would make sure Matthew regretted his actions.

But Matthew had the last word. "Stay away from me and mine, Banny. I won't forgive so easily again."

All grew strangely quiet as the town watched the print shop with its fine oak desk, work table, typesetting cabinet, and visitor's chair burn to the ground. Most prayed the fire wouldn't spread, taking out half the town. They had no fire engine and no way of forming a bucket line. They could only watch and wait.

Soon, it became apparent the fire would not spread. It was far enough from the freight office that it didn't jump the gap to reach there. On the other side of the print shop was a vacant lot. Without much of a breeze and plenty of rain lately, the danger passed in less than an hour. The problems for the rest of the town were over. But they were only beginning for the *Choctaw Tribune*.

CHAPTER FOURTEEN

RUTH ANN QUIETLY PREPARED BREAKFAST next morning. Della had gone upstairs to tend Matthew's burns, insisting he stay in bed for the day, or at least until his cough subsided. Instead, it grew louder and Ruth Ann heard Della fussing at him. The *clump clump* of his boots sounded on the stairs and he appeared next to the stove where Ruth Ann was scrambling eggs.

She wanted to cry when she saw him. His eyebrows were singed in a haphazard pattern, along with bits and pieces of his hair. A large bandage covered one cheek and jaw. His eyes were bloodshot, and he continued to hack and cough. He didn't look at her, just took himself to the kitchen table and collapsed in the chair, folded his arms and laid his head in them.

Della came down behind him, rattling in Choctaw about how stubborn and crazy he was, about how he was going to get himself an early grave one way or another.

Matthew coughed so hard he had to push himself away from the table and fling open the back door, vomiting. Della continued to rant as she wet a rag from the kitchen pump and shoved it at him. Ruth Ann wanted to scream for silence, but instead she let her tears fall and sizzle on the stove.

She scooped the eggs onto a plate and slammed it in the middle of the table, then set out plates and cutlery. She plopped in her seat and stared blankly. Matthew retook his seat with a shaky breath. Della fell silent and they all knew she wouldn't say anything for some time. Maybe days.

No one ate much of the simple breakfast. Finally, Matthew pushed back from the table. "I'm taking the train down to Paris."

Della's head came up sharply but she said nothing. Ruth Ann choked on the tears in her throat. "Wh-why?"

Matthew put both hands on the table and pushed himself up. "Business," he rasped before turning away. He managed to cross the front room and lift his hat from the peg by the front door. He also lifted his gun belt and strapped it on. He shut the door firmly behind him.

Ruth Ann's shoulders slumped and she dipped her head between them. The *Choctaw Tribune* was doomed. It didn't matter what scheme Matthew was going to try in Paris. That city wouldn't have the equipment he needed, nor did he have the money to purchase any. Uncle Preston, though not enthused about the paper, had staked Matthew in getting started. There was no one else who would loan him that kind of money. They would have to shut the paper down awhile. Probably forever.

◆◆◆

Matthew didn't come home on the afternoon train, meaning he'd have to stay the night in Paris. Doing what, Ruth Ann didn't bother to guess. From the train depot where she'd waited for him, she found herself wandering outside in the gloomy overcast and down the street to the charred remains of the newspaper office. Mr. Levitt had helped Matthew drag the printing press into the vacant lot next to the former storage building, and they covered it with the ruined blankets. No one had bothered the press. The image of

Matthew with his six-shooter had warned everyone off for the time being.

Ruth Ann stood in front of the ashes, trying to comprehend the loss. It was no use. On one hand, it seemed not much could have been lost in the sparse building—on the other hand, the loss was incalculable.

She wondered if she should send for Uncle Preston. It wouldn't be long before he'd hear, though, and come to see about things. That would be soon enough. Matthew hadn't gone to him first, so there was no use interfering with his plan now. If he truly had one, or if desperation had driven him to look for solutions in Paris.

It didn't seem like anything would do much good. Maybe the *Choctaw Tribune* had been doomed from its start. More than once in the past week, they'd faced head-on confrontations, even deadly ones. How could those be a sign God wanted them to continue on?

A sprinkling of activity went on around Ruth Ann as she stood in front of a place she had grown to care for. Without realizing it, she'd fallen in love with the little newspaper, and she felt keenly Matthew's determination to keep it. But there wasn't much could be done, and certainly not by her.

Of all the footsteps she heard avoiding the area, a pair coming toward her on the wood boardwalk caught her ear and she pulled herself down into her shawl. She peeked over her shoulder, fearful to see Banny or Maxwell, come to gloat over the defeat.

But it was neither of the arrogant men. Instead, Mr. Levitt, with Beulah on his arm, came toward her. She was glad to see he didn't appear harmed by the fire, and she wanted to thank them for helping in the late-night terror. But she felt no gratefulness for anything in her heart. She merely nodded to them and turned back to the mess. Mr. Levitt sighed behind her. "A sad thing. How is your brother?"

Ruth Ann shrugged but knew that wasn't a sufficient or polite answer. "Stubborn. Burned up some. He went to Paris this morning to take care of business. Don't know what."

Beulah came to stand beside her. She reached out and rubbed one hand briskly up and down Ruth Ann's arm as if to infuse her with courage. "You must not give up. You cannot let them defeat you. You will not have peace if you—"

"Daughter." Mr. Levitt spoke softly but with authority. He looked at Ruth Ann. "She is much like her mother, not one to back away from a fight, be it over the price of a side of beef or taking a gun after horse thieves. Ah yes, she did that. But me..." He shrugged. "I take night walks to remind myself I have nothing to fear. It is my own conquering, small it may be. At least it resulted in some good, or perhaps bad. I was able to alert my new town of the fire, but..." He gazed over at the printing press, still draped in blankets. "Tell me, Ruth Ann Teller, could it have been an accident?"

For this, Ruth Ann had no provable answer. She wasn't sure if Mr. Levitt had witnessed the incident with Jake Banny right before the execution of Silas Sloan. Banny certainly had motivation if he was running illegal whiskey. Though he wouldn't want more bad news coming out of Dickens, would he? Still, the smell of whiskey all over the press was enough to convince Matthew. But without the *Tribune*, he couldn't do anything about it or exposing Banny as a whiskey runner.

Mr. Levitt wouldn't know of Carter's pressure concerning the building itself. In a flash, Ruth Ann wondered if he had gone so far as to burn his own building down with Matthew's equipment just for spite. But no, Mr. Carter wasn't that kind of man. And he would not have endangered his own freight office with such a rash act.

If not Banny or Carter, that left Mr. Levitt's question of a possible accident, but Ruth Ann was certain of the malice toward the newspaper and shook her head with no definite answer. "Thank you, sir, for helping last night. Matthew would have killed himself trying to save that press. I don't know why though. We can't put it in our home, and it's not likely anyone will lease to us with all these happenings. Not that there are many vacant buildings to be had. And we lost most everything but the press. I suppose Matthew's looking for replacements in Paris, but…"

She didn't want to talk about their lack of funds or the concern that the city might not even have what they needed. Paris was far in advance of Dickens to be sure, but it wasn't like St. Louis. And sending off for an order there could take weeks.

With a quick glance to her father, Beulah spoke up, keeping her voice more subdued than before. "What of that large building off the main street? It stands alone and neglected. Who owns it?"

Ruth Ann sighed. "That would be Mayor Warren. He staked claim to a fair bit of Dickens, even appointing himself mayor from the beginning. He built that building in hopes of putting in a furniture shop. He hired an experienced manager from the States, but that man came, took one look at Dickens, and went on down to Paris. The mayor hasn't done anything with the building since. He never stocked it, so it's only a big empty building full of false hopes…."

The more she envisioned it, the more perfect Ruth Ann saw it being. Large picture windows in the front, an open floor plan with ample space…

But there was no way the mayor would lease it to them. He was part of the group who wanted to rid the town of the *Choctaw Tribune*, leaving only the *Dickens Herald* to report the kind of headlines he wanted. "Even if the mayor would lease it, there's no way we could account for that much cost and space. We were barely able to do this little place with its papered walls." Ruth Ann smiled to herself, thinking of how quaint the shop seemed now that it was gone.

"The mayor, you say?" Mr. Levitt was staring off in the distance, and Beulah had a strange, knowing smile on her face. She squeezed Ruth Ann's arm. "I think my father has a plan."

CHAPTER FIFTEEN

THE NEXT AFTERNOON, RUTH ANN spruced up in her pale yellow gingham dress and folded her hair up in the old way with a ribbon, tying it in the center back. She didn't often wear it that way but this was a special occasion.

She checked her image in the mirror, examining it from all sides. She was a young lady indeed. Her bright dove eyes still held a shy look, but her dusty rose lips had sharpened with quiet confidence.

After informing Della she would be gone a bit, Ruth Ann picked up her tablet and headed out and across the street to the train depot. The tablet was in case she heard a snippet of gossip or news. Her real reason for visiting the depot was in hopes that Matthew was on the train back up from Paris.

She could scarcely contain herself at the news she had for him, but she waited patiently—at least on the outside—along with an assortment of characters on the platform. A few looked to be meeting relatives. Then there were a couple of workers from the freight office, hauling a cart up the ramp and to the other end of the platform in anticipation of unloading a delivery.

A small group of ranch hands stood off to one side of

the platform, all in town on various excuses and all waiting to see the train and if any special mail had come in for the boss. Among these, Ruth Ann recognized G.W., the old cowboy she had met who reminded her it didn't matter what color skin a person had. He was free to act the way he wanted and defend anyone he pleased.

At the same time she noticed him, G.W. glanced around and saw her. He tipped his hat and wiped away a stream of tobacco juice that had seeped from the corner of his mouth. Ruth Ann cringed but politely nodded back.

Aside from regular townsfolk waiting on the mail, there was one last group who stood out more than they realized. The unmarried young women of the town made a regular appearance at the depot around the time the train was due. They weren't there to welcome anyone home. They weren't watching for a special letter or catalogue to come in the mail. Truth told, they didn't even know exactly why they were there. It just seemed a good idea to an available young lady to let others know she was available by making a regular appearance at the depot, dressed in her finest with hair done up and cheeks pinched rosy red.

Summer parasols abandoned for winter gloves and scarves, the young ladies were overdressed for the cool but sunshiny day. They did look the part of available young women, cooing to one another and occasionally glancing about with batting eyelashes.

Though Ruth Ann knew most of them and attended church with their families, she only exchanged cordial nods with them. She had no intention of ever wasting such time as they did on a daily basis. There was too much to do, too many responsibilities and challenges and...*life* to be about. Ruth Ann knew she was settling into and embracing that life.

A train whistle brought her back to the task at hand, the reason she had come to the depot. She anxiously watched the hissing, smoking engine as it pulled its load closer to the platform. The engineer blew the whistle in short spurts, alerting horse and foot traffic alike to clear the tracks.

A farm wagon had already crossed, and the team of horses pulling it spooked. The team lurched and ran against the restraining hands of the farmer, who stood from his seat as he pulled full back on the reins, yelling, "Whoa! Whoa now, settle down! It's just a blasted train!"

The team was halfway down Main Street before they calmed, but Ruth Ann paid them little mind. Matthew should be on this train and she had the best news to share with him. Something that would cause him to really understand she was indeed a young woman now, not just a tagalong baby sister as he and Philip had always seen her.

The train whistled once more before the screech of brakes sounded, slowing it to a stop with its passenger cars lined up with the platform. The cargo car doors further down slid open, and the freight office men went to work transferring their shipment onto the push cart. They seemed in a great hurry, but Ruth Ann paid them little mind as she watched each passenger disembark. Matthew wouldn't be the first off, always content with watching others and letting them go first. "Reporters have to be observant, Annie," he would say. "They're the ones who see all the things others don't. That's the kind of news you want."

Ruth Ann tried to practice her skills now, watching and observing everyone, but really, she was only waiting for Matthew. She paid the gaggle of girls little mind as they chatted with a young family that had disembarked. A few more people got off, and the mail was brought forward. Most of the people around the platform began the usual huddle, waiting to see the mail distributed by the postmaster inside the depot.

Agitated, Ruth Ann walked the length of the platform, peeking at the doorway of each passenger car. No sign of Matthew. He hadn't come home yet.

A sudden chill gripped her. What if something had happened to him? He'd traveled by train, not on a lonely mountain road like Daddy and Philip had, but still. What if he'd gotten into a shoot-out with some drunk or outlaw down in Paris? The city was supposedly civilized, but who knew what might happen if there was drink there? What if Matthew had even found whiskey and decided to drown out his troubles…?

Ruth Ann clenched her hands together, neglected tablet tucked under her arm. No. Matthew would never drink. He'd sworn against it like most of the men in her family, knowing how detrimental alcohol was and had been to their people. There was a reason it was illegal, and Matthew would always stay on the side that fought to keep it so. She knew this. But where was he?

Desperate for any news or rumors from Paris, she approached the young man helping unload the freight office shipment. "Excuse me." With all the noise on the platform, he didn't seem to hear her soft voice as he hefted a large wooden crate.

Ruth Ann tapped his shoulder. Startled, he fumbled the crate and one end hit the platform with a thud. The sound of glass clinked inside the crate marked *Linens, Custom Order for Josiah Carter*.

Liquid seeped from one corner. The young man glared at her over his shoulder. He quickly lifted the box and clunked it on the push cart. "What do you want?"

Taken aback, Ruth Ann stuttered, "I…I wondered if there were any special happenings in Paris. Any trouble or—"

"How would I know?" the young man snapped. He glanced around as the freight workers hurried off with their loaded cart. "Look, miss, I work the loading docks. That's it. I don't know nothin' about nothin', you understand?"

The whistle sounded again and the young man hopped back into the cargo car and yanked the door closed.

The train started and soon disappeared from sight. The gaggle of girls sighed and drifted away, cowboys mounted their horses and rode off, townsfolk wandered on, most reading a letter or an Eastern newspaper.

Ruth Ann might as well pick up her family's mail. But as she stepped forward, a strange odor struck her. It was a smell she felt she should know, but with all the people and shipments that had been on the platform, there was no telling what it was. She picked up the mail and started down the steps. The smell was fainter, but still with her. She paused and sniffed. Sudden realization halted her. Sickened her.

Whiskey. She smelled whiskey.

Ruth Ann turned onto the boardwalk leading to the freight office. The smell was stronger here, and a wet line led right to Mr. Carter's place of business where his workers had hauled their push cart with the crate marked *Linens* that actually contained glass.

Glass bottles of whiskey, to be exact.

CHAPTER SIXTEEN

BE SURE YOUR SINS WILL FIND you out. Whether it was a paraphrase he'd heard the preacher use or if it was an actual scripture verse, the words rang far too true for Josiah Carter. The problem was, he'd never seen himself as a bad man. Never set out to be one. It just happened.

No. Things didn't just happen. They resulted from a chain of choices that eventually grew so long they shackled a man. Such was the place he found himself as he sat in front of his fireplace the evening after seeing Matthew Teller face down the gunslinging Banny. The young man had spunk. More than Josiah had at the moment, maybe more than he'd ever had.

He truly never set out to do anything bad. He just hadn't set out to do anything good. Maybe that was the heart of his problem. If he'd been about doing good in the world, maybe that would have kept the bad from ever coming across his path—the temptations, the pressures from the kind of company his mother had warned him to stay away from.

At one point in his life, Josiah had been happy. He adored his Choctaw bride and she him. Their little son was a blend of two cultures, two worlds come together as one, as he and Lucy had. His family and business grew, and so did his happiness. Then the fever struck and ravaged his life in a matter of days. The remnants of his happiness were represented by two graves.

His business suffered in his heartache and lack of will. The mayor and Banny knew his weaknesses and vulnerabilities, taking full advantage of them. Now he was their slave, at their beck and call, night and day. Blackmail was the greatest threat they held over him now, exposure of his fine reputation to all the town and before his church.

Josiah set aside the coffee he realized had gone cold long ago. When had he poured it? Probably before supper. He made it a point not to drink coffee too late in the evening and prevent sleep. He had enough internal enemies who did that.

It took a moment before he realized he'd set the cup on a copy of the latest edition of the *Choctaw Tribune*. Since the paper's founding, he'd read each edition as soon as it was released, as did the other leading men in town. Especially now, with the controversies heating to a boiling point.

Moving the cup aside, Josiah lifted the paper and skimmed past the headline about the execution, and focused on the article alluding to whiskey-running right there in Dickens. If only Matthew Teller knew the rest.

Josiah sighed and rubbed his tired eyes. He never set out to do anything wrong. But he hadn't set out to do anything right, either. He lifted the copy of the *Choctaw Tribune* again. At least someone in the world was willing to do what was right.

◆◆◆

The next day, while the afternoon train came and went, Ruth Ann busied herself with Beulah and Mr. Levitt. She'd left word with her mother for Matthew—surely he had been on *that* train—with instructions on where to find her. Though she was determined to finish the task before he arrived, she couldn't help glancing out the large picture windows often, looking for him.

But when he finally did arrive, near dark, his face was grim and tired, his hands full of leaflets. He swung open the door and stepped inside Mayor Warren's unused building.

Granted, there was little for him to be impressed with. The press sat near the back right corner, all polished and oiled after its scrape with death. Next to it sat a small round table with two tablets and pencils on it. It was far less than the work table and desk they had before, but Mr. Levitt was a carpenter as well as a repairman, and had already offered to help with new furnishings as time and money allowed.

While the newspaper side of the large open room was sparsely furnished, the Levitt Repair Shop was set up for business. As it turned out, Mr. Levitt's wagon had been loaded with all his belongings, primarily for his and Beulah's businesses.

Along the back wall, he had rigged a long table and workbench where various projects already sat, including Matthew's damaged camera. Odds and ends of furniture created by Mr. Levitt filled in the majority of the ample floor space. A huge grandfather clock sat ticking along the wall, an impressive piece in the frontier town. A simple desk with a swivel chair sat close to the front door as if ready to greet customers. Two violins were elegantly displayed in their cases near the desk and picture windows to interest anyone passing by in lessons from Beulah. She would give them in the back room that was to serve as storage.

A newspaper office, repair shop, and music lessons…all under one roof. Ruth Ann couldn't help the proud smile on her lips as she faced Matthew. "Welcome to the offices of the *Choctaw Tribune* and the Levitt Repair and Music Shop. We're all ready for…" Her voice drifted off when Matthew stared at her, lips pinched. Ignoring the Levitts, he strode up to her.

"Ruth Ann, we cannot afford this."

Matthew never called her by her full name unless he was really, really upset with something she'd done. Like the time she'd tried to run off the rest of an edition while Matthew went home for a nap after an all-night effort to get the paper out. They were late but he simply could not finish. Ruth Ann then over-inked the press and ruined the last of the printing paper to the point he couldn't meet the distribution quota he'd promised advertisers.

Matthew didn't speak to her the rest of the day, though later apologized, knowing she had tried to help. They printed the remaining copies on meat-packing paper from Mr. Bates and distributed them a day late, but they still went out and Matthew eventually got over the humiliation and jabbing from his former coworkers at the *Dickens Herald*.

He had that same look on his face now as when he'd seen the ruined copies a few months ago. But Ruth Ann squared her shoulders, determined not to back down. He wasn't the only one allowed stubbornness in this family. "Matthew, it's all arranged. Mr. Levitt is actually the one on the lease at his own insistence. He approached Mayor Warren in a way that, well, we'll just say the mayor paid no mind to the clause Mr. Levitt added in the five-year lease agreement about subleasing to whomever he wished. And he wishes to lease to us. I've been dying for you to get back to sign the papers."

"I can't sign anything." Matthew looked at the press the three had disassembled, brought over, and reassembled inside the new shop. Then he met Mr. Levitt's eyes, as the smaller man stood quietly during the exchange. "I appreciate what you're trying to do, but we have no funds right now." He glared at Ruth Ann. "And what my sister doesn't know is, I've been in Paris arranging to print mini-editions of the *Choctaw Tribune* until we can regroup. It'll be a slower process, but I can make it work. Here's the remaining copies, already distributed through most of town. The boys should be finishing soon."

Matthew tossed the leaflets down on the makeshift table desk then handed them each a copy. He halted when he offered one to Beulah, staring at her. Ruth Ann frowned. Mr. Levitt smiled. "You have not been properly introduced to my daughter, Beulah Levitt."

Beulah tugged the single page from his hand and scanned the headline. "Well, you are not afraid to print your truth."

Ruth Ann looked down at the paper, a simple printing of the *Choctaw Tribune*. But the headline made her gasp.

JAKE BANNY RUNS ILLEGAL WHISKEY, BURNS DOWN NEWSPAPER OFFICE

"Matthew…" Ruth Ann could only murmur as she sought out the plain wooden chair Mr. Levitt had loaned them. She sank into it and dropped her forehead onto her arm on the table.

"The pen is mightier than the sword!" Matthew's voice was strong. "I may not have shot Banny, but now everyone will know him for who he is. And you don't need to worry about being involved, Annie. Stay home. Since I'll be going to Paris to make the runs and we won't be printing a full edition, I don't need your help like before."

"Yes, you do," Ruth Ann muttered. She lifted her gaze to him. He looked pitiful with his burnt eyebrows and hair. Didn't look like he'd slept in a few days either. She hardly had the heart to tell him what she'd revealed to no one, but circumstances demanded it. She rose and looked around at the little group. "It isn't Mr. Banny running the whiskey. He may be the seller, but it's Mr. Carter who has it shipped in, right through with his regular shipments on the train."

Stunned, it was Matthew's turn to fumble for words. "How do you…how could you know…?"

Trying to lighten the moment with a smile, Ruth Ann shrugged. "My brother taught me to be observant. 'The best stories are the ones no one else sees. That's what people want to read.'"

Matthew shook his head in astonishment. Mr. Levitt asked, "Should we go to your police?"

Matthew barely answered. "I suppose." He crunched the leaflet in his hand and waved it around the building. "All this. You arranged it, Annie?"

She dipped her head, blushing. "It was mostly Mr. Levitt. He offered to help us get started again. But I figured you'd gone to Paris to get equipment. We can go right back to printing if we had supplies."

Matthew shrugged. "I tried to get a loan at the bank, but they turned me down. Said the business wasn't established, and I'm sure my appearance helped nothing. That's why I went to the newspaper there and created these. It will cost all of our revenue to handle it this way." He looked down at the stack of leaflets, knowing the rest of them had already flown in his hasty work.

A retraction might be in order, but for now, Ruth Ann went back to a more pleasant though hard subject. "Matthew, Mr. Levitt has agreed to let us stay here—rent-free for now—if we will help them in establishing their business. He also wants to build a house a few blocks from here. I figured you could help, and Mama already agreed to help with linens and doilies. I'll work here in the shop with Beulah, tending customers and drumming up business for them on my advertisement rounds. We can make it work, Matt. Really."

She grabbed his hand and winced when she felt the blisters and scabs on his unbandaged skin. Their mother would surely fuss at him most of the night for not taking care of his burns for two days.

Matthew withdrew his hand carefully and spoke to Mr. Levitt. "What have we done to earn this?"

Mr. Levitt smiled, one of genuine trust and happiness. "You write about truth. And you make us welcome. It is enough. I am certain we can help with supplies to start you printing again."

Beulah cleared her throat. "I am to blame for wrangling you all into any work. My father would let you off on nothing for eternity. I am the one who keeps his business going." She winked at Ruth Ann, who returned it, knowing Beulah's heart was every bit as golden as her father's.

Mr. Levitt opened his mouth to speak, but hesitated. Ruth Ann watched him closely, knowing he was about to ask something difficult, but she was unable to imagine what. They'd already arranged all the details, and the Levitts seemed grateful to have made these Choctaw friends.

Mr. Levitt finally sighed. "I do have one demand you may find difficult."

Ruth Ann held her breath. *No. Everything is already agreed on.* Still, she held herself in respectful silence as did Matthew.

Mr. Levitt pointed with a trembling finger at the six-gun on Matthew's hip. "You are not to bring that into my building or my home. I abhor guns and violence of any kind for any reason."

"Papa—"

Beulah's protest was cut short when Mr. Levitt raised his hand in the air to cut her off. Perhaps he seemed like a weak man, but there was no denying he was still in authority. Beulah obviously recognized that and fell into a pensive silence.

"No, daughter. This I will have." He looked to Matthew for his answer. So did Ruth Ann.

After several quiet moments, no one feeling the need to rush, Matthew nodded and offered his hand to Mr. Levitt. "You have a deal, sir. Rest assured, we will keep our end of the bargain and then some."

Mr. Levitt looked at Matthew's damaged hand a moment, but then clasped it gently with his own small one. "God be with us all."

CHAPTER SEVENTEEN

THE TELLER SIBLINGS WAITED UNTIL morning before approaching a Choctaw Lighthorseman about the whiskey running. One of the men was visiting relatives about a mile outside of town. Matthew and Ruth Ann rode out early, long before the town was rumbling with gossip stirred by the leaflet.

Whiskey running and brewers that produced Choctaw Beer, known as *Choc*, were something the Indian police force dealt with on a regular basis. But when Matthew informed Jeremiah, the young full-blood Lighthorseman, about what had happened in Dickens, Jeremiah backed off. He said the Lighthorsemen's jurisdiction was limited to Choctaws and more so since a new town sheriff for the whites had been appointed. After the execution of Silas Sloan and bad reporting done by the *Dickens Herald*, the Lighthorsemen needed to stay away from the primarily white town.

Jeremiah stood on the front porch of the cabin, leaned against a post that supported the overhanging roof while he looked down at them. Hands in his back pockets, he shrugged at Matthew. "We've stopped our fair share of whiskey running the past several years. Caught shipments coming in from St.

Louis wholesalers disguised in most every package. But the railroad put a stop to our inspections."

Ruth Ann sighed in frustration as Jeremiah continued to explain the various issues the Lighthorsemen faced in the changing times. She interrupted. "And just who is the new sheriff for the whites in Dickens? When did this take place?"

Jeremiah cocked an eyebrow at her. "The mayor appointed him last night. The hotel owner, Jake Banny, is the sheriff now."

Ruth Ann took a step back, mouth agape. She sputtered, but no words emerged.

Matthew had plenty, and he started to lay them out but halted mid-sentence, realizing he was shooting at the wrong target. He motioned to Ruth Ann. "Let's go."

♦♦♦

Back in town, a surprisingly large crowd had gathered in front of Carter's freight office. Mayor Warren stood on the platform next to an abashed Mr. Carter. Jake Banny, boasting a tin star on his chest, stood on his other side.

The sight of Banny with a badge was preposterous. How could the townsfolk let such a ridiculous declaration stand? Should they send for the Indian agent? Without bothering to ask the question aloud, Ruth Ann knew the answer. The agent dealt strictly with affairs involving the Indian tribes, not whites. Town mayors were given the right to appoint town law enforcement.

Since Mayor Warren's claim to office had never been openly challenged, his law stood. Sheriffs were restricted to crimes committed by whites only, and were supposed to collaborate with the U.S. marshals and courts.

The mayor was making a grand speech of some kind when Matthew and Ruth Ann halted their horses behind the crowd. They drew more attention than either of them wanted.

But the mayor kept talking. "I did not intend this to be such a public embarrassment to my friend and one of our leading citizens, Mr. Carter. But word does get around, and this deed we must do may as well be seen by all so we understand the great strides we are making as an advanced, civilized town in this Indian Territory wilderness."

As he spoke, Banny—rather, the sheriff—motioned to two of the freight workers, who hefted the large crate marked *Linens* onto the platform and stepped back. Sheriff Banny took a hammer and splintered the wood lid, sending pieces flying. The crowd gasped and stepped back.

The new sheriff reached into the crate and withdrew a full long-neck whiskey bottle. He turned, drew back his arm, and threw the bottle against the wall of the freight office, smashing the bottle with a dramatic crash. This elicited more gasps from the crowd, which included women and children. Straightening, Banny pointed a finger at Matthew, still mounted at the back of the crowd.

"I think you'd best get busy writing a retraction, boy. If you can manage to do that right."

Silence fell over the crowd. Matthew wasn't wearing his gun belt, but most of the people there had witnessed his threat against Banny and had read the bold accusations in the makeshift *Tribune*.

Matthew, still looking rough even after a night's sleep, shave, and fresh bandages, leaned forward in his saddle. "A good show, Banny, but I still say what I printed is true. I just didn't include your accomplices."

They had witnessed enough of the charade that featured Carter as a scapegoat with no actual punishment. At least the whiskey running in Dickens had been exposed, thanks to the *Choctaw Tribune*.

The story was finished. But there were still more to be done.

Matthew and Ruth Ann turned their mounts away from the scene and trotted off toward their new office. They had a newspaper to publish.

There was nothing, short of God Almighty, more powerful than the press.

CHAPTER EIGHTEEN

"YOU CAN'T GO WITH ME, Annie. You're a woman." Matthew had said this before, and it irritated Ruth Ann. The last time was about attending town council meetings. In Choctaw culture, women had long been respected for their wisdom, and participated in council. But they lived in a mixed world now, Matthew said, and white men didn't see women that way. They had their place, and that was in the kitchen. Her brother wasn't adopting that attitude, but with the trouble the *Choctaw Tribune* had stirred up lately, he didn't need the added controversy of his sister making her way into white-man politics—yet.

Still, Ruth Ann knew that wasn't the reason Matthew forbid her to go to this meeting. This had to do with the dangers of riding through the mountains and attending a potentially riotous temperance meeting held by Choctaws who were tired of the ill effects whiskey had on their people. It had been over a month since the debacle with Carter and Banny but the whiskey issue in Indian Territory was far from resolved. It likely never would be. The *Choctaw Tribune* continued to fight it and other problems in the Nation with their most powerful weapon—words. As long as they could keep the newspaper in business, they would use it for good.

This particular temperance group Matthew was headed to see was known to stretch the law in their favor, not abashed about killing if they had to in order to stop a wrong deed. They were rumored to be behind the death of an elderly Choctaw woman they claimed was a witch.

Matthew was attending the meeting in hopes of capturing some faces on camera, uncovering who these men were and proving it before the Choctaw judicial system. Whiskey running needed dealing with, yes, but not in the way it was being done.

Matthew checked the cinch on his gelding, Little Chief, one more time before securing the fragile camera behind his saddle. "This has to stop, Annie. Our people are doing each other in without the proper channels of our own justice system. What kind of civilization is that? Not the kind our ancestors died for."

Ruth Ann had followed him to the barn, still trying to talk him into letting her ride with him. She was tired of being left behind the past month. She'd stayed busy arranging the new print shop with Mr. Levitt. Then there was helping Beulah settle into their freshly built box-house. The Jewish family was able to erect it in a few weeks, thanks to Matthew's help and favors called in from cousins on Uncle Preston's farm.

But all those things were tiresome and nothing at all like investigating a good story. Since they'd faced brushes with death lately, Ruth Ann should have been glad for the relative peace. But instead, she was left with a strange thirst to step out of her shelter and see more of the world, even the evils of it that could be changed by the power of the press. The things she believed Matthew was doing, but she could only be a sideline participant.

"Matt, I write as well as you, can ride as well as you—"

"And be as stubborn as me." Matthew reached out and snatched a pin from her bun.

The neatly pinned hair threatened to slide loose.

"Matthew!" She tried to catch it in place. He took the opportunity to swing up onto his mount and cross his arms on the saddle horn, reins dangling between two fingers.

"You stay here, look after Mama, and keep the Levitts happy. I want that print shop to still be ours when I get back in two days." He winked at her but then grew very, very serious. "And you stay away from that so-called sheriff Banny. Don't go out at night. I saw the way he looked at you when he passed in front of the print shop and didn't know I was there."

Ruth Ann blushed and fumbled with her hair. "He won't bother me."

"Humph." Matthew waved her hair pin in front of her. She snatched it with a scowl and finally got her hair back in place.

"I still want to go with you."

"Uncle Preston is expecting you and Mama for the day. Go. It'll do you both good to get out of town for a while and away from all these whites."

"The Levitts are white. Sort of."

Matthew smiled and adjusted the reins. "You know I was joking. We can't judge all by a few. If only certain whites would do the same." With that, he shook the reins and nudged Little Chief into a soft lope. He crossed the railroad tracks and kicked dust as he melded with the road and sunrise.

Ruth Ann put her hands on her hips, staring after him, wishing he weren't leaving her behind. Or maybe it was she wished he weren't leaving at all. He'd been right about the look the sheriff gave her, and it wasn't the first. She'd be happier than anyone for a peaceful day or two at Uncle Preston's.

She just didn't know it wasn't to be.

CHAPTER NINETEEN

LATER THAT MORNING, RUTH ANN showed Beulah around their barn and gave her instructions on the feeding routine for the Teller animals. It was possible Ruth Ann and her mother would spend the night at Uncle Preston's, so she prepared by asking Beulah to tend the livestock.

Ruth Ann hitched the horse to their modest buggy. They were already getting a late start, and the sky held the possibility of a snowstorm. The weather rarely turned severe this far south, but storms were always a chance they took when traveling in winter.

Ruth Ann chose not to worry over Matthew. He had proven he could take care of himself. Still, Daddy and Philip should have been able to do so, especially together, but they were both dead.

Della appeared in the doorway of the barn, and Beulah gave her a big hug of farewell. Ruth Ann smiled as she thought of the dinners Beulah and her father had partaken of in the Teller home. She noted a special kinship developing with her mother and Beulah, and Ruth Ann wondered if Della reminded Beulah of her own deceased mother.

Whenever the Levitts came to supper, Ruth Ann made

sure they prepared no pork. It took some time to learn the Jewish diet, but after over a month with their new friends, Ruth Ann felt comfortable she could do well each time they sat at a kosher meal together.

Once the Teller women were in the buggy, Beulah waved goodbye. Della clicked to the horse, directing him onto the road leading toward Uncle Preston's large farm down near the Red River, nine miles south of town.

The leaves had long since fallen after the Thanksgiving holiday. Soon, Christmas would be upon them, with more family gatherings and a special service at the church. Thinking about glowing candles and homemade fudge kept Ruth Ann's mind off the ever-increasing wind as she tucked the lap-blanket more firmly around her legs. Della kept the horse calm and at a good clip.

Ruth Ann had never liked driving the buggy since the time the train whistle had spooked their horse. He had taken the bit in his teeth and run off with her halfway to the river it seemed. She would drive if she had to, but her mother enjoyed it.

Once they were miles outside of town, Ruth Ann leaned back in the springboard seat and watched the wind as it did battle with the trees lining the dirt road. She imagined the invisible fight taking place as nature clashed with itself, screaming and taunting.

The scream grew louder. Della pulled back on the reins, bringing the buggy to a stop. She cocked her head to one side, listening. Ruth Ann straightened and listened too. It *was* a scream. An unearthly scream coming from the treetops. Or maybe the trunks.

The report of a rifle sounded. And again. The buggy horse shied to one side, but Della held a steady hand on the reins, keeping him much calmer than Ruth Ann felt. She twisted around and leaned partly out of the buggy to look. It sounded like the shot had echoed off the bluff behind them, almost lost in the thick woods. Two more shots followed in rapid succession. Della shook the reins and started the buggy horse off at a fast clip, but something on the bluff caught Ruth Ann's eye.

"Stop!" She grabbed her mother's arm, and Della pulled up again and looked where Ruth Ann pointed to the right and behind them. A woman was scrambling down the steep bluff. Ruth Ann had no idea how she kept from tumbling to her death. Perhaps it was the tiny child she clutched in her arms that gave her special human abilities only a mother knows.

Della turned the buggy around on the wide road and urged the horse to a lope. They drew even with the disheveled young woman who skittered to the bottom of the bluff with a scream as she scrambled up the ditch to the buggy.

She spoke rapidly in Choctaw. "They tried to kill...they are trying to kill my son...please! Help me! I am not a witch! I am not a witch!"

She lunged forward and grabbed the seat on Ruth Ann's side, collapsing against the buggy. Ruth Ann stared, stunned, at the woman and dirty-faced toddler in her arms, both wailing less than a foot from her. Della elbowed Ruth Ann to gain her attention. "Take the trail through the woods as you and your brothers used to go to the farm. I'll drive fast and go east at the fork. The hunters will think she's with me. Now go. Go!"

Della all but shoved Ruth Ann off the buggy. Ruth Ann numbly complied, gathering herself and her full skirt away from the wheel. She turned her attention to untangling the exhausted woman from the spring of the seat she clung to.

"Come. Come with me. We have a safe place until this gets straightened out. Come on." Ruth Ann barely had the young mother clear of the wheels when Della snapped the reins over the back of the buggy horse and shot away, dust swirling. In the distance, more dust stirred as riders came down the road toward them.

Panicked with the knowledge they would be spotted, Ruth Ann dragged the woman toward the ditch and pushed her down among the sharp rocks, urging her to keep the child quiet. Carefully, Ruth Ann peeked over the edge of the road, praying her mother made it to the east fork before encountering the men.

And then realization struck her like a lightning bolt. Her mother! She was alone, unarmed, and about to incur the wrath of men bent on killing a young mother and her child. What had Della been thinking?

"Please, God, please," Ruth Ann whispered, unable to grasp onto anything specific to say. "Please, please, God, please."

The buggy swayed onto the east fork road and veered away from the riders, who cut through the grass in an effort to catch the buggy. It disappeared from sight in the dust and bend in the road.

Knowing the diversion that might cost her mother's life would not buy them much time, Ruth Ann turned back to the shaking woman who had curled herself in a ball around her toddler. Ruth Ann spoke in Choctaw. "We must go, now. To my uncle's farm. Let's go."

When the woman didn't respond, Ruth Ann cupped her hands under her armpits and pulled with all her strength. She set the woman on her feet while she clutched her whimpering child. "Let's go. We haven't much time."

With a moan, the woman didn't even look at her steps as she let Ruth Ann put an arm around her shoulders and guide her over the rocks that had tumbled down the side of the bluff over the years. Ruth Ann wasn't exactly sure where the old trail began that she had often taken with her brothers, or how much of it still existed. She wasn't sure she could find it.

But one thing she knew. If the witch hunters found her and the woman before she found their way to Uncle Preston's, they were all as good as dead.

♦♦♦

The buggy horse could keep a good pace, but Della knew he couldn't outrun the three stout mounts chasing her. Still, she coaxed all the remaining heart from the horse as they flew along down the road. The wind was heavy against them, looping under the buggy awning and attempting to rip it loose.

Della alternated her words between urging the animal on and a prayer for her child and the ones she helped. "Please, God, be with them."

A shot sounded behind her, a warning fired into the sky perhaps. Della took it as such and brought her horse to a trot, knowing the men would shoot him next. The other horses thundered up from behind her, heaving and shaking as they found footing and a stop.

"Halito," was Della's simple greeting as she gazed over the men who were looking at the bench seat occupied by her alone. She recognized one of the men. "Why are you chasing me?"

The man held a chokehold grip on the double-barrel shotgun across his lap. He lifted his chin. "You should not help one so wicked as she."

Della laid her hands, still holding firm to the reins, on her blanket-covered legs and leaned forward. "My daughter is not wicked. She does well. You leave her be."

Understanding passed between them, but no more words. One of the other two men spurred his mount away and into a gallop. Della shook her head. The horses were spent and would collapse soon. The man must have known this, because he moved his horse off at a slower pace, the third man following.

They'd have to find water and feed soon or fresh horses altogether. The chase after the buggy had accomplished that at least, and would give Della a chance to make it into town for help. The men were moving off on the road between her and her brother's farm. The road that might lead them to Ruth Ann.

Della flicked the reins and started her horse off at a fast trot. She needed to pace him, but if she had to drive him to collapse, she would. She'd walk the remainder of the way.

Her people knew how to walk.

CHAPTER TWENTY

THE WIND GUSTED THROUGH THE trees, insisting on finding the women in their vulnerable state. It carried the threatening sense of snow. The woman stumbled so, Ruth Ann had a hard time paying attention to finding the way. She had to concentrate on keeping the woman on her feet and moving.

Twice, she offered to take the child from the mother's arms to relieve her of that burden so she could walk, but the woman shrieked to the point Ruth Ann was afraid they'd be discovered.

They pushed on through the woods and small rock outcroppings, always heading downhill. The terrain around Uncle Preston's farm was gently rolling pastures and woods but always south, down toward the Red River. As long as they stayed on the west side of the road and going down, they were bound to find it.

The old trail she had taken with her brothers when they were young was the quickest route, but Ruth Ann found herself confused as she looked at the trees and overgrowth of ten years. Philip and Matthew had never waited for her, always rushing ahead to where her shorter legs and long skirt barely let her keep them in sight. They'd laugh and yell, "Slow poke! Crawling along like a little *luksi*."

She hadn't taken heed of the trees, the rocks, the streams. She hadn't known where she was going, only determined to keep up and terrified of being left behind in the woods where the Grandmother had told her stories of the little people and how they came after children who didn't behave. As a child, Ruth Ann was never certain she was good no matter how hard she tried. It was only just prior to her teens that she fully embraced the saving grace of Jesus Christ.

That memory warmed her now and she knew it wasn't a mere memory. The words her father often spoke whispered to her as branches whipped her face, stinging her cheek and tearing her flesh.

God knows.

"Please, please, God," Ruth Ann murmured to herself, not sure if she prayed for herself or her mother or this woman and child. Perhaps all of them, encompassed in one pain-filled breath.

The woman collapsed and used her body to shield her child as she shivered and sobbed. Ruth Ann tried to get her up, but the woman was incoherent.

Ruth Ann lifted her torn skirt high and navigated back over their path a short ways. She silenced her own heavy breathing and listened. No sound of horses or men followed them. They were leaving an easy trail to track, but perhaps the men had given up.

No. They would not, not after chasing the woman this far, bent on killing a witch they likely believed had done them great harm.

Superstitions still ran high among some Choctaws, even those who went to church and professed Christianity. They claimed they found confirmation in Bible scriptures about what should be done to witches.

Ruth Ann didn't hold to it, but stories the Grandmother told, tales of owl-men and shape-shifting panthers, made her skin prickle. It didn't help now with the screech of the limbs tangling and ripping apart from each other in their battle with the wind. How much truth was there in the tales?

She shook her head and hurried back to the woman still lying on the ground, eyes closed, shivering. Ruth Ann took off her coat and experienced the chilling assault of the winter storm in full. She coughed and laid the coat over the woman and child. She briskly rubbed the woman's arms and the toddler's back. It took a few minutes, but the woman finally opened her eyes.

"What is your name?" Ruth Ann asked the woman in Choctaw. She looked full-blood. Ruth Ann didn't recognize her, though she knew most of the families around the area. How could she have traveled far on foot with a child?

"My...my name is Harriet Anoletubbee. My child is Samuel. We rode and rode. They shot my pony. I am not a witch...." Her eyes drifted closed.

Needing to keep her conscious, Ruth Ann persisted. "Why do they think you are? Why are they after you?"

Harriet shook her head and left it resting on the ground. A single snowflake made its way through the limbs above them and landed in her hair. If she stayed there, she might die.

Standing, Ruth Ann tripped her way over to a rock outcropping ahead of them. It was steep, but Ruth Ann scrambled up the sharp rocks, poking around in the crevices until she found one large enough for them to squeeze into and hopefully shield them from view. It was free of any varmints taking shelter. She went down and forced Harriet to her feet by lifting her and the child with a grunt. She pushed and pulled them up the incline until they reached the crevice.

Ruth Ann carefully guided Harriet's head to keep her from hitting it on the rocks as the woman pitched forward into the slight space. With a little situating, Ruth Ann managed to get them all inside the warmer shelter. At least the wind no longer battered them and the snow would not accumulate on their clothes.

But they couldn't stay long. The storm was bound to get worse before better, and those men would hunt the woods until they found them. But maybe if Harriet had a few hours of rest, she could go on at a good pace.

Once Della was free from the hunters—and Ruth Ann had to believe she was—she would go for help in town, or more likely to Uncle Preston's farm if she could get to it. The men from there would come up the old trail looking for Ruth Ann, but if she wasn't on it, there was no reason for them to find her before the witch hunters did.

♦♦♦

"Moved on?" Matthew repeated the words in hopes they would be refuted. But the cheery-faced boy who had spoken them paid Matthew's displeasure no mind as he pressed his nose against the glass of the general store.

After an unsuccessful hunt through the woods near where the temperance meeting was to have taken place, Matthew had ridden into the nearest town. It was a small place with hardly a name yet, but a general store always held the best promise for information. On the porch, he'd seen the barefoot Choctaw boy sticking his tongue on the glass in front of the candy display in the large picture window. Matthew repeated his question. "How do you know about it?"

"Was there." The boy lifted his tongue off the glass long enough to answer, then added, "Whole bunch of them. They meet there all the time and talk about who needs shooting next. They went on after the witch who's been killing babies down the creek from here. I lit out and took a shortcut to warn the family. I like them. She don't seem like a witch. Told her husband, and I reckon they high-tailed it fast. Likely go on down to the Red. If they make it across, I reckon they'll be okay."

Since the group had moved on, Matthew had wasted a ride up to make his attempt to photograph the leaders. He'd planned it well, but the plan unraveled and it looked as if he would have been better off staying close to home, since that was the way the party went anyway.

Home.

Sudden realization struck him, but he quickly dismissed it. His mother and sister were safe at Uncle Preston's farm, enjoying chats with the Grandmother and cousins. They wouldn't even hear about the witch-hunt until he returned and told the story. It was about the only usefulness this trip had been.

The boy closed his eyes and dragged his tongue up the glass. Matthew could imagine what it was like to taste the freezing cold glass as if it were a peppermint stick. Sweet with sugar to ignite the taste buds, taking one to a blissful place.

Matthew clasped the boy's shoulder, shaking them both from their daydreams. "Come on. I think we've both earned a peppermint. My treat."

"You mean it, mister?" The words were barely out of the boy's mouth before he darted inside.

At least Matthew had accomplished one significant thing this day.

CHAPTER TWENTY-ONE

THE STORM WASN'T ANGRY BUT still held steady as the temperature dropped lower. It brought to mind stories the Grandmother had told of the long walk she endured as a young adult.

Elizabeth Homa, Ruth Ann's mother's mother, had lived in the homelands of Mississippi. She had visited the sacred mound, *Nanih Waiya*, often with her relatives. They lived in the old ways of the Choctaws, though blended with ways brought by the missionaries who taught them who God's Son was. Most of their clan accepted Him as their Savior.

But none of that stopped leaders of the American government from forcing a final treaty on the Choctaw Nation to trade their homelands in Mississippi, along with *Nanih Waiya*, for a new country in the west, a country to be theirs forever. Getting to the new country proved disastrous for the tribe, causing the deaths of thousands.

The Grandmother, Elizabeth, had walked and walked. Snow on bare feet, burying loved ones every mile it seemed.

Drownings. Frostbite. Disease. None of it was fair; none of it was easy.

These were the things Ruth Ann told herself with each shiver as she snuggled closer to the woman and child to give them the warmth she sought herself. Her layers of stockings and petticoat made her ashamed of wishing for an easier time. She wasn't starved, diseased, or frozen. But she *was* worried about burying a loved one when this trail ended.

That thought spurred her to rise as much as she could in the cramped space and shake Harriet's shoulder, hard. The woman had rested better than two hours, snuggled with her toddler in Ruth Ann's coat, scarf, and gloves. If Harriet couldn't travel now, they would never make it to Uncle Preston's farm.

Ruth Ann worried where the witch hunters might be. If they followed their trail even now, only minutes away with their shotguns and Winchesters, it wouldn't be hard to find the three frightened runaways sheltering among the rocks.

Harriet moaned at the intrusion to her sleep and shook her head as if disoriented. But then she snapped. Eyes popped open wide, she screamed in Ruth Ann's face with gagging foul breath. Harriet blindly clawed and scratched Ruth Ann's bare cheeks and neck.

"Stop!" Ruth Ann pushed away, her backside to the steep outcropping they had climbed. The woman lunged over her toddler with a wild yell and Ruth Ann shoved herself backward, tangled in her heavy skirt as she tried to find footing. But it was too late.

She slid and tumbled down the rock outcropping, skirt flying over her face, rocks tearing her sleeves and bare hands as she tried to grasp something to stop her plunge. Nothing worked. The world spun around and around until it finally thumped into a star in the dark universe. No sun was shining. All was black. Black and white. And then nothing.

CHAPTER TWENTY-TWO

A WOMAN'S PLACE IS IN the kitchen. That way of thinking about women caused a giggle to bubble up through Ruth Ann's chapped lips before she opened her eyes. The thought was ironic now...in the kitchen was exactly where she wished to be. But she wasn't. And with consciousness came roaring pain through her head and intense cold throughout her body.

Nausea washed over her. With a moan, Ruth Ann pried her eyes open, only to blink away the snowflakes landing on her lashes. Mentally, she took inventory of the pain that still managed to shoot through the numb parts of her body. Her head throbbed as if a severe cold was coming on, and it did roar to the point she didn't want to think or stay awake. If she rested a bit longer...

But no. She had to get up. Shifting her feet, she yelped when a thousand needles stabbed her left ankle. It had tangled in her skirt and twisted severely. She didn't have to look at it to know the swelling was already past help. It was sprained.

Ruth Ann lifted her head a little, waited for the nausea to pass, then lifted it a little more from where she lay flat on her back. The more she moved, the more aware she was of her body's condition. The bed of rocks under her stabbed her lower back and shoulders. She gasped, but forced herself to sit up. Every part of her body felt beaten on.

Propping herself up with weak hands splayed behind her, she looked up the rock outcropping to where she knew the crevice was, mostly out of sight from her angle. But she could see enough to realize Harriet and her child were gone. She panicked and tried to move her legs, but her ankle screamed in protest and so did Ruth Ann, though it came out as a whimper.

A glance around revealed no one in sight of the lightly snow-blanketed woods, so she tugged her skirt above her knees and gazed down at her left ankle. Her lace-up boot bulged with impossible strain. Surely she would never be able to take it off, but still she loosened the strings and tongue, pausing every few seconds to rest her head on her knee to allow the dizziness to pass. The cold leather seemed frozen in place.

It took Ruth Ann several minutes of tugging and crying before the boot was fully off. She wasn't sure that was the best thing she could have done when her pain level doubled. She moaned and sniffed as her nose dripped. Her eyes hurt. She wanted Matthew or Uncle Preston to find her and carry her home. But they weren't there, nor would they find her so far from the farm.

The witch hunters might. That thought caused Ruth Ann to whip her head around again, though she regretted her fast actions. No one was in sight, but if they did find her in the now approaching dark and snow, they could easily mistake her for Harriet Anoletubbee. And where had that woman gone? She had been so weak.

Ruth Ann touched her cheek and scraped away dried blood with her numb fingers. Correction. Harriet was exhausted, but still had plenty of fight in her. Perhaps it was special powers...

She shook her head. This was no time to make up her mind about witches or shape-shifters or anything else. She had to use every bit of mental resources she had to get herself to

Uncle Preston's farm.

Ruth Ann braced herself and pushed up to stand on her good foot. Or tried. Instead, she pitched forward on her knees as the world spun before coming to rest against a star again. But at least everything didn't go black this time. She scrambled until she was on her foot, clenching her right shoulder while balancing on one good boot, with her stockinged injured foot held above the rocky ground.

Breathing deeply in the cold air made Ruth Ann cough, and her head ached worse than ever in her life. But she forced herself to study the woods around her and the outcropping beside her. That was when she saw it.

The split pine tree, two in one that formed an eerie fork in its middle. It sat high on a cliff further past the outcropping. That always marked a turnoff in the trail to Uncle Preston's home. There should be a creek under the outcropping on the other side, and then it couldn't be more than a mile or two from there.

Even with the throb in her ankle, it seemed a short distance to the now relieved Ruth Ann. At least she wasn't lost, and there was a good chance someone familiar and friendly might come up that trail at any time. Why they hadn't already, Ruth Ann refused to consider.

It was possible her mother had been forced to go into town for help instead of the farm since that was the direction the east fork would have taken her. Ruth Ann didn't want to contemplate anything else. All she needed to do was follow the path to Uncle Preston's and find help.

She took a tentative step and hop, though it proved more than she could handle. Ruth Ann wind-milled her arms for balance, only to fall to her side with a yelp. The light layer of snow offered no cushion, but the resulting tears were ones of frustration and not only pain. She wiped them away, knowing they would freeze on her face. She no longer had a coat or gloves or scarf. At least they would keep Harriet and her child warm until the witch hunters found them.

Shamed by her cruel thoughts, Ruth Ann asked God's

forgiveness as she crawled toward something she saw that would help. A pine branch had fallen victim to the storm. It would flex too much, but maybe it would give her enough balance to hop and drag herself along the trail before the witch hunters found her.

With the pine branch grasped in both hands, Ruth Ann hobbled her way toward the split pine that stood guard over the old trail. But she halted to stare at irregular footprints in the mud and snow ahead, leading the opposite way of the trail to the farm. It was the path Harriet had taken, one that would lead her toward the road, the last place they'd seen the men who'd shot at her.

Ruth Ann tried to ignore the footprints, tried to forget the innocent face of the child. Little Samuel. She had tried to help them and was nearly killed for it.

What could she do now? She could hardly walk herself, much less be any use to the hunted pair. The best thing she could do was find Uncle Preston and have him send men to help. Men with guns who could do some good.

But as Ruth Ann came to the point where the footprints went one way and the old trail went the other, she couldn't make herself go on.

There was only a breath of time between life and death.

Harriet and her child couldn't be far ahead. And Ruth Ann was hobbling along fine with the bending pine branch. Maybe she could still find a way to save them before that breath was taken and gone.

God knows.

Feeling a sudden urgency, Ruth Ann abandoned her trek toward the split pine tree and hurried along the opposite direction at the best pace she could. She paused to lift her skirt and tuck it in at her waist to give her complete freedom of movement. The action allowed the wind in around bare spots on her legs, but she didn't care, and it didn't matter if anyone saw her in such a despicable condition.

Lives were in danger, and if she could do something about it, she would. It was what her father would have done.

Or Philip, or Matthew. And what her mother had done. Ruth Ann could do no less and call herself a Teller. They were a family who cared for others. It was how their tribe had survived the trail of tears. The invasion of whites onto their new lands. It was what the *Choctaw Tribune* fought for. Ruth Ann prayed she could always be a part of that fight, even to the death.

She swallowed, sniffed, and coughed as she staggered over the uneven terrain in the footsteps of the accused witch. The footsteps, the fight—they might lead to her death at that.

CHAPTER TWENTY-THREE

RUTH ANN TOOK A STEP and hop in the snow, her eyes on the frozen ground. The Grandmother—Elizabeth—took the next step on the frozen ground. Ruth Ann hopped again, her vision blurred as she stared at her boot and stocking-covered foot. The Grandmother's bare feet moved forward again. They were young feet, but red and black in the snow.

Ruth Ann stepped. Elizabeth. Ruth Ann.

Elizabeth took another step, wondering if it was to be her last. Her toes were frozen. Her flesh was torn from the underside of her feet. Each step brought pain, but she'd long ago stopped complaining. Stopped crying. She would never need to cry again. Her mother. Her father. Buried with her tears. There was no one left.

Eyes on her feet, Elizabeth took another step and halted. She would stay there. Let her feet freeze to the earth from which they came. *Nanih Waiya* called to her, the sacred mound she had left behind.

Then a little cry sounded, a baby's wail. Elizabeth lifted her eyes from her feet and saw her people. Young, old. They stepped forward on the trail. They kept their moving spirit within them. It was time to move. She must move with her people, with their spirit. *Chihowa* would guide them. He was with them.

Elizabeth took another step, eyes on the horizon ahead. Ruth Ann took another step, thinking of her mother. Elizabeth stepped. Ruth Ann stepped in the Grandmother's place, feeling the presence of her spirit as she gazed about the darkening woods.

It was an exhausting hour later and Ruth Ann knew she was near the road again, though further down than when her mother had pushed her from the buggy. She had seen no signs nor heard anything as the storm had calmed with the coming darkness, gentle snow falling at a peaceful pace. Somehow, the snow created an unnatural yet perfectly natural, eerie light around her as the woods broke and a field opened up before her.

The road lay on the other side of the field. Between it and the woods stood a lone figure. Just standing there in the shimmering light of the field sparsely layered in snow. As if in a trance, the figure stayed unmoving, unflinching until suddenly it stumbled back, turned and ran toward Ruth Ann.

It was Harriet Anoletubbee, still clutching little Samuel in her arms.

Then Ruth Ann heard them. Saw them. Riders on the road. At full gallop slinging snow and mud, it was obvious they had spotted the figure as well. The snow-light reflected on the glint of their rifle barrels that lay across their saddles. Ruth Ann stood paralyzed after tossing aside the pine branch for fear they might think she was a witch too.

Harriet ran up to her, her face twisted grotesquely from the cold. For a moment, Ruth Ann couldn't help but wonder if it was the face of an ancestor who had died on the long trail.

But it was Harriet, sure enough. She had wrapped the coat around her child, but had lost the scarf and gloves somewhere along the way. She shoved Samuel into Ruth Ann's arms without a word before turning again and running toward the men, who had slowed their horses, rifles in hand. One clearly held a double-barrel shotgun.

THE EXECUTIONS

♦♦♦

Pain. That was all he felt, all he knew. Not the blasting wind—his face had numbed to that long ago. Not the darkness around him—that paled compared to the darkness within him. Not the voices of the men who rode with him—only the voices of his dead loved ones did he want to hear.

Pain. It rode before him, it rode behind him, it rode with him. It *was* him.

The only light on the earth was from the moon that teased him from behind the clouds, sometimes showing itself and the way to go, other times hiding and leaving him to ride blindly. He'd known the light of God to be like that. And at this moment, that Light was hidden away behind the clouds of death and curses.

Pain. It was all he had left of his baby and his wife. His family, the ones God had given and then taken away. No. God had not taken them, but a witch. And that witch had to be stopped.

That witch was near him now. Ahead, running toward him through the field. His exhausted mount slowed. He was barely aware of easing back in the saddle. Then he saw the other one. The innocent one. She now held the other innocent one. These were the ones he was not to harm. But they were a part of the witch. They all must die, be purged through death as he had been.

He halted his mount. He heard words of pleading. For forgiveness, for mercy, for life. Whatever they were, they could not be granted. Only blood could bring relief from the pain. Only death could stop death.

He cocked the hammer of the shotgun and raised it.

♦♦♦

Harriet Anoletubbee had stopped halfway toward the horsemen and spread her arms wide. She screamed something in Choctaw, but Ruth Ann couldn't understand it over the cries of the child straining in her arms in a fit of temper.

The man with the shotgun leveled it on Harriet Anoletubbee and squeezed the trigger. The blast of buckshot hit her square in the chest. It lifted her off her feet to land backward on the snowy ground, arms spread to each side of her.

Ruth Ann swayed, the life of the child the only thing keeping her on her feet. For how long, she did not know. The men rode toward her.

When they came close, Ruth Ann was shocked when she recognized the shotgun carrier. She was so surprised she said his name aloud in the frosty air.

"Reverend Anoletubbee?"

The grim-faced man looked her and the child up and down, perhaps recognizing her from the camp meeting thousands of Choctaws had gathered for last spring. He had preached a stirring sermon on the love of God and how the people should follow Him in all their ways. Afterward, the full-blood Choctaw reverend, who had graduated from a Presbyterian seminary, spent half the night at their fire, speaking with Matthew and Della about the latest developments with the Dawes Commission. Somewhere along that time, Ruth Ann had drifted off to sleep, but she remembered she liked the man.

Now he sat astride a paint horse with a shotgun still smoking after shooting a woman dead in front of her.

One of the other two men, both younger than the reverend, muttered something to him, motioning with his rifle barrel toward Ruth Ann. She clutched Samuel in one arm while she fumbled to straighten her skirt with the other. Thankfully, it had mostly fallen into place in her tramping so she wasn't caught bare-legged in front of the reverend.

Reverend Anoletubbee looked her over a few seconds before tugging on the reins, pulling his horse's head away from her and leading the other two men in a slow lope across the pasture, past the body of Harriet Anoletubbee and back to the road, heading south. Probably for the Texas border at the

THE EXECUTIONS

Red River. Or maybe to join the western road leading them back to where they'd come from.

Ruth Ann didn't venture many guesses. She was too focused on trying to give thanks to God, and trying not to think about Harriet Anoletubbee lying dead a few dozen paces from her, and trying to pray for her mother.

All she could whisper was, "Please, God, please."

The child in her arms went strangely still, as if life had been stolen out of him. Ruth Ann rubbed up and down his arm and shook him before holding him tight to her chest, softly singing one of her favorite hymns.

> *Gracious Lord, incline Thine ear;*
> *My request vouchsafe to hear;*
> *Hear my never-ceasing cry;*
> *Give me Christ, or else I die.*
>
> *Wealth and honor I disdain,*
> *Earthly comforts, Lord, are vain;*
> *These can never satisfy:*
> *Give me Christ, or else I die.*

Samuel's little heartbeat was hardly discernible against her own. She swung back and forth, continuing to hum as she waited. For what, she didn't know. She could not make the trek back through the woods and down the old trail to Uncle Preston's. She could not make herself move forward to the road, past Harriet Anoletubbee's body. She could not walk one way or the other without the help of the pine branch, and she could not hold it and the child. So she stood still. Sang. Prayed.

The clouds parted and a full moon glowed from behind them, making the snow blinding. Somewhere beyond it, though, thundering hoofbeats sounded, and Ruth Ann knew they'd come back for her. The reverend may have felt he had a special word from God about her, that she was an accomplice, a witch like Harriet. If so, he would not hesitate to shoot her with the child in her arms. Then she would have done no good this day. She had helped no one. Her life—her death—served no purpose.

Realizing her eyes were squeezed shut against the blinding moonlight on the snow and her coming doom, Ruth Ann cracked them open and blinked. A single rider galloped toward her. He wore a cowboy hat and chaps that flapped loud in the stillness of the dead field. Ruth Ann put a protective hand around Samuel's head.

"Please, God, please."

The moon making the man a silhouette, Ruth Ann could not see his face as he reined to a stop in front of her, dusting her with snow. The dark spot where his face was came alive with images of Sheriff Banny.

Ruth Ann gasped and tried to step back. The man dismounted quickly, dropping his reins to the ground.

"You all right, miss?"

Something about the voice was familiar, and now that he was eye-level with her—well, taller by a good foot—she recognized something about him that let her breathe easier, but she couldn't answer.

The old cowboy, G.W., looked over his shoulder at the body of the woman, then back at Ruth Ann, sizing up her condition with a frown. "I were on my way out of town when I seen your ma. She was walking the streets, trying to get help...." His voice drifted off as he raised an eyebrow in concern to her reaction.

Tears dripped down Ruth Ann's cold cheeks. They were tears of pure relief that made her shake all over. "My...my mother is well?"

Instead of answering, G.W. carefully took the child from her arms. "Best get you both into town to the doc. This little feller don't seem to have much life left in him." He glanced again to the body of the woman and frowned. He spoke to Ruth Ann. "You reckon you can hang on behind me?"

Before she could answer, a wagon rumbled up the road from the south at a good clip, and the woods Ruth Ann had emerged from came alive with voices and lantern light.

Startled, she jerked and looked between the road and the woods. Those in the woods got to them first, a small band of armed men. They were led by Uncle Preston.

He came straight to her, took a look at G.W. and the body in the field before speaking in Choctaw to Ruth Ann. "Did he harm you?"

Ruth Ann hurried her reply, though she watched the wagon veer off the road and fly across the snow-covered field toward them. "No, no, not at all. He's a friend my mother sent from town to find me...."

Peter, her fifteen-year-old cousin, half stood in the wagon, urging the team along before using all of his young strength to bring them to a clattering halt near the group. Before the wagon came to a full stop, his passenger hopped off and ran to Ruth Ann.

Ruth Ann couldn't run to meet her, so she just opened her arms wide to embrace her mother as Della nearly tackled her in joy. Della chattered about her brave girl, not stopping for a breath. Somewhere in the commotion, Uncle Preston asked G.W. to take the child into town to the doctor, and said they would take Ruth Ann to the farm.

After being alone for so long, praying, wishing, hoping for help, Ruth Ann was overwhelmed and her head lightened impossibly. The world spun around and around before finally bumping into a star and stopping suddenly. Everything was black and white. And then just an endless black universe.

CHAPTER TWENTY-FOUR

WHEN THE WORLD GREW COLORFUL again, Ruth Ann expected to awake in her own bed. She didn't, but the surroundings were familiar when she peeked out at them between droopy eyelids. She was vaguely aware of opening them once or twice before and having a spoonful of nastiness forced between her lips. With this memory, Ruth Ann pressed her lips tight and opened her eyes wide, but it was her ears that picked up the presence of someone in the room.

"I've seen that fish on a riverbank look before, when you were little and the Grandmother tended your cold."

Turning her head on the pillow produced pain in her stiff neck and shoulders, but she wanted to see her brother's face. He looked somber now as he reached to rub her right shoulder lightly. "You were supposed to be safe. That's why I left you at home. Instead, I find the group had already moved on at the news of witches putting spells on children, supposedly killing them. Then I find out you and Mama faced some of the men and saved a child's life." Matthew smiled a little. "And what was it I said you were supposed to be doing while I was away?"

The tease was poorly delivered, but Ruth Ann managed

to return the smile. She wanted to tease back about the front-page story she had lived so he could write it. When she tried to speak, though, a hacking cough overcame her. Her head exploded with pain and she pulled her knees toward her chest, only to send a thousand needles through her sprained ankle. She was aware of Matthew calling for help.

A warm hand lay across her cheek. Too warm for Ruth Ann's hot face, and she tried to pull away. But the hand gripped her jaw firmly and a spoonful of nastiness was in her mouth, down her throat, and into the pit of her empty stomach before she could gag.

She coughed once more then rested her spinning head against the pillow. When she opened her eyes, Matthew's presence had been replaced by their grandmother Elizabeth. She seemed ancient, in body and in soul. Della was her youngest child, younger than her only son, Preston. It made her more the age of a great-grandmother to Ruth Ann, but in all her growing-up years, the Grandmother never seemed old. That had happened suddenly. Just in the past few years did she seem to age too quickly.

But that had not depleted her strength or her wisdom. The Grandmother leaned over Ruth Ann and roughly stuck a thumb under one eye at a time, pulling the skin down and examining the pupil. She muttered to herself in Choctaw, words Ruth Ann could not distinguish, but it was the Grandmother's way. Finally, she sat back and folded her hands together, hands so crinkled they looked to have spent a lifetime in water.

Ruth Ann tried to roll to her side to better face her, but her shoulder warned her not to move. She settled for adjusting her head to the point before pain could not be endured and said, "Your stories kept me alive."

Her voice sounded like a sick bullfrog. Clearing her throat didn't help, but she continued. "When I was cold and lost, I thought of you and our people. How they came bravely to this new land, but mostly, how they suffered and died trying to get here. Will you tell me the story again, Pokni?"

THE EXECUTIONS

The Grandmother rocked herself a few minutes, staring a hole through Ruth Ann. She never told stories unless the listener truly wanted to hear. That had taught Ruth Ann greater patience than anything in life. When she was young and all the children gathered around to beg the Grandmother to tell a story, it became a game to see who could sit still the longest. The boys always lost, poking each other and wrestling on the floor. But soon, even they settled down as the circle of brothers, sisters, and cousins sat cross-legged before the Grandmother as she rocked in her rocking chair. Minutes would pass. Half an hour. She spent that time looking into each of their eyes, getting to know them without words and imparting the wisdom of patience and understanding to them. Letting them know it was good and right to bring themselves to complete stillness and silence for a time, to get to know their surroundings, but more importantly, to hear the voice of Chihowa. God.

The Grandmother had been a child when the missionaries came to their homelands in Mississippi. Her father had embraced the Book the white men taught from as it completed his belief in the Creator, and passed these teachings on to his children. He had died of cholera on the long trail, but his faith remained alive and well within his family. The Grandmother had often said that was when she learned to be still. That was when she could know her father's wisdom as a little girl, and share in the faith he'd had. One day, it became her own.

Instead of telling the story again, the Grandmother began to sing softly in Choctaw, then English. It was a familiar tune to all people, regardless of race or social status. Ruth Ann knew the hymn in both languages. They were not quite the same, yet exactly the same. It had been a song sung by her people on the long journey of death and life.

Through many dangers, toils and snares
I have already come;
'Twas Grace that brought me safe thus far

and Grace will lead me home.

The Lord has promised good to me
His word my hope secures
He will my shield and portion be,
As long as life endures.

Yea, when this flesh and heart shall fail,
And mortal life shall cease,
I shall possess within the veil,
A life of joy and peace.

When the Grandmother finished singing, she began the old story of leaving behind the sacred mound, Nanih Waiya. Of leaving relatives and friends who still refused to move. Of crossing great rivers on ferries and even a steamboat. Of wagon drivers who took small Choctaw boys, too little to keep up, into the woods and bashed their heads against a tree. Of soldiers who fed the starved people rancid meat and spoiled vegetables. Of the good white farmers who gave of their pumpkin crop to the starving Choctaws.

The Grandmother talked of her bare feet every time. She spoke of how they must move, always move or be frozen to the ground. Only at night could she find a fire to sit by and be still. These were the better times.

The more she spoke in her slow way, the more the discomfort seeped from Ruth Ann's body. It was as if the words had the power to absorb pain and carry it in the way all words go. Those words and the Grandmother's spirit had moved with her on her own trail of tragedy.

At the end of the Grandmother's story, Ruth Ann closed her eyes and forced herself to allow a time of respectful silence. But soon, she opened them again and had to ask the burning question on her heart. "Pokni, was Harriet Anoletubbee a witch?"

The Grandmother had not known the woman to Ruth Ann's knowledge, but it wasn't really what she meant by the question. She had wrapped a dozen questions into one inconsequential one, and the Grandmother would understand.

The Grandmother swayed in the rocking chair for several minutes before she spoke again. "When I was four years old, before we had to leave *Nanih Waiya*, our neighbor Tobias came for me. But he did not come as a man. He flew on the wings of an owl in front of our home. The owl grabbed me by the shoulders. My father shot him. Next morning, we went out there. There was Tobias with my father's musket ball in him."

The Grandmother stared at the wall behind Ruth Ann. "Those were in the old ways, but ways do not know time."

And that was it. The Grandmother rose and tucked the blanket under Ruth Ann's chin like she was a little girl again before leaving the room, closing the door softly behind her.

Despite the swirling thoughts and confusion, Ruth Ann gave in to her gritty eyes and drifted off to a fitful sleep.

◆◆◆

Four weeks later, Ruth Ann was still hobbling around on the crutches Dr. Anderson had provided. She hadn't gone out much and was sick of being tended to by everyone from Matthew, to Beulah, to her mother. They fussed over and pampered her through the Christmas holiday and into the New Year.

Matthew had moved her bed to Della's sewing room just off the front room so she wouldn't have to be carried up and down the stairs. Or chance breaking her neck if she fell while attempting to go up on her own. She sorely missed her work at the newspaper office. How could Matthew manage without her? They had to keep the *Choctaw Tribune* going strong.

One advantage of being cooped up, though, was missing the questioning looks and whispered rumors firsthand. Plenty of folks were wondering about the Choctaw woman, Harriet Anoletubbee, accused of being a witch, and Ruth Ann's part in trying to help her and little Samuel. Beulah kept her abreast of the latest gossip without overdoing the drama.

Samuel had recovered and gone home with his father, a sad man grieving over the events but accepting them as though they were divine. Reverend Anoletubbee and the two young men with him were arrested in their homes one district over and taken to Paris, Texas, until a federal hearing could be arranged. It was another sign of the changing times that they were taken away instead of tried by the Choctaw justice system.

Anoletubbee didn't fight the move, having a well-revered lawyer on his side. It was rumored he would plead emotional insanity. Anoletubbee's wife and young daughter had died mysteriously of a spinal infection—or so the doctor nearest them said. Ironically, it was rumored he was more a witch doctor than anything, and it was he who claimed Harriet Anoletubbee was a witch who had cast a spell on the reverend's wife and daughter, along with several others in their community. The only way to stop the curse was to kill the supposed witch, who happened to be the reverend's sister-in-law.

Reverend Anoletubbee somehow mixed this old way with his Christian faith. So he calmly saddled his horse and enlisted the help of two young Choctaw men. They rode to Harriet Anoletubbee's home, but his brother had been warned ahead of time. He saddled a pony and sent Harriet away with the child, fearing the reverend would kill them all. She had made it as far as the bluff before the pony was shot from under her.

Ruth Ann had lived the rest of the nightmare.

She fidgeted in the chair by the window, looking out at the bustle of the ever-growing town. Three families had moved in since Ruth Ann's confinement began and she hadn't gotten to meet them.

At least she had managed not to miss all the church meetings, but even being there was difficult. The white and the black families had trouble understanding the events and often cast odd looks at Ruth Ann as if wondering if Harriet

Anoletubbee had indeed been a witch and perhaps cursed Ruth Ann before her death. Other than being holed up in the house, she didn't feel cursed. She just wasn't sure how she felt about what happened, whether to feel grief for Harriet's death, which she did, or feel sorry for the former reverend, which she did. Somewhat. It was all unsettling.

Matthew came in late, right before supper that evening, and stomped the mud from his boots. The early snow they'd gotten wasn't a sign of continued severe weather. It was cold but the snow had turned to rain most of the time. He joined them at the kitchen table, where Della fussed at him for being late. They said grace then he announced, "I'm going to Paris tomorrow. A lot stirring about the witch hunt. Probably some news worth reporting in the *Choctaw Tribune*."

Ruth Ann unconsciously stiffened at any talk of the witch incident, and Della frowned at her son. But Ruth Ann quickly said, "I want to go with you. I want to see Reverend Anoletubbee."

Matthew shook his head. "You're still recovering. Besides, jails are a harsh place for a..." He halted and looked between a silent Della and a determined Ruth Ann before finishing, "...a woman's place is anywhere God puts her."

And that was how Ruth Ann came to be on the train the next morning bound for Paris, Texas.

CHAPTER TWENTY-FIVE

IT WASN'T RUTH ANN'S FIRST time across the Red into the state of Texas. She'd attended Kidd-Key College in Sherman before deciding she could better spend her time at home when Matthew urged them to move into town and start a newspaper. Truth told, she hadn't liked being away from home and her relatives. That was last year, and Ruth Ann was glad she made that decision. Although they'd had their own set of troubles, she wouldn't have wanted Matthew and Della to face them alone.

Besides, she knew she was attached to the newspaper during her four-week absence. She couldn't wait to get back to work. But first, she had to put things in her past, obtain a settling in her mind about the whole witch incident. And that meant leaving behind the familiarities of Indian Territory to do it.

Paris was a booming city in its own right. With the cotton industry, it had briskly evolved before the War, suffered and survived Reconstruction, and thrived as the nearest city to Dickens on the south side of the Red River.

The train depot was more crowded with purpose than the Dickens depot, which was more an attraction to most that loitered around. Here, everyone had somewhere they were going, a job they had to do, or an important trip they were making. The train now made two runs a day up to St. Louis instead of one. Another change that had taken place during Ruth Ann's confinement.

Matthew stayed protectively at her side as Ruth Ann tried to navigate the heavy crowd with her skirt and crutches. Mercifully, Della had pinned a few of Ruth Ann's dresses and petticoats up slightly above her ankles and taken in some of the fullness to make it possible for Ruth Ann to modestly use the crutches in public. Her mother was such an artist when it came to clothing, no one could notice the adjustments without close examination. And Ruth Ann never stopped long enough for that.

Matthew guided her along the platform, staying in front of her to make a clear path through the crowd. They went down a loading ramp instead of the stairs, and Ruth Ann managed it without falling. She had become experienced in the use of the crutches, but the city noises and hurrying jarred her nerves. There was little relief when they reached the sidewalk, and she had to pause to catch her breath. Dr. Anderson had ordered a wheelchair from St. Louis for her family to take her to church and such, but it never arrived, leaving Ruth Ann to gain stronger muscles in her arms than she thought possible.

But the muddy streets beyond the brick around the depot, the fast-trotting horses and foot traffic were beyond what she wanted to handle. She lifted her chin, but it still quivered when she said to Matthew, "I don't think I can make it across town."

He nodded, squeezing her shoulder. "Stay here." He helped her settle on a wood bench by the depot then left.

Soon, Matthew returned, riding in a hack with a friendly faced man sitting high atop the enclosed vehicle. The man bounced down from the seat and tipped his hat to Ruth Ann. "Name's Aaron Greiner, but folks call me Cabby. I can get you anywhere around these muddy roads you need to go."

Ruth Ann dipped her head with a smile, shy and also ashamed she'd insisted on coming, which caused extra expense. But Matthew didn't complain as he introduced her while getting her loaded in the carriage.

Trying to set her embarrassment aside, she took to looking through the window of the enclosed vehicle, thankful to be out of the cold and yet hoping the ride didn't cost too much. But when the carriage had to plod through the muddy roads leading away from the depot, Ruth Ann figured the fare was worth it.

They arrived in front of the Lamar County Sheriff's Office a short time later. After disembarking, Matthew paid Cabby and informed him they might be awhile. The driver assured them he'd be around unless he was waved down.

With nothing but wide steps leading up to the door of the jailhouse, Matthew had Ruth Ann hold the crutches in one hand as he scooped her into his arms. She gasped and tried to make sure her skirt was lying properly, embarrassed to be carried up the steps. But they were to the top and she was back on her one good foot before anyone seemed to notice.

Inside, she let Matthew get the proper permissions while she looked around the large interior—at least what she could see—of the sheriff's office. She'd noted from the outside that the jail was in another section further down. The building felt cold and lonely, and Ruth Ann wondered why she was here.

Soon, Matthew came to her, shaking his head. "You can't speak with Reverend Anoletubbee. You were the only witness to the actual killing, and your testimony will count heavy against him."

This, Ruth Ann had not expected. She had given a deposition about the incident and knew she'd likely be called to testify in court, but she hadn't realized that would have a bearing on seeing the prisoner. An idea came to her. "Matt, I don't need to speak with him. I just want to see him."

An understanding smile touched Matthew's lips and he nodded, re-entering the office. He would find a way for her to see the reverend.

And he did.

Not much time passed before Ruth Ann stood outside on the cold lawn filled with dead grass in the space between the jailhouse and the majestic two-story courthouse across the lot from them. Matthew found an empty crate behind the jailhouse and turned it on its side for her to sit on. They waited. Before long, a face appeared in the barred window with its soiled glass.

Reverend Anoletubbee.

He looked more at ease than he had that night in the field after shooting Harriet Anoletubbee, but still sorrowful. He stood at the window, his face showing recognition of Ruth Ann, but he made no gestures or effort to communicate. He stood and watched her. She stared back.

Time slipped away, and Ruth Ann's good foot grew numb from pressing her toe against the dirt to keep herself balanced on the crate. Matthew said nothing, just watched and waited. He had always been more patient than she, learning that lesson better than any of the children who had sat at the Grandmother's feet. Ruth Ann didn't yet know the secret to being still. She had to find her own way to stillness as she spent this time with Reverend Anoletubbee.

Nothing happened at once. But in those minutes that grew to a half hour, a knowing, an understanding took place. Nothing that could ever be put to thought or words, but it didn't need to be. It just was.

Slowly, Ruth Ann pulled herself to stand balanced on the crutches. She felt older, as if years had passed and age-old wisdom had visited her soul. She was glad she'd come to see Reverend Anoletubbee. Nothing was resolved or changed except the peace in her heart. Perhaps that was one thing it took to get to know someone. Perhaps that was why scripture said to *be still, and know that I am God*.

That was the old way to know someone. Not with words or even thoughts. Just being still.

Ruth Ann nodded to Reverend Anoletubbee. He nodded back. Months from now, maybe a year, she would likely return

THE EXECUTIONS

and give testimony that would sentence him to death. But it was understood by them both. That chapter of Ruth Ann's life was closed.

Since they were both shivering, Matthew took Ruth Ann over to the courthouse to seek warmth from a large stove in the hall. There were people he had come to speak with to get more information about the rumors going around about the trial of the witch hunters. It was said one of the young men might be released soon, charges dropped.

But before Matthew made any rounds, a clerk popped out from an office. "You're Matthew Teller, right?"

He approached where Matthew had settled Ruth Ann on one of the long benches that ran half the length of the wide-open halls. Matthew turned to the clerk and nodded while accepting a slip of paper. The clerk said, "Telegram came for you. The boy left it here per the instructions. I guess they knew you'd be here."

"Thank you." Matthew sat next to Ruth Ann while he opened the telegram and read it. He popped back up. "We have to go!"

Caught off guard, Ruth Ann frowned. "I thought we were spending the night and going to a play while we're here—"

"Sorry, Annie." He pulled her to her feet and shoved the crutches under her arms. "There's more trouble brewing over that last election for chief. A standoff is going on right now up at Barnes mansion."

Ruth Ann struggled to follow his long strides toward the courthouse door. "But what...how...?"

"Beulah Levitt caught wind of the story from a passing peddler, who hightailed it out of Springstown when the shooting started."

"Matthew, do you mean we're going *toward* trouble again?"

"Not we, me." Matthew opened the courthouse door, a blast of freezing air striking them. Ruth Ann stopped and refused to cross the threshold as she narrowed her eyes at him. He put up one hand as if surrendering. "Okay. Not me, we. Now let's move."

Ruth Ann grinned. "There's nothing more powerful than the press…"

"Short of God Almighty." Matthew grabbed her crutches and put them in her left hand before swooping her into his arms. Her skirt caught wind and flapped almost to her knees, but Ruth Ann just held on for the ride.

God Almighty was all powerful, and He'd given them a mighty tool if they stayed alive long enough to make good use of it.

CHAPTER TWENTY-SIX

RUTH ANN SAT ON THE edge of her train seat, flexing her ankle and hoping it would bear more weight than she had tried on it since the sprain occurred. She couldn't let the crutches hinder her, with Matthew feeling he had to constantly look after her. If she was a burden, she'd need to stand aside while he did his work on the story happening right now.

Compared to her pensive state, Matthew was calm, reading a copy of the *Paris News* he'd bought while they waited for the train to Springstown. They would pass through Dickens, but Matthew had already wired Beulah and asked her not to mention to Della the fact that her two children were heading into a local feud. When the Dickens stop came and went, the people who knew they'd left for Paris would think they were staying there as planned to watch a stage play and spend the night.

But the Dickens stop did not merely come and go. When passengers boarded, Beulah Levitt was among them. Ruth Ann saw her first and stood, gripping the seat in front of her to stay balanced on one foot. Matthew raised his eyes from his newspaper and frowned.

Ruth Ann hissed as soon as her friend was close, "Beulah, what are you doing? Is Mama all right?"

Beulah had her reticule in hand and her feathery hat perched perfectly atop a womanly bun, but her expression was one of girlish delight. "You two always have the fun. I thought I would be a sightseer this time. Please, you don't mind?"

She directed this question at Matthew, who tossed the newspaper and caught the floating pieces in midair. "Of course not. This shouldn't be much more rowdy than a Sunday picnic when deacons disagree with the sermon."

"Good." Beulah motioned for him to move his feet which he had propped on the seat in front of him. Sighing, Matthew dropped his boots to the floor and sat up straight, Beulah taking the seat across from him. Ruth Ann settled back on the edge of her own seat as the train jerked into motion again. "But what about your father?"

Beulah drew a dainty watch from her rose colored lace pocket on her vest and checked the time. "He should be home soon and will see my note that I have gone to meet with friends. He will understand."

"About the note or why you've come with us?" Matthew was back to reading his newspaper, barely muttering the words loud enough for them to hear.

Beulah continued to speak with Ruth Ann. "I am sorry, but I'm certain your mother is aware of where you are and what you must do. She came to the house after the news spread about the shooting in Springstown. She did not say anything, looked at me awhile before leaving again. I wanted to apologize to her for sending you the telegram, but she appeared to understand why."

Ruth Ann finally leaned back in her seat. It would take over an hour for the train to reach Springstown and there was no use being anxious about her mother. Della knew her offspring were as hardheaded as she was—as their father had been—and what had to be done, would be done. No use fretting over things. Pray and see them happen.

THE EXECUTIONS

The train lazed its way through the foothills of the Kiamichi Mountains, plowing ever closer to Springstown. That was where a militia of a hundred or more Choctaws were rumored to have surrounded the Barnes mansion, threatening to massacre the whole lot of those inside.

◆◆◆

He was the Captain. Entrusted with authority and responsible to bring back the guilty. Where had things gone wrong?

In the cover of darkness, he eyed the swaggering, swearing men who stumbled around the makeshift camp on the edge of town. They were incoherent, insensible and rude. Nothing of the orderly militia he'd been promised by those from the Progressive party. But it was too late to back them out of the situation. Shots fired. This was the place. Not tonight though.

While the Captain watched, Ramsey, a mixed-blood Choctaw, upended a forbidden bottle, his tongue stuck out to touch the tip of the glass rim as he drained the last drops. The bottle caught the reflection of the quarter moon as the man took a step backward and toppled to the ground.

The Captain growled as he strode over. He latched onto the front of Ramsey's jacket with one hand and hauled him to his feet. He shook the nonsensical man until his head snapped back and forth and he howled. "Cap'n, cap'n! I don't do nothing."

The Captain backhanded him across the face. "You don't do nothing? You don't! Quit the drink or I'll level you where you stand."

Ramsey's head bobbed, though it was impossible to tell whether from the shaking he'd been given or in agreement. The Captain gave him a hard shove to the merciless ground before turning to the next drunken militia man.

Not all Progressives were mixed-bloods, same as not all Nationals were full-bloods. But in this drunken mess, it didn't matter what blood flowed in whose veins. Their blood would be flowing out, hard and heavy, if they didn't come to their senses.

One by one, he tried to conform his men with little success. The train whistle sounded. The last train of the night would roll into town in a few moments. Not all his men were accounted for.

With a few choice words under his breath, the Captain jerked the reins of his horse loose from the tree it had been tethered to and mounted. He urged the horse into a lope before fully finding the stirrups with the tips of his boots.

The whistle blew again, timid and afraid as if too long a blast would awaken a monster. He passed the empty depot, his head ducked low as he scoured the shadows. No sign of his missing men, the ones supposed to be on a mission of justice.

The train screeched to a stop. Gunshots sounded up the street. A gasp, maybe a scream off in the darkness. The Captain turned his horse in the direction of the shots.

Something had gone wrong. He was the Captain. He would set it right. Or die trying.

♦♦♦

When the train let off a final whistle for Springstown, darkness had fast closed in on the small town. The train pulled to a stop. A few passengers peered through the windows, though there wasn't much to see besides the depot and a road leading out of town. It wasn't until Ruth Ann, Matthew, and Beulah disembarked from the train and moved across the platform that they saw riders. The air chilled Ruth Ann as she adjusted the crutches under her arms, thankful for the cape over her shoulders.

The train puffed away from the station. A shot sounded, and Matthew herded the young women into the depot.

A slight man, middle-aged and graying, jumped from his place behind the ticket counter, its bars not appearing to

THE EXECUTIONS

provide much security or comfort to the man. He pressed a hand to his chest. "Land sakes, I didn't know anyone got off the train. You addled? We got shooting going on by a militia of Choctaws. Some kind of tribal war. You all best stay in here until they ride on out to the Barnes place like they've threatened all day to do."

Matthew, after making sure the young women were away from the windows, went over to the counter. "They aren't out at the mansion now?"

The sound of glass breaking and another shot served as an answer. The ticket master wiped moisture from his forehead with a bandana. "They may have gone out there, or tried to. From what I saw, the whole bunch of them were so drunk they couldn't sit their horses. Their captain feller keeps trying to get them sobered up and thinking straight. I don't think he's looking for a fight, but what else do you expect from a bunch of drunken Injuns?"

The way he said *Injuns*, Ruth Ann knew he did not realize they were Choctaws too. Dressed in a suit and tie, Matthew could pass for a white man, and Ruth Ann was in Beulah's shadow.

Beulah opened her mouth as if something sharp might come out, but Ruth Ann managed to elbow her despite the crutches, and shook her head. They weren't out to convince every white man that all Indians weren't drunken heathens. He could find that out by reading the *Choctaw Tribune*.

Matthew conversed with the man a few more seconds before seeming to make a decision. He came back to the young women and motioned toward the benches. "Get comfortable here. I'm going to rent a buggy and head out to the Barnes mansion."

Beulah replied, "Be sure the buggy is large enough for three."

CHAPTER TWENTY-SEVEN

IT WAS PAST DARK WHEN their rented buggy rolled up to the Barnes mansion. Even with only the moonlight, the structure was impressive. Three stories high with an equal width, it boasted a wraparound porch with white columns, large picture windows for the parlor, and a fenced-in yard. Mr. Robert Barnes, a white man, had come from a ruined Southern plantation after the War and settled in Indian Territory where he married a Choctaw girl and reared a number of mixed-blood children. Some of them already grown and married, two others at school and little ones likely in bed, the house stood quiet and peaceful. Hardly welcoming to late night visitors who wanted a news story.

But the Tellers had known the Barnes family for years. Mr. Barnes had been particularly fond of Jim Teller, grieving when he heard of his death. He ordered and paid for a tombstone from New Orleans with the family's permission, along with the writing they wanted on it. Sissy Barnes, smart, adventurous, fearless, but beautiful and sweet, had been Ruth Ann's roommate at Kidd-Key College. Ruth Ann admired her spunk, maybe envious of it, but the girls always got on well. Sissy was the only reason Ruth Ann regretted leaving school.

Her friend was still at the college, entering the winter semester.

A lantern shone near the barn and two men walked toward them. They were easy to recognize. Mr. Barnes walked with a limp from an old war injury never healed, though he strode tall and proud on land he'd claimed as his own through his marriage within the Choctaw Nation.

Next to him was a humble black man called Uncle Solomon who had worked there since before most of the children were born. He had shown dear love for the family, grieving when they grieved, laughing loud when they did. He truly was more an uncle to them than a hired hand, and Ruth Ann always enjoyed listening to his wild yarns when she was a young friend of Sissy's.

Now though, with grim faces, Mr. Barnes and Uncle Solomon carried Winchesters under their arms and Colts holstered on their hips.

Matthew called out, "Halito, it's Matthew Teller." He hopped down from the buggy to shake their hands.

Barnes nodded, still solemn. "I saw who you were coming up from the road, otherwise I might have blasted you out of the seat. Bit of trouble around here abouts. You heard?"

Matthew nodded and Uncle Solomon went to the buggy to help the ladies down. Beulah was introduced and Ruth Ann fussed over about her ankle, which served as an embarrassment as she tried to exit the buggy properly, a difficult task even with Uncle Solomon's help. She finally abandoned etiquette, opting to let Uncle Solomon lift her by the waist and swing her and her skirt free of the wheels to settle her gently on the ground. He retrieved her crutches and handed them to her. "You sure grown up to a fine lady, Miss Ruth Ann."

He winked at her, teasing, and she blushed. "I'm trying, but you wouldn't believe the difficulties."

Uncle Solomon laughed and untied the small trunk Matthew and Ruth Ann had packed for Paris. "Reckon y'all are staying the night then?"

Barnes adjusted his Winchester and nodded. "You're more than welcome to. I know my Sissy will be glad to see you, Ruth Ann. We heard about your scrape and she's been pestering to see you since she got home."

Surprised, Ruth Ann started moving toward the mansion, hoping to get an unnoticeable head start on the rest of them. "Sissy is home? What of school?"

Barnes led the way to the steps. "Seems her mother thought it best with all the trouble stirring to have her brood close to home. Pepper's back, too." He looked at Ruth Ann but she focused on navigating the steps to the mansion.

A few years ago, there were rumors that Pepper was courting Ruth Ann. He made frequent trips to the Dickens area and people said what a handsome couple they would make. But Pepper never came to see Ruth Ann. There was a white girl on a farm out near Uncle Preston's he had his eye on until her father threatened to disown her if she didn't break off the relationship.

These things Pepper had told Matthew in private, though he intended for Ruth Ann to know. It was somewhat an apology for letting the rumors continue and even promoting them. He didn't want his mother to know he was seeing a white girl. Not that Mrs. Barnes, who was full-blood Choctaw, had any prejudice. Her husband was white. She merely had picked out someone else for her middle son and wanted to see him married within the tribe for political reasons. And she had admired the young woman Ruth Ann was becoming. His father saw it the same way, but never once had Pepper shown interest in Ruth Ann. It certainly wasn't something she wanted to think on or discuss.

Once they'd navigated through the double doors leading into the mansion, they saw it was alive with activity despite the dark exterior. The curtains were tightly drawn and the family was gathered in the parlor. The baby grand piano sat quiet, something it was not used to in the evenings. Mrs. Barnes was fond of music and had obtained piano lessons for herself and all their children after Mr. Barnes ordered the baby grand from St. Louis.

Though not a real mansion in Eastern terms, the Barnes estate exceeded any in the district and maybe half of Indian Territory. Its wide staircase leading to the second floor was graced with a polished oak banister and rich red carpet. The second floor held bedrooms and guest rooms, while the third was consumed almost entirely by a ballroom. A second baby grand piano was housed there with a small stage for other musicians.

The Barnes family had often held dances there leading well into the night, but things had changed. Since their oldest were married, two young adults in school and the youngest too little to appreciate such socials, the times of youthful celebrations had taken a rest in the Barnes mansion. They likely would have anyway with all the controversies upheaving the tribe and forcing everyone to take sides.

Despite having no Indian blood, Mr. Barnes was fiercely protective of the tribe's rights and sovereignty. He took a strong stance with most full-bloods against the Dawes Commission and the talk of joining the Territory with the United States. The last election for chief had ended in violent disagreement, both sides claiming victory. Secret meetings were held, and it was around that time several Nationals banded together for a shooting rampage. This was the band Silas Sloan had joined.

After more fighting, negotiating and threats, the joint session of the council declared the Progressives had won by a mere eight votes. Barnes had been a strong backer of the Nationals candidate and his loud protests over the results hadn't gone unnoticed. The fact that he sided with the Nationals, mostly full-bloods, against the Progressives, primarily mixed-bloods, brought the tribal feud to his front door. The newly re-elected Chief Jones had turned vindictive, looking to squash Robert Barnes any chance he got. At least, that was how the story went.

But the atmosphere in the parlor was a pleasant one,

though with tense undertones. Mrs. Barnes welcomed her guests in with a smile and Ruth Ann noted they were not the only ones.

She recognized Edward Combs, a mixed-blood who owned the mercantile, and also an older white doctor, William Caldwell. Mrs. Combs was settled comfortably on the sofa nearest the fire, a blanket laid primly over her lap. She was a frail woman, but still offered a smile as greetings were exchanged. Dr. Caldwell asked after Ruth Ann's injury and seemed pleased with her progress.

Mrs. Barnes had laid aside the book she'd been reading aloud to embrace Ruth Ann in a careful hug. "So glad you are doing well, young lady. I'm sorry we haven't come down to see you. There's been trouble..."

The fading words didn't dim her greeting, but she did cast an unconscious glance at the last person in the room, who stood near the entrance, speaking with Matthew. Ruth Ann tried to keep her eyes down, but she still caught Pepper Barnes' glance toward her. He nodded briefly then went back to speaking with Matthew.

Pepper Barnes was a fine-looking young man, ambitious and amiable. He was destined for tribal politics, everyone said. At twenty, he'd seen more of that world than the average Choctaw man. Thanks in part to his father, he already had connections in high places.

All in all, there were plenty of reasons the Barnes parents kept looking between their son and Ruth Ann to the point of embarrassment. Thankfully, a high squeal disrupted the looks as Sissy Barnes literally bounded into the parlor.

"Ruth Ann!" Sissy skidded to a stop beside her and leaned over the crutches for a tight hug.

Ruth Ann returned it gladly, excited to see her friend home. "Oh, Sissy, I've missed you with you being away at school. We didn't even see each other at Christmas."

Sissy nodded, her loose black braid falling over her shoulder. She'd obviously already retired for the night, with a simple calico dress quickly thrown on and her hair already down in a braid. But it didn't diminish her enthusiasm as she greeted the new guests and got acquainted with Beulah. While they chatted, Ruth Ann noticed Pepper's frequent glances toward the conversation and she was sure it wasn't his sister or her he was looking at.

Pepper had gotten his nickname at the ripe old age of six when the family took a trip down to Mexico. In broken Spanish, he'd finagled a local vendor into giving him a bright red apple. After taking a large bite, Pepper gagged and turned red the rest of the day. His family teasingly took to calling him Pepper when telling the story back home, and it stuck so well most folks didn't remember his real name.

Watching him now watch Beulah made Ruth Ann a little red, though she couldn't tell why. She focused her attention on finding a place on the sofa to sit and let Beulah retire her crutches against the wall for the rest of the evening.

CHAPTER TWENTY-EIGHT

THE NEXT MORNING DAWNED COLD and dreary, but Sissy's chipper behavior lightened the mood. She entertained the group with college stories through breakfast, then Dr. Caldwell went to sit on the front porch and the Combs left for home. Mr. Barnes, Matthew and Pepper went into the large office off the main hall that Barnes used for business.

No doubt the men had plenty of business to discuss. Aside from being a friend, Barnes was fully aware of the influence the *Choctaw Tribune* had and how it would only grow. It didn't hurt for a prominent man to court the publisher who controlled what went into the news. Two Indian newspapers had already taken sides in the political turmoil.

Meanwhile, the young women were hosted by Sissy on what she wanted to be a grand tour of the place for Beulah. But she quickly recognized Ruth Ann's limitations, so she took them onto the back porch of the mansion. She settled Ruth Ann in one of the wicker and cane rockers, making sure she had a lap blanket to cover her legs. Beulah tucked it more snugly around her waist and Ruth Ann was almost upset with her friends for treating her like an invalid.

Her ankle could hold some weight that night, and she'd even managed the wide staircase up to the guest room to her own surprise. Determination to not be a burden had only lasted as long as it took Sissy and Beulah to take over her care, which was worse than her own mother in terms of fussing.

From the back porch, Ruth Ann took in the cold view of the bright red barn and stables. Pastureland graced most of the property and this part in particular was especially impressive. Corrals made with mill cut boards separated off areas for Mr. Barnes's prize possessions and primary source of income: horse breeding. He raised top quality stock which had started with selling to the cavalry remount stations. That grew into such a reputation for fine horse flesh, he was soon shipping stock back East, as well as selling individual colts and race horses locally in Indian Territory.

Contrasted with the standard breeds was his herd of Choctaw ponies. He'd started his stock with a stallion and mare he bought from a full-blood man who claimed the horses were descendants of those who crossed on the long trail of tears from Mississippi. Mr. Barnes had taken a liking to the sturdy animals and started raising and selling them. Ruth Ann's own paint pony, Skyline, had come from this herd.

It was a special pony Sissy wanted them to see that brought them out on the back porch that morning as the sun tried, unsuccessfully, to break through the morning clouds and mist.

Inside the corral nearest the back porch, Sissy clicked her tongue, but already, one fine black pony had lifted his head and trotted toward her. She laughed and rubbed his nose before offering him the carrot in her other hand. She slipped a halter with its rope over his muzzle and led him to the gate.

In spite of her sour disposition from being pampered to the point of embarrassment, Ruth Ann leaned forward in the rocker and admired the pony's movements. He pranced to one side of Sissy, showing a great deal of spirit, though a willingness to submit to his mistress's bidding. His shapely ears were up and alert to his surroundings, taking in sounds coming from the barn, to noises of the other horses asking for attention and treats.

When Sissy opened the gate, he didn't bolt but allowed her to lead him through while she turned to latch it back in place. Overall, he was a fine animal and Ruth Ann anticipated riding alongside him when Sissy was home again in the spring and summer.

Sissy led the pony up to the porch. "Christmas present from my daddy. Isn't he something?"

Ruth Ann nodded. "He certainly is."

"I haven't named him yet. Nothing is special enough."

When Beulah made no comment, Ruth Ann glanced up to see her friend's white face. Beulah was wringing her hands. When she realized they were staring at her, she forced a nervous laugh. "I, well, I never learned to ride. Really, horses terrify me, except when they are hitched to a buggy or wagon. I thank God for trains!"

At this, they all laughed and Sissy tied her pony to a hitching post before joining them on the porch. "You cannot live around here and not ride horses!" Her eyes twinkled with mischief. "Why, when I was just a little thing, I climbed up and took off on my daddy's saddle horse. My feet couldn't even reach the stirrups. Took them a quarter of a mile to catch me, and when Daddy pulled me off, I promptly announced, 'I ride, Daddy, I ride!'"

They laughed again as the wind picked up, sending a gusty chill over them. But Sissy put her hands on her hips with a set look in her eyes. "When the weather warms, we're going to get you over here for a week and teach you how to ride." She waved toward the corrals. "We have plenty of horses to choose from!"

While Beulah shook her head and tried to excuse away any such notion, and Ruth Ann thought of how Pepper would like the idea, the back door opened. Actually, it was pulled inward so hard, it nearly banged a hole in the wall while the screen door was shoved out and into the porch wall with a sickening thud.

Beulah, who was closest to the door, spun around. Before anyone could scold him, Matthew grabbed Beulah by the arm and pulled her toward the door. "Come, now!"

"What is it?" Sissy grabbed Ruth Ann's crutches and was moving to give them to her, but Matthew didn't give her a chance. He quickly pushed her along behind Beulah while he lifted Ruth Ann into his arms. She gasped. "What has gotten into you, Matthew Teller? What's happening?"

"Riders," was all Matthew said as he kicked the door shut behind him and told Sissy to bolt it.

CHAPTER TWENTY-NINE

IN THE PARLOR, CHAOS REIGNED. Mrs. Barnes had the two youngest children seated by her on the baby grand piano bench. The children whimpered and Mrs. Barnes soothed them in her motherly voice.

Dr. Caldwell, who had sounded the warning from the porch, fidgeted near the fireplace. He spoke with Mr. Barnes, who shook his head as he loaded a Winchester. A second one was tucked under his arm, and Colts were holstered on both hips. "All I can say, Doc, is there ain't no talking with hot heads, 'specially when they've had drink. Their captain won't be able to hold them. Every man better get a gun and get ready to defend."

Pepper and Uncle Solomon entered the parlor with more Winchesters. Matthew set Ruth Ann steady on her feet and took one of the rifles while he met Ruth Ann's eyes. Matthew hadn't done much shooting lately, except a hunting trip with cousins a few weeks ago. He'd taken to not wearing his six-shooter since Mr. Levitt's request he not bring it into the new print shop combined with the repair shop.

Banny had mostly left them alone since becoming sheriff and having no legal jurisdiction over Choctaws. He seemed content with harassing other people. Because he hadn't been able to run the *Choctaw Tribune* out of town or kill it off, he realized it was gaining in popularity and its influence could and would be used heavily against him, so he steered clear for now.

Seeing Matthew with a gun, and probably having to use it, heightened Ruth Ann's senses and memories. Her daddy and other brother, Philip, were killed with guns in defense of the money entrusted to them. This day, more Tellers might die by bullet. Yet Ruth Ann felt a natural security in seeing the armed men preparing to defend them.

When she glanced at Beulah, she was surprised at the anticipation she saw—as if this really were what she'd expected when she boarded the train at Dickens to join them on their adventure. Ruth Ann knew Beulah and her father disagreed on many things. The use of guns was one of them. If only Beulah had experience with weapons, Ruth Ann wouldn't doubt seeing her Jewish friend take up a rifle alongside Mr. Barnes himself.

But neither protest nor enthusiasm would make a difference this day. The stage was set and the players for catastrophe were in place. Ruth Ann could do little but watch it play out.

Matthew had put her down near the sofa away from the front windows where Mr. Barnes and Pepper were taking positions, peering through the lace curtains. She gratefully collapsed on the sofa, and Sissy settled on one side while Beulah took the other as if they still intended to care for her. Ruth Ann was too frightened to get flustered at them. She held her breath as things settled into deadly silence.

The faint rumble was distinct now, and when Pepper pulled one curtain to the side, Ruth Ann caught a glimpse of a sight that made her heartbeat double. Dozens of riders—maybe a hundred—were on the road leading up to the mansion, kicking up dust and waving rifles in the air.

A loud whoop sounded from what appeared to be a primarily mixed-blood group. Progressives. They didn't like

Barnes, a white man, butting into their politics. They mostly didn't like the Nationals candidate he had supported for chief at the last election and the ensuing fiasco. Threats had flown between the two political parties, and too much blood had been spilled already.

The unorganized riders started drifting apart, coming ever closer to the mansion. Ruth Ann saw one take a swig from a long-neck bottle before another man rode by and knocked it from the man's hand. The rider kept moving back and forth in front of the others, waving an arm at the men, who ignored him as they checked their rifles and tried to steer their horses in a straight line.

Then it happened.

A shot rang out, shattering the window Pepper had been looking through. He jumped back before hitting a knee and taking aim through the broken glass and returning fire.

Mrs. Barnes pushed her young children to the floor. Ruth Ann did not need any assistance in scrambling off the sofa and behind it as more volleys were exchanged, glass shattering from the windows. Dr. Caldwell, a rifle in hand, knelt behind an armchair, glancing around as if to determine if his help was really needed.

Mr. Barnes pumped off several shots and quickly exchanged the empty Winchester for a loaded one on a side table. Uncle Solomon laid aside his own rifle and started reloading one Pepper passed off to him.

Matthew, braced against the far corner, took aim and fired in a steady pattern. Ruth Ann, watching the action from behind the sofa, could not help but believe Matthew, and probably the other men, were aiming to dismount, injure and divert the riders, not to actually kill anyone. She prayed so.

A rapid succession of gunfire splintered the wall behind the sofa, well over head height, but still, Beulah gripped her arm and Ruth Ann heard her whispering prayers.

Pings sounded to Ruth Ann's right, and Mrs. Barnes groaned as fine China doll figurines on the mantle were struck, the pieces flying across the room.

Then Barnes shouted, "Cover the back! They're riding around there!"

Pepper responded, Uncle Solomon not far behind. Sissy, quite calm until this moment, suddenly screamed, "My pony!"

She leaped to her feet despite the gunfire all around her. Uncle Solomon shoved her back down. "I'll get him safe, don't you worry." He bolted into the hallway toward the back door the young women had used only minutes before. The far end of the parlor faced the back porch where they had sat and Sissy scrambled over to those windows.

"Sissy!" Ruth Ann gasped, limping after her while staying bent at the waist. She pushed her friend from behind, forcing her lower as the window she'd aimed for exploded from a bullet.

"Ah!" Sissy tumbled to the floor, Ruth Ann on top of her. At first, she thought her friend had yelled from the shove, but when she rolled face up, it was Ruth Ann's turn to scream at the sight of blood trickling from Sissy's forehead. Blinking her eyes and trying to sit up, Sissy touched the wound and a nervous giggle bubbled through her lips. "If you hadn't pushed me, it would have hit my heart. I'm glad we're friends."

But the near brush with death didn't stop Sissy from going—more cautiously—to the broken window. Ruth Ann crawled along behind her, trying to avoid getting glass in her skirt or palms. They peeked out together from where the window let in a gust of cold air.

Amid eight or nine riders now in the back area of the mansion was Uncle Solomon at the barn, hurrying the black pony inside. Once he'd secured the doors with a cross timber, he ran back for the mansion, shots flying past him from all sides. Some of these were coming from Pepper as he tried to offer the older man cover. It almost worked.

Sissy screamed when the bullet struck Uncle Solomon in the side, knocking him to the ground. Matthew was beside them almost instantly, brushing the young women aside as he propped the Winchester on the windowsill and aimed before squeezing off a round, jacking the lever and firing again.

Pepper darted out and hauled Uncle Solomon to the porch. The back door slammed open. Sissy rushed to the hall and came back moments later tucked under Uncle Solomon's arm as she helped the bleeding man to the floor behind the sofa. Beulah moved to help lay him down while Dr. Caldwell crawled to them and took over the emergency care.

Ruth Ann stayed in a stunned state against the wall by the window, watching the events unfold as if in a dream. A warm hand on her shoulder brought her head slowly around and she looked into Matthew's concerned eyes where he crouched below the shattered window, bullets pinging off the mansion's outside walls. Ruth Ann reached up and covered his hand. Unable to speak, she managed a smile and a nod. They would do what they had to do.

The sounds of gunfire tapered off as both sides reloaded and regrouped. Pepper came back into the parlor for ammunition, another rifle and to check on Uncle Solomon. The older man was laid out behind the sofa, eyes closed but conscious the doctor said, and he expected he'd be all right. Dr. Caldwell turned to tending the bullet scrape on Sissy's forehead.

Mr. Barnes circled the room with his limping gait to check on everyone and paused by his wife and youngest children where they huddled beneath the baby grand piano. Mrs. Barnes was teary eyed but still had her chin up, her strong Choctaw jawline more pronounced than ever, assuring her husband they were all right and that he should tend to the others. He and Pepper conversed a moment before he made his way over to Ruth Ann and Matthew, who held guard on the back window.

Barnes bent to look out. "They come around this way again?"

Matthew shook his head. "Not since they all headed back to the main road to figure out what they're doing next."

Barnes nodded and glanced between the siblings. "Awful sorry you two got in the middle of things, but I reckon you're getting one humdinger of a story out of it."

Matthew chuckled, but it wasn't an appreciative one. In truth, he probably wouldn't mind being in this fix, but having his sister and Beulah in the middle of it tipped the scales considerably. Still, he must not have been too worried to begin with since he let them come along in the first place.

Ruth Ann asked the next question. "Mr. Barnes, what do you suppose they'll do? When will they go away?"

Barnes frowned, bending to look out the window again, probably trying to check on his horse herd which had run off to the far side of the corrals. He had several hired hands but they didn't live on the ranch and had likely steered clear of the day's work when they heard about the coming troubles. "Them hooligans won't stop until they run out of liquored up courage. Or I'm dead. Running out of liquor ain't likely to happen."

CHAPTER THIRTY

ABBY BARNES SUCKED IN A deep breath after the rapid climb up two flights of stairs. She was unaccustomed to such strain, at least since her children had grown and she no longer rushed about and worried over their care as she had when they were toddlers on these very stairs of the mansion. This day, she rushed for a different reason. They were under attack in their own home, and already wounded had to be tended.

Abby lifted her skirt and skipped down the hall to move as quickly as possible without running. Even alone, her womanly graces wouldn't allow for such behavior. Contrary to some beliefs about Indians, she was refined, a delicate Choctaw woman with a strength only the burial of infants could instill.

At the end of the hall, she flung open the linen closet. Scooting the step stool close to the shelves, she selected sheets from the uppermost one. These older, near threadbare ones would do for bandaging. She never threw away old sheets or clothing. Such waste was not permitted in her rearing or the rearing of her own children. And now it proved useful, in the most horrible way.

Stepping carefully from the closet, Abby buried her face

in the well-pressed sheets. She breathed the faint scent of lavender she'd used to wash them in before carefully storing them away last summer. A hint of dust chided her, but she added a few tears to anoint the sheets.

Come what may. Though her own interest in the politics of her tribe had waned, she would stand by her husband's side as she had through countless conflicts and disasters and death. She at his side, he at hers. They had weathered great storms this way.

Still, Abby hesitated by the linen closet, lifting her face slowly from the sheets and to the ceiling of the great home her husband had built.

"Father, protect them."

With one corner of the worn sheets, Abby absorbed the last of her tears and fright. She moved forward.

♦♦♦

Noontime came and went with the mounted men circling about with their captain still trying to get them under control. Pepper had fetched blankets and pillows from the upstairs bedrooms to make the trapped guests and family more comfortable.

Ruth Ann settled in one corner of the parlor away from the range of any windows. Beulah and Sissy took turns at her side, or checking on Uncle Solomon. Dr. Caldwell didn't seem to think he was in grave danger and had given him something to help him sleep.

When the quiet lingered, Mrs. Barnes and Sissy went into the kitchen with Matthew as a guard. They returned before long with ham sandwiches and distributed them to the antsy but hungry group huddled in the parlor. Ruth Ann politely took a bite of her sandwich but it went down thickly in her dry throat despite the hot tea Mrs. Barnes poured for everyone. Ruth Ann's throat felt raw as if she'd been screaming for days, though she'd said or done very little since the ordeal had begun three hours before.

The tension didn't lesson as minutes ticked away. In fact, the quieter things were, the more anxious the mood of the room grew until it seemed a fight was destined to break out among them for no reason. It stirred in the air, especially between Pepper and Matthew.

Ruth Ann became aware of it when she heard the familiar pitch of her brother's irritated tone. She craned her neck to see the two by the fireplace hearth. She laid her sandwich down on the napkin in her lap, appetite forgotten.

Everyone in the room seemed to notice at the same time, but Matthew and Pepper were oblivious to the stares as their voices rose.

"You can't shoot your way to the top anymore. The War and the Wild West are long over and that way of doing things is past." Matthew had leaned his Winchester by the mantle, but Pepper held his in both hands as he stared back, hard.

"You may think you've got some class now with your own newspaper, but you're still as mixed-blooded as the rest of us. I don't look for fights, but I sure won't run from them either."

Why they had found an argument on that topic, Ruth Ann couldn't guess but she didn't like the sarcasm in Pepper's voice, as if he was accusing Matthew of being a coward. Mr. Barnes watched the conversation from his post by the front window where he was monitoring the gang of riders who seemed to be taking a rest. Matthew's comment could have been meant for him, a Civil War veteran and one who had seen his fair share of the "wild west." He was known to have a murky background with the law.

Rumor had it that Robert Barnes left his home in sunny Georgia to come west and seek a new beginning. Other rumors went about that he participated in the killing of several Federal officers who were taking part in the South's reconstruction. The officers might have been doing more than taking part. They were taking everything in sight, including the plantation Barnes had grown up on, and the farms of several local boys who came home to nothing. The stories varied, with some saying Barnes had merely been riding with the killers, while others said he led the attacks.

Ruth Ann never ventured to ask Sissy about her father's past, though she was sure her friend would have little to say. The Barnes family hosted lots of people, always opening their home for social gatherings to friends and strangers alike. But they didn't discuss family business outside of family.

Now, Barnes did not interfere in Matthew and Pepper's argument. He watched silently, keeping one eye on them and one on the window.

Matthew's voice went up a notch. "Sometimes running from a fight is the braver thing to do, though not from what folks see on the outside. Of course, that's all some people are concerned with—what shows on the outside."

Some underlying message must have been packaged in Matthew's words, because Pepper exploded. He shot his fist forward—the one that clenched the back of the Winchester—busting Matthew across the jaw with the wooden stock. Matthew's head whipped to one side as he staggered away a few steps, tripping over a footstool and crashing to the floor.

Ruth Ann shot up against the wall from the floor, her ham sandwich tumbling off her lap. Beulah drew back, as if retreating into a shell, her eyes frozen wide open in shock. Sissy remained seated, shaking her head as if she'd seen this scene one too many times.

Mrs. Barnes stood from where she'd settled on the sofa. She looked undecided on what to do, not wanting to sit but, after glancing to her husband who seemed unconcerned, she lowered herself down and clenched her hands. The younger children slid to the floor to watch.

Matthew jumped to his feet, wiping blood from his lip with the back of his sleeve. He charged Pepper, who pulled the rifle back for another strike, but Matthew was ready for the upward swing. He was able to duck lower and barrel into Pepper's stomach, lifting him off his feet and throwing him into an elegant arm chair, splintering the back legs as it tipped over.

Mrs. Barnes shrieked and jumped up again, hands on her hips. "You two boys fight outside!" She winced when she realized the foolishness in her demand. They didn't hear her anyway.

Matthew kept up his charge, grabbing Pepper by the front of his shirt and hauling him to his feet as he lost his grip on the Winchester. Pepper pushed back and they both rolled to the floor, neither getting a clean strike as they battered each other with fists from close range. They rammed the low tea table, sending a teacup crashing to the floor.

At the shattering sound, Beulah screamed. Not a small cry of being startled or of disapproval. It was like the scream of someone who had witnessed a horrific murder.

Ruth Ann stared at her Russian Jewish friend to see her with fist to lips as she screamed again, tears in her eyes. "Stop! Stop it!"

They did. Matthew pulled back when Pepper quit whacking him, and looked up from the floor with a bloody lip. Pepper sported a black eye. They scrambled to their feet and stared at Beulah. But Mr. Barnes took command.

"They're coming back, boys. Better quit lollygagging and take a position. It's time for some real fighting."

Without a word, the two young men grabbed their guns and Matthew went to the back window, Pepper to the front with his father.

When the shooting started again, Ruth Ann wanted to cover her ringing ears. She could no longer stand the sound of gunfire, and Beulah's haunting scream left her head hurting. Why the gunfire and violence hadn't affected Beulah the way the parlor fight had puzzled Ruth Ann. She looked at Beulah again to see her changed from before. She sat with her back straight against the wall, eyes staring blankly ahead, lips white. Ruth Ann reached to rub her arm, and Beulah didn't turn her head, but responded by wrapping her fingers around Ruth Ann's hand.

Bullets flew as the small group took cover the best they could. The gunfire was different this time, more intense.

Whatnots in a corner curio that had previously seemed safe shattered. A shower of ceramic rained around Ruth Ann and she covered her head with her arms, telling Beulah to do the same. Slowly, Beulah came out of her dazed state and responded to the instructions Ruth Ann or Sissy gave her.

The shooting grew louder, more rapid. Pepper shouted for Matthew to come up front and help, but Matthew didn't respond, too intent on steadily shooting out the back where bullets flew past him through the window. Ruth Ann recognized the grim determination on his face. It was the kind of look he had when he knew the odds were stacked impossibly against him, but he would go down fighting. Like the time he'd faced off with Banny when he didn't stand a chance of outdrawing his opponent.

Did those inside the mansion stand a chance against the onslaught? What if the men rushed the house? They might be drunk and stupid, but one hundred men against three weren't good odds in any situation.

Without thinking, Ruth Ann got to her good foot and hobbled to Matthew, very aware of the volley of bullets flying over her head as she stayed low. At his side, she knelt in the shattered glass and picked up the empty Winchester he dropped on the floor to grab a loaded one. He glanced down at her. "Annie, get yourself back! These bullets are going wild everywhere—"

Another series of shots coming through the window cut him off as he leaned away before pumping off two shots in defense.

With strangely steady hands, Ruth Ann took the cartridge box from the small side table and began loading the rifle. She couldn't help but wonder if the bullets she selected would end a man's life.

The first round of attacks had done damage to the house and injured Uncle Solomon and Sissy, but it still hadn't seemed necessary to kill anyone. That was what Matthew had told her when things settled a bit. This time, though, it was more intense, as if the men outside truly were set on not letting up until Mr. Barnes—and the rest of them—were dead.

The firing at the back part of the house tapered off, probably so the horsemen could reload. Matthew dropped to one knee and reloaded his rifle while Ruth Ann finished the one she still held. In the sudden quiet, Ruth Ann lowered her voice when she asked, "What were you and Pepper fighting about?"

Matthew didn't answer until he'd finished reloading and held the gun lightly between his scraped knuckles. "Seems the reason this militia is here is because they were sent by the chief to arrest a Nationalist, Darby Smith. They say he killed one of the Progressive leaders and dumped his body in Dead Man's Lake. They think Barnes is hiding Smith here. Pepper says they let them go on thinking that to give Smith a chance to get away. They gave him a fresh horse day before yesterday."

Ruth Ann fumbled the box of cartridges, spilling them on the floor. She stared at Matthew. "You mean to tell me we're helping a criminal escape?"

"Who's to say?" Matthew rose slightly from his crouched position and peeked through the lower half of the window. "Mr. Barnes told me this morning that the Lighthorsemen were going to shoot Smith rather than bother with taking him back. Smith said he killed in self-defense. Aside from that, Smith is Mrs. Barnes's cousin." His jaw tightened. "But Smith isn't what this is really about. This is about two parties who want to have each other's hide over political differences. Some civilization."

Matthew glanced at Ruth Ann. "What happened with Beulah?"

Ruth Ann opened her mouth to say she didn't understand her friend's outburst over the fight, but her words froze with the next round of gunfire. From this close, Ruth Ann could almost feel the bullets striking inches from her on the other side of the wall. She hunkered lower while Matthew rose and returned fire. She wondered how much ammunition was left. The box she had was nearly empty.

Then a call came from the front of the mansion. The voice rose in volume as the gunfire ceased. Mr. Barnes hugged the wall and gazed through the parlor window. He whistled low. "Looks like the captain is laying down his gun and wants to talk. Won't do no good. Them polecat Progressives won't stop until they see me six feet under."

Dr. Caldwell, who'd done little more than cower in the corner after tending Uncle Solomon, suddenly leaped to his feet and sprang out of the room. Ruth Ann heard the front door fling open and bang the wall. Pepper started after him, but Mr. Barnes halted him with a wave of his hand as he continued watching through the window. "They got nothing against the doc. Neither do we. Let him go."

Ruth Ann pulled herself up to see better. Through the window Pepper guarded, she watched the doctor wave his arms at the man who approached the mansion from the crew of horsemen. The two halted in the middle and a few words were exchanged.

The man, apparently the captain of the militia, glanced toward the house a long moment. Finally he motioned at the men behind him, shouting words that were met with protest. But in a few moments, the wounded were gathered together and the horses turned back toward the town a few miles from the mansion.

It was over.

CHAPTER THIRTY-ONE

WITH THE SETTLING DUST, THE doctor came back in the house. Barnes pushed away from the window and stared at him. When the doctor merely headed toward the sofa where they had put Uncle Solomon after the shooting stopped, Barnes barked, "Well, confound it man, what did you say to them?"

Dr. Caldwell lifted the bandage on the groggy man's wound and looked the bloody spot over careful before replying, head down, "I told them you were dead, that there was no sense in shooting the rest of us full of holes."

Ruth Ann hovered near the wall, using it to support her weak ankle as she glanced around at the worn faces in the room. Mrs. Barnes looked relieved, but still frowned. Pepper kept watch through the window, shaking his head. Matthew sighed and combed his fingers through his hair. Sissy smiled a little, looking like she might dissolve into uncontrollable giggles at any moment. Ruth Ann felt the same way, the release from the threat of death almost too much for her trembling body. She needed to either laugh or cry. But she did neither, just glanced at Beulah, who hadn't moved from her spot on the floor, leaned against the wall.

Barnes finally broke the remaining tension in the air with a booming laugh. "Well, sir, thank you. I'm feeling mighty fine for a dead man. I don't reckon there will be much laughing going on with them polecats when they find out they've been had. They might even take to calling us Nationals 'foxes' instead of 'buzzards.'"

Sissy joined her father's contagious laugh, and everyone started moving around the room, setting furniture upright and sweeping the broken glass and ceramics to the side. Beulah finally stood and, wiping tears from her cheeks, began helping.

Dr. Caldwell, who was changing Uncle Solomon's bandage, muttered loud enough for them all to hear, "You'll quit your laughing when you see what the outside of your mansion looks like."

♦♦♦

Several hours later, with the coming dusk, Matthew helped Ruth Ann and Beulah into the buggy that had remained safe inside the barn along with Sissy's pony. The Barnes family and Dr. Caldwell came out to bid them farewell.

Barnes gripped Matthew's hand. "You've turned out to be your own man, Matthew Teller. You and that sister of yours keep a-going and telling the truth about your people. I reckon that's what you'll do about what happened here, and I know it may not shine well for me, but you do what you got to do." He raised an eyebrow at the buggy and added quietly, though Ruth Ann still heard, "Your sister sure is a fine Choctaw girl. But that lady friend of yours could use some backbone if she's going to stay around here."

Matthew opened his mouth as if to correct him, but nodded and offered his hand to Pepper. Despite their tussle, Pepper shook his hand firmly with a quiet yakoke. But his eyes were more on the young women in the buggy and Ruth Ann slid lower in her seat, knowing who he was looking at. He had to have heard his father's comment as well, but Beulah paid no mind, keeping her eyes on the bullet-riddled mansion. It was shot to pieces.

Sissy climbed partially into the buggy to give Ruth Ann another hug and whisper to them, "I'm going to hold you both to coming back for a visit real soon. We'll have Beulah riding across the mountains in no time. And wait until you see Solomon's Victory run." She winked.

Mr. Barnes raised his hand in farewell as Matthew took his place on the buggy seat next to Ruth Ann and off they went toward the depot and home.

The three remained quiet during the ride and wait for the southbound train, due in another hour. They had intentionally missed the one earlier they could have caught, knowing many of the Progressive militia might have been on it.

Even now, Ruth Ann kept her eyes on the men milling around the depot. From their dust and blood-splattered clothing and wobbly movements, she guessed they, too, were part of the militia that had been shooting at them not long before, but thankfully, she didn't recognize their faces and knew they didn't recognize her either.

When Matthew moved to one corner of the depot to study the wanted posters pinned to the wall, Ruth Ann shifted and realized her ankle didn't hurt as much as it had yesterday. Or maybe it felt that way because the rest of her body ached and protested against not being in bed. Beulah stirred next to her, but was silent and staring at nothing. Ruth Ann leaned toward her and asked, "Are you all right?"

Beulah's lips parted and Ruth Ann was sure she caught the sound of a soft laugh from them, as if the question was ironic. "By most definitions, yes, I am well. Now. You must think you should be ashamed of my fears."

Ruth Ann shook her head. "Pay no mind to what Mr. Barnes said. He's a rough man himself, and you shouldn't—"

"We were young, foolish."

It took Ruth Ann a moment to recognize the far-off look in Beulah's eyes, the look of a story in them. And it had nothing to do with what had happened at the mansion. Ruth

Ann folded her hands in her lap and let the depot's dank interior and its occupants fade around them as she listened.

"We should not have been out that night, but we wanted to be together before my family left for America. He was to come too, someday. We would be together forever but we wanted forever that night." Beulah bowed her head, clenching her hands.

"Soldiers found us. They had just gotten off duty and feeling frisky, as Americans say. They knew we were Jews. How, I cannot explain. People know. Especially the soldiers.

"They taunted us, then one of them struck him with the butt of his rifle. Another hit him from behind." Beulah was shaking and looked as if she might vomit. "When he fell to the ground, they started kicking him. But it wasn't fast or furious. They did it slow, as if they knew how to make it hurt the worst. One of them held me back, clamped a hand over my scream. I watched the blood drain from the body of the one I loved, drop by drop, moan by moan."

Ruth Ann felt trapped herself, but she managed to reach out one hand to cover her friend's. Beulah turned hers over to grasp Ruth Ann's. She swallowed visibly and caught her breath, staving off tears. "Oh, Ruth, I was not afraid when the guns were firing. I was not afraid when that man was shot. I was not afraid when I knew I might die. It was all exciting, even thrilling, and I was glad to be there. But that fight…when he struck Matthew with the gun and they started hitting and kicking…"

Beulah used one hand to cover her mouth and closed her eyes. "I have refused to relive that night for many years. But in an instant, it attacked me, rendered me utterly helpless and completely alone. I have lived in that aloneness since Albert died." Beulah dropped her hand. "I have not even spoken his name since then."

Ruth Ann squeezed her hand again, praying for the right words to come. She finally said weakly, "You were so young."

The soft laugh came through Beulah's lips. "Yes. Young and foolish teenagers. I sometimes wonder if I am much more than that now."

"You are more." Ruth Ann's reply came quickly this time. "You've been a wonderful friend, a woman I look up to. Please know that."

For the first time in several hours, Beulah met Ruth Ann's eyes and smiled. "You are someone I admire greatly, Ruth. Like your namesake, you are strong and gentle and loyal to those you love. Do not ever change."

And with those words, Ruth Ann moved a little more away from the insecurities of youth and into the responsibilities of womanhood.

A train whistle sounded and Matthew came over to them as the others in the depot picked up gear and even saddles in preparation to board. Ruth Ann stood with her crutches, thankful to not be assisted but grateful for the lessons in humility learned through her injury. Matthew lifted one handle of their trunk and hesitated before offering Beulah a hand. She looked up briefly then placed her hand in his, rising gracefully and with a smile.

CHAPTER THIRTY-TWO

WHEN THE TRAIN CAME TO a stop at the Dickens depot, Ruth Ann noted a lone man standing on the dark platform. He was small, slight of build. Anyone else would have taken him for a weak man. Ruth Ann knew better.

When they disembarked from the train, Beulah trotted into her father's waiting arms. They said nothing, but Ruth Ann noticed the wetness on his cheeks and recalled his telling of his own fears of being out at night, of the things that had happened to the Jewish family in Russia.

Quiet goodnights were exchanged. Ruth Ann and Matthew waited together on the platform as they watched their friends depart, arm in arm. Matthew turned to her. "Need a hand?" His smile was teasing.

Ruth Ann adjusted her crutches under her arms, scarcely feeling the need for them anymore. She gave him a wink. "No. I do believe I can manage."

But before they could take a step, heavy boots echoed from the darkness at the other end of the platform. Ruth Ann jerked in surprise, trying to turn swiftly around and hoping not to see Sheriff Banny coming toward them. Matthew didn't have his gun and she for one had heard enough shooting for one day.

But it wasn't Sheriff Banny.

Josiah Carter, owner of the freight office and accused whiskey runner, came toward them with steps that exuded a confidence Ruth Ann didn't know the man to have. When she saw the uncertainty in his eyes, she knew the truth of his demeanor as he gave a brisk nod to each of them. "I've been wondering when you two would get back. I need a favor, and I have a business proposition."

Matthew sighed and rubbed the back of his neck. "Mr. Carter, we're exhausted and our mother hasn't had word of us yet. We can talk in the morning—"

"No!" Carter hesitated as if his raised voice had spooked him. The pitch of his tone went up. "I need your answers now. You see, I'm leaving on a business trip in seven weeks. The problem is, my telegraph operator quit on me, so I've had to man it myself. The thing is a nuisance and the constant clatter is bad for my digestion."

Ruth Ann did her best not to let her smile show in the dim light given off from the lantern hanging from the pole above them.

Carter continued. "Because of where your, uh, new shop is located, we can easily run the wires to it. Telegraphy isn't difficult to learn, and with it, you would be the first to have any outside news that came through. I really see no reason for you to say no…" He let his words jumble together and stop. He looked at them expectantly.

Matthew stared back at him and Ruth Ann knew he was having a difficult time containing his anticipation. But he kept his eagerness in check for the sake of professionalism. "I don't know, sir. We're very busy with the newspaper, but…perhaps we can help you out."

Carter frowned. "That was the business proposition, not the favor. I'm doing you a service."

Matthew cocked his head. "Which is interesting considering our previous business dealings. Why not ask the *Dickens Herald?*"

"That's my affair," Carter snapped, then added slowly, "I mean, like I said, your building is in a better location for running the wires."

When Matthew looked at Ruth Ann to get her opinion, she spoke to Mr. Carter. "So, you're doing us a favor by letting us take your clattering responsibility off your hands. It will bring us additional income and give us first chance to break outside news. But you want a favor. What exactly are we exchanging?"

Carter cleared his throat and looked quite uncomfortable. "It's a personal matter. I need you to meet someone coming in on the train while I'm gone. Hotel room is already reserved, I just want you to make them feel...welcome. Give them a good first impression of Dickens."

"*Us?*" Ruth Ann and Matthew said together then chuckled.

Carter unbuttoned the top of his shirt and tugged on his collar. "I'll be frank. You are the only ones in this town I know to be trustworthy. Honorable. Even with someone who has been...less than courteous to you."

Like trying to kick us out of your old storage building so our newspaper would go out of business? Ruth Ann kept this to herself. "Who is this person? A business associate? If they're coming from outside the Territory, they may not like Choctaws. Especially with what just happened up in Springstown."

Carter's Adam's apple bulged. "What happened?" He raised his hand, palm out, and shook his head. "Never mind. Don't want to know. And no, I don't believe this person will be hostile toward In—um, Choctaws."

Matthew crossed his arms, showing the deal wasn't sealed yet. "You didn't answer my sister's question. Who is this person and why are they special?"

Carter punched a fist in his other hand. "Oh, I might as well say. You have to know." He paused a long moment, as if hoping they would take pity on him. When neither said anything, he sighed heavily. "She's my bride-to-be. Of all things, she's coming here to marry *me*. Josiah Carter."

Ruth Ann stared. Matthew rubbed a hand over his mouth as if hiding a grin. "A mail-order bride?"

"We've written letters...I have them all. She's willing to come here and marry me and that's that. That is, unless she takes one look at this shabby town and heads on down to Paris." At this, Carter looked Ruth Ann in the eyes, as if knowing where the sympathy in the Teller family could be found.

She sighed and glanced at Matthew, who shrugged. She said, "We can do our best, Mr. Carter."

The man nodded briskly. "It'll be enough. You won't regret it. And I'll have you trained on the sounder before you know it. You'll be right smart with it, what with working with typesetting all the time."

"The sounder?"

Carter's face lightened with a smile. "I'll tell you all about it. You'll love it, really you will." He reached out and shook Ruth Ann's hand then Matthew's. "I look forward to reading the next edition of the *Choctaw Tribune*. Goodnight."

As he hurried off the platform toward his home, Matthew chuckled. "Me too. What do you think of adding a love letters column? You'd be good at it."

Ruth Ann swatted his arm. "This is very serious business for Mr. Carter. You'd do good to remember that."

"Oh, of course." Matthew kept a straight face as he hauled their small trunk up by one handle and settled it over his shoulder on his back. "Just don't let this romance stuff go to your head...or your heart. You're a businesswoman, you know."

Ruth Ann's cheeks flushed from both the praise and the thought of romance. For a second, Pepper Barnes came to mind, but she quickly dismissed the thought. She was a businesswoman now. Newspaper, telegraph...what kind of chapter did God plan to write in her life next?

♦♦♦

THE EXECUTIONS

A week after the mansion shoot-out, the *Choctaw Tribune* ran a follow-up story.

Violence still brews following this year's elections among the political parties. Indian Agent Bennett sent a scathing report of the mansion shoot-out incident to Washington, D.C., much to Chief Jones' disapproval. A copy of the report reads in part:

"...the acts of said so-called militia have been contrary to the laws and the constitution of the Choctaw Nation, and the conflict precipitated by them was the act of a drunken, irresponsible, and uncontrollable mob, who were banded together as militia for the evident purpose of murdering men, women, and children, thereby removing their political opponents, and so intimidating others that the powers of the present party in authority may be perpetuated."

The United States military have been called in to squelch the conflict, though with much objection from the leadership of the Choctaw Nation, which claims the U.S. government has no say in their affairs. Regardless, the militia to arrest Darby Smith has been disbanded, as well as supporters of Barnes and his followers. Special Agent Faison ordered the arrest of Darby Smith. Smith was apprehended yesterday and placed in jail.

While casualties and arrests overall were few, the tension created by the incident sets a dark tone for the Nation. More conflict is foreseen in the future for the Choctaw Nation—from without and within.

Prayers to the Almighty are going up from homes throughout our land.

CHAPTER THIRTY-THREE

RUTH ANN'S EYEBROWS KNITTED and she pressed her tongue against the back of her teeth. Her finger was poised over the key on the sounder, trembling. Holding her breath, she opened the key and signaled station *Rn*, twenty-two miles up the line. She squinted at the slip of paper held carefully in place by the tips of her fingers. The writing was almost illegible but Ruth Ann made out the words in her mind slowly. Then the signal came from *Rn*.

They were ready to receive.

Dots and dashes, dashes and dots.

Ruth Ann was halfway through the message when a voice boomed behind her. "You sure you know what you're doing?"

Her finger slipped, adding a dash too many. She sighed and tried to answer without stopping her work. "Yes, sir. It's almost through and—"

"Ol' Josiah never had any trouble. Always zipped that thing off like magic. I don't have all day, missy."

Eyebrows still knit, Ruth Ann completed her message.

Received, came the reply. She took her first breath in fifteen seconds. "Your brother should have that message delivered to him shortly, Mr. Newton. He'll be able to tell you if the storm looks like it's coming this way."

Ruth Ann looked up and smiled at the man from her seat, hoping he would leave. Mr. Carter warned her the poor but eccentric farmer would come in once a week, spend a few precious coins to wire his brother twenty-two miles north of them and ask about the weather. What she hadn't known was, he would be her first customer on her first day to man the telegraph alone.

The sounder clacked with a message for down the line, but Mr. Newton stood on his toes and leaned partway through the cutout window and stared at the sounder. "That his answer?"

"No, sir."

"What is it, then?"

"A message for on down the line. Would you like to do your errands and stop back by before you leave to check for your brother's answer?"

"No. I'll wait." Mr. Newton leaned back, but still crowded the space in front of the window, staring at the sounder. "We shore could use the rain. Mighty dry heading into spring."

It hadn't seemed so to Ruth Ann, but then, she wasn't a farmer with a lifetime of work invested in what the fickle weather might or might not do.

Still, it wasn't easy having him stand there, listening to everything and blocking the window. She didn't expect many customers, but his bulky frame still made it look like a line had formed. But Ruth Ann remained gracious and stood to move around the small room. She straightened perfectly straight bits of paper, checked to see that all the pencils were sharp, stirred the fire in the tiny stove, and noted an out-of-place ink can on the desk that held the sounder. It must have migrated from the adjoining print shop. She should take it back in and cover it, but she was certain Mr. Newton would throw a fit if she ventured far from the sounder.

When Carter informed them he was turning the telegraph wire over to them, Matthew and Mr. Levitt set to work on a plan to incorporate it with their shop. Since Mr. Levitt had a five-year lease and a clause that he could make modifications to the building, they enlisted the help of Peter, Uncle Preston's son, to add a small room to the right side of the shop, a lean-to. Peter, at fifteen, was already a master carpenter and practically built it himself. And he didn't mind pointing out that fact in a loving, younger cousin type way.

A doorway was cut to connect the lean-to with the print shop side, with no outside door. Matthew believed the room would be more secure that way. Ruth Ann felt better in there alone, the window with its shelf the only access to the outside street. Anyone else had to come in through the print/repair shop and past Mr. Levitt, Beulah and Matthew.

Except only Mr. Levitt was operating the shop today. Matthew had gone to Paris to check on a story and Beulah had gone with him to shop for new dress material. Dickens had limited options.

The sounder clattered again, and Ruth Ann calmly explained to Mr. Newton that the message wasn't for their station. The noise that had bothered Mr. Carter so much was an exciting sound to her. To think, the world was connected through telegraphy. She could contact people back East in no time at all. They could contact Dickens. If there was a reason.

Important—and not so important—communications were in her hands. Ruth Ann didn't take the responsibility lightly, so when a signal came through for their station *Tn*, she dropped into her chair and signaled she was ready, pencil in hand.

But the dots and dashes were almost drowned out by Newton's booming voice. "That him? What's happening with the weather? You sure you know what you're doing there, missy?"

Ruth Ann didn't answer, tongue pressed against the back of her teeth again. When she finished writing the message, she shook her head. "No, sir. It's for—oh, I'm sorry, I'm not supposed to mention who receives a telegram. But it's not from your brother."

Newton put a fist on the tray, grumbling, "Ol' Josiah would've had an answer by now."

"Ol' Josiah," Mr. Carter, had left that morning on his three-day business trip. But he hadn't operated the wire for a week now, turning it fully over to the staff of the *Choctaw Tribune,* Ruth Ann and Matthew. And today, Ruth Ann alone. She would make good on her promise to Matthew that all would be well while he tended important work of the newspaper.

"Gracious, if one man can gum up the works, it's this one." A shrill voice accompanied the woman who elbowed Mr. Newton to the side as she stepped into Ruth Ann's limited view. Ruth Ann smiled and greeted her, recognizing her as the wife of the mayor. Mayor Warren hadn't exactly been the nicest man to her, but Ruth Ann wouldn't judge his wife based on that.

"May I help you, Mrs. Warren?"

"My, my, but if you aren't a smart little whip for an Indian. Running the telegraph all by yourself. Yes, I want to send a telegraph to St. Louis. Right away." Mrs. Warren placed her reticule on the shelf, further pushing the irritated Newton back. She withdrew a slip of paper and glanced at the man but spoke to Ruth Ann. "This is confidential, is it not, my dear?"

"Yes ma'am. Only the telegraphers and the recipient will know."

"Splendid." She slipped the folded paper to Ruth Ann who opened it and read the pristine handwriting: *Please check the sizes remaining at Claremont's regarding the aforementioned undergarment. Purchase according to my prior measurements. Though I have gained a tiny bit, I am confident in my abilities to make do.*

Ruth Ann wrote out the cost on a slip of paper and handed it back to the woman who wanted confidentiality. Mrs. Warren gasped and her shrill voice echoed into the small room. "Land sakes! That is outrageous! Just to inform my sister to purchase…*something* for me?"

"Perhaps you'd like me to shorten it," Ruth Ann offered, face warming from embarrassment. Two unhappy customers standing at her window was not how she'd hoped to start the day.

"Shorten it! Good grief, at this price rate, you'd have to send only three words. And every single one in my message is vital." Calming herself, Mrs. Warren looked Ruth Ann in the eyes and smiled sweetly. "Now, my dear, I am certain we can do better than this on the cost. Woman to woman."

Ruth Ann doubted the sincerity of Mrs. Warren's words, but before she could explain she had no control of the prices, Newton pushed his way to fill half the window. "Hey now, if you give her a discount, you gotta give me one too!"

Clatter from the sounder alerted Ruth Ann of an incoming message. "Excuse me, I must take this."

Mrs. Warren sputtered, "But what about my message? You have customers to attend, young lady!"

"Hey, is that from my brother? Sounds like the kind of message he'd send."

Ruth Ann furiously scribbled the message from station *Xn* in Paris. She sighed with relief when she realized what it was. Beulah had taken a bit of her shopping money to send a message to Ruth Ann: *Wish you were here, but know you are doing well. God's blessings on my sister.*

Savoring the message a moment, Ruth Ann carefully pocketed it and wired back: *You as well.*

"Well? Well?"

"Well?"

"Someone must be awful thirsty." A third voice joined the group around the window. Mrs. Warren frowned at the poor joke, Mr. Newton folded his arms and scowled, but Ruth Ann hadn't needed to see their reactions to recognize the voice and know who had come to add to the chaos.

Sheriff Banny stood behind the other two, thumbs stuck in his gun belt. His presence made them part but not give up their valued spots in front of the window.

Uncertain whether to ignore the man or acknowledge him, Ruth Ann pretended to have already been in the process of speaking to Mrs. Warren as she moved back to the window.

"Would you like to send the message in its entirety?"

From the corner of her eye, she noted the sheriff move off and she took a quick breath. Mrs. Warren grumbled, "I suppose it will have to do. But I will speak to Mr. Carter about this as soon as he returns. I'm certain *he* would never charge me so much."

Ruth Ann didn't reply as she took the money, made change and sat at her little desk across from the window. Matthew said they needed to place the desk there so the operator would have easy access to the customers, but it made Ruth Ann nervous to have two sets of eyes watching her every twitch.

Before she could open her key to transmit to St. Louis, she was hailed with an incoming message from *Rn*, the station twenty-two miles up the road. Ruth Ann made the fatal mistake of commenting aloud, "That will probably be from Mr. Newton's brother."

"It is? What's he say? A storm coming? Tornadoes? Hail? God knows we just need rain. Well, speak up, missy! What's he say?"

During Mr. Newton's outburst, the message rang through rapidly, so sharp and harsh Ruth Ann couldn't get it down. She was forced to "break" the operator's dots and dashes by lifting her key and informing of the last word she'd received.

The operator immediately picked up at that point but didn't deliver more slowly. Mrs. Warren whined in the background, "You are supposed to be sending my message, not taking them! Gracious, why did Mr. Carter turn this thing over to a child?"

At almost nineteen, Ruth Ann hardly considered herself a child, but she was too busy breaking the operator's message again to make a comment.

Please slow down. I'm having difficulty getting your message.

Oh! came the rapid reply and then the sounder clattered impossibly slow. So slow, Ruth Ann could make no sense of the Morse code she'd learned not long before. On the verge of tears, Ruth Ann broke once again: *Please transmit at a normal speed. You are too fast and too slow. Last word: fever.*

Oh! Is it that I am too fast and too slow or are you too slow and too fast?

Ruth Ann gasped at the insult. But she calmly replied with: *fever*

You have a fever?

Fever was the last word received.

Oh! The correct way to say this is G.A..

Ruth Ann cleared her throat, remembering Mr. Carter had taught her the same, G.A. meaning "go ahead." *Thank you. G.A. fever.*

I did not send that word.

"Well? What's wrong with you, missy? What's he say?"

Ruth Ann lifted her eyes enough to see Mr. Newton's red face and Mrs. Warren's impudent expression. "Young lady, you had better send my message this instant, or I shall be forced to mention your blatant inconsideration to the mayor!"

"One moment. Please." Ruth Ann's voice trembled but she was determined to make a success of the morning. She replied to *Rn*: *I am neither fast nor slow. I am new. Please begin your message again.*

Oh! Why didn't you say so?

And with that, the dots and dashes of the actual message started, still sharp and clipped but at a speed Ruth Ann was able to interpret.

Weather is good. If ever bad coming, will wire you. Charles.

The bell in the print shop rang, but Ruth Ann knew Mr. Levitt could manage for a moment. She acknowledged receipt of the message with a deep breath and prepared to rise to deliver her successful message. From the corner of her eye, she saw someone looming in the doorway of the lean-to.

Ruth Ann jumped from her seat, banging the desk and tipping the misplaced open ink can back and then forward to topple full down the front of her skirt. Black ink streamed down and dripped from her hem.

A chuckle sounded from the doorway, Mr. Newton

reached through the window and snatched the paper from Ruth Ann's hand and Mrs. Warren backed away and sputtered. "What a disgrace, what a disgrace!"

And then they were both gone, leaving the window shelf open and Sheriff Banny standing in her doorway.

CHAPTER THIRTY-FOUR

"GOOD DAY, MISS TELLER." THE sheriff took off his hat and held it in one hand while he withdrew a white handkerchief with his other. "Sorry if I startled you." He stepped into the tiny room, seeming to fill it as he offered the cloth to her.

Ruth Ann took a step back and made no move to take anything from him. "There's a sign outside the door. No admittance. I must ask you to leave."

Sheriff Banny smiled, a gentle one uncommon to him and said, "I'm just trying to be friendly. Seems you could use more friends."

"The ones she has are sufficient." A soft voice came from behind the sheriff, who turned enough for Ruth Ann to see Mr. Levitt standing in the doorway. He was holding the wooden leg of a table in one hand, fresh shavings on his gray apron.

Sheriff Banny turned back to Ruth Ann. "And I got to say, you pick interesting friends at that." He laid the white handkerchief on her desk and backed away and past Mr. Levitt before putting his hat back on and tipping it. "See you around, Miss Teller."

The bell rang when he left and Ruth Ann shuddered. She gazed down at her ruined dress. She should have worn her printing apron, but she wanted to look sharp and professional for customers.

A hail came from *Rn*. Speaking of sharp...

Ruth Ann looked desperately at Mr. Levitt, who smiled and nodded encouragingly. "You are doing well."

With a sigh, Ruth Ann plopped into her chair and signaled she was ready to receive.

Oh! No message. I wanted to ask if your day has improved?

Confused, Ruth Ann replied, *Not so much. But thank you for asking.*

That's a shame. When you get used to it, it's quite interesting. All the people and their quirks. Is it not?

Perhaps. Ruth Ann halted and marveled. She was having a casual conversation with someone she could neither hear nor see. Fascination took over. *What is your station like? Are people so rude there as they are here?*

Oh! To be sure. You should see the man Charles who sent the last message. Quite the character. He gets annoyed at his brother's wires, and takes it out on me, cussing the wire like it was the devil itself!

Oh, that is terrible! Mr. Newton, the brother, gets excited and all, but still somewhat of a dear. At least I hope so. He's said to come in every week, so I have that to look forward to.

You will adapt, I'm sure. Young women are generally quick to do so.

Ruth Ann opened the key to reply, but halted. How would she answer someone in person who said such a thing to her? Who was this person at *Rn* anyway? An elderly woman? A leering man like Sheriff Banny? Ruth Ann thought a moment then replied, *What makes you think I am in that category?*

Oh! It's quite easy when you've been on the wire awhile. Everyone has their own style with the dots and dashes. And your flustered response earlier made it quite clear.

But you were! Going too fast. Ruth Ann tried to emphasize her point, but realized too late it likely pegged her gender and age once again.

Haha. I bet you are a pleasant little lady in person. What is your name?

You first.

Oh! Becoming clever, are we? Picture a beautiful young lady with locks over her shoulders and sparkling eyes when someone looks her way, yet shy and modest.

I can hardly picture you as such.

Oh! That was a description for yourself, was it not? For me, simply call me "D."

Before Ruth Ann could reply, Mr. Levitt reentered the room with her apron and a clean rag. "Oh! Thank you!" Ruth Ann's voice was a little too loud, a little too excited.

Mr. Levitt offered the apron and rag to her with a soft smile and raised eyebrow. "Certainly a great deal of messages to send on this day."

"Oh, well, I..." The sounder interrupted her.

Well? No greeting or introduction of yourself?

Ruth Ann quickly replied, *Call me R.A.. Customers.*

Very well, but tell them to hurry. We are chatting so well now that we've clarified who we are and at what speed we like to transmit.

While Ruth Ann tied the apron over her soiled dress, Mr. Levitt lifted a pristinely penned piece of paper from the floor where it had fallen victim to the ink disaster as well.

Ruth Ann gasped. "Oh dear! Mrs. Warren's message. I must send it right away."

Mr. Levitt placed a hand on her shoulder and looked at her, concern on his face. Ruth Ann realized she must look flushed and too excited. How long had he been standing in the doorway while she and "D" were...chatting? "Yes, sir?"

The smile returned and Mr. Levitt said, "Caution, child. The world is a tempting place, lovely but cruel sometimes. You have it all at your fingertips now. Be wise."

Ruth Ann took Mr. Levitt's hand, squeezed it and smiled. "Thank you, sir. I will."

As Ruth Ann returned to the business of sending "important" telegrams, she wondered how Mr. Levitt had known she was jesting with a person she could neither see, hear, nor judge their character. Not even knowing their gender? Had he suspected it or was he simply leery of such communications in general?

Mr. Levitt was such a kind, gentle man, oft overlooked by everyone but always seeing and knowing things. In many ways, he reminded her of her own father who would say to his children, *"God knows. God knows and He will tell me."*

With the message sent to Mrs. Warren's sister in St. Louis, Ruth Ann was preparing to clean the office when the sounder went off again.

Oh! Hello! Where is the shy girl at Tn? Where's my R.A.?

Ruth Ann hesitated then replied, *Sorry, busy.*

Do hurry and finish. I want to hear more about your station and the rude customers you had this morning. Chatting will be good practice for you.

Ruth Ann didn't reply.

♦♦♦

Where did she go? Daniel drummed his fingers on the table that held his old sounder. He balled his other hand against his cheek, resting his elbow on the table as he lounged, bored. No one interesting on the wire in months and now the little sweet thing at *Tn* had disappeared on him. Surely she wasn't too busy in such a little town as Dickens.

Why, ol' Josiah Carter used to run his freight office, poke his nose in other peoples' business *and* run the wire all at once. But then again, this little gal was new. A plug operator. Handling more than a customer at a time every hour or so was probably enough to frazzle her hair.

She was young, for sure. Insecure. Uncertain of her own abilities. But she'd make out fine with his help. He'd show her the ropes. Or the wires, so to speak.

The sounder clattered and he received the message, jotting it down. For the postmaster in the train depot.

Giving a good shove with both feet, Daniel sent his rolling chair across the rough wood floor and to the side door one step up where he banged with a plump fist. "Telegram, George!" He banged until he heard the familiar grumblings on the other side.

"All right, all right, Danny boy, I'm coming. Quit your bellyaching." The door jerked open and George poked his head through.

Daniel waved the paper under the postmaster's nose. "Something mighty important, yes sir."

George snagged it hopefully and scanned the short message, frowning. "Mighty important, all right. Folks up the line forgot to properly address a box for delivery to the correct millinery shop. As if we had us more than one."

Daniel sighed and pushed his green visor back up his slick forehead. "Yep, 'bout the most exciting thing of the day."

If he had a mirror, he was sure to see his eyes twinkling. George was a good mirror though. He eyed Daniel and barked, "Sure, sure. I suppose that's why I've been hearing that clatter go on and on to beat the band. Who you pestering over the wire now? One of these days, a big man's going to get you for that."

"Aw, ain't no fuss needed. Why, there ain't nothing else for us operators to do, so why not get a little friendliness out of a thankless job?"

George shook his head, still the only part leaning into Daniel's lonely hole. "You just watch it, Danny. One of these days...but who you got on the line this time?"

Daniel grinned. "A sweet sounding thing who's getting all flustered down in Dickens. Sounds like she's having a time, a real splash of cold water on what dealing with folks is like. But she'll make out fine—with my help. And my, but I'll have a real funny story to entertain Bertha with tonight."

At the mention of his wife's name, an uncomfortable silence settled in the room. George mumbled something about, "Sure 'nough," before quietly closing the door.

Daniel slowly rolled his way back to his table, a darkness settling over the room. He twirled a pencil stub in his hand.

Someday, his funny stories would make Bertha smile again. Someday, as she lay on her back, immobile and unresponsive, a twinkle would sparkle in her eye and in that way, she would smile at him again.

Using the kind of sweet words he liked to read aloud in the evenings to Bertha, Daniel lifted the key and transmitted—slowly for him—a message to R.A.: *Oh! Hello! Where is the shy girl at Tn? Where's my R.A.?*

♦♦♦

Before Matthew and Beulah returned, Ruth Ann had delivered all telegram responses and filed the paid telegram records, but stuffed the personal ones from *Rn* into the stove to burn. She felt like a failure, like she'd abused power and privilege and didn't deserve forgiveness.

D had hailed her several times, unofficially, but she'd put the person off. Once, another operator broke in and scolded the "scoundrel" for chatting over the wire. D had replied that the operator should mind her own business and that as long as there were no paid wires breaking in, the telegraph should be used to keep a pleasant atmosphere and make friendships.

Ruth Ann never joined in these messages and tried to concentrate on writing her newspaper columns, due Monday. She had only one other customer the entire day before the train whistle alerted her that she would soon be able to go home with Matthew while the telegraph closed for the night. She sighed and had put her writing aside when the sounder clattered for her.

Rn to Tn. Where are you, R.A.? It's almost time for the evening to end and I wanted to say goodnight.

Ruth Ann hesitated, finger over the key. The lure of chatting with someone unseen was fascinating, but was it proper? She made a quick reply, *Good evening. I am leaving now.*

Such a shame! Just when we've made acquaintance. But we can resume tomorrow. Goodnight!

Ruth Ann jumped when she heard the bell over the

THE EXECUTIONS

doorway. Beulah's pleasant laugh floated into the little room. She stood and started to remove her apron, but thought better of it, recalling the stain down her skirt front.

Beulah peeked in. "I know you're hungry, but I want to hear all about your day. Give me a moment to take this plunder to the house." Beulah held three white boxes in her arms and twirled away before Ruth Ann could reply.

Ruth Ann heard Mr. Levitt greet her, then they left through the back door. The Levitt dwelling was only a few dozen yards from the shop.

Matthew, who had stood back out of Beulah's wake, stepped into the telegraph office and glanced around. "Well, seems everything is in one piece still. How about that? No fires or anything?"

Ruth Ann turned briskly away. "Of course not. Didn't you think I could handle one day here alone?"

"Hey now." Matthew came up behind her and turned her around to face him. He tilted her tight chin up until she was forced to look him in the eyes. He frowned. "That bad, was it? What happened?"

"Noth...nothing. Well, maybe a few things." Ruth Ann stuttered then forced a brave smile. "All is well now."

Matthew raised an eyebrow at her. "You sure? I need you fresh and chipper in the morning. I want to be able to show off Dickens' finest when we meet Mr. Carter's bride-to-be at the train. We have Peter trained well enough to take over the wire while we're gone."

"Oh!" Ruth Ann stepped back and hurried to gather her things. "I'd forgotten all about the train. I need to hurry and help Mama with dinner preparations for tomorrow. I want it all done so I won't have to get steamed up in the kitchen in the morning..."

Matthew halted her scurrying with a hand on her arm. "Are you sure you're all right? Did Banny come by?"

"What makes you think that?" Ruth Ann's cheeks burned as she avoided Matthew's eyes. If only he knew it wasn't Sheriff Banny's visit that had her blushing. But before he could get anything more from her, the sound of the back door opening and Beulah's call interrupted them. "I have something for you, sister!"

Beulah appeared with one of the boxes, lid off. "Here, you must try this color ribbon in your hair. It will go well with—"

"Thank you." Head still down, Ruth Ann took the ribbon and stuffed it in her reticule before hurrying by. "I'm sorry, Beulah, we'll talk tomorrow. I have to prepare for meeting the bride at the station. The lady. Miss Viona Blake, that is."

Behind her, Ruth Ann heard Matthew muttering an explanation for her behavior to Beulah before following her out the door. As they walked quietly along, Ruth Ann pulled the lovely pink ribbon out and fingered it while thinking about the woman coming to be Mr. Carter's wife.

How could she have not thought of it all day when that had occupied her mind since the man had first told them of his mail-order bride? Not even the intense training for the telegraph had wholly distracted her thoughts on the matter.

But she'd not thought of it one time since this morning. And now all she could think of was how she'd forgotten to tell D she wouldn't be on the wire in the morning because of it.

CHAPTER THIRTY-FIVE

THE MORNING WAS GORGEOUS. Sunshine and fair temperatures. No storms on the horizon, at least not the kind Mr. Newton had been looking for.

Ruth Ann fidgeted with her sleeves, uncertain if adding lace to them had been a good idea. Perhaps she shouldn't have worn this dress and the pink ribbon in her hair. Perhaps she shouldn't have come at all.

Before leaving on his business trip, Mr. Carter had emphasized how important he thought it was for Ruth Ann to be at the station and make a good first impression and show how fine the ladies were in Dickens. He must not have thought much of the young women who generally congregated around the platform, decked out in their best to show how available and amiable they were.

The arrival of the train was a big deal to several groups of citizens and folks from the outlying farms and ranches. It created a festival type atmosphere Ruth Ann could not hope to compete with in her current mood. She had no excuse for her jitters, no reason to not be calm and kind, other than the fact that she couldn't stop wondering if D was a scoundrel as the one operator had said, or if he was a pleasant fellow.

A fellow she was sure he was, based on things another operator had said. Apparently that operator knew him. Perhaps they had had their own chats and quarrels before Ruth Ann made the acquaintance of D. She would have to ask Mr. Carter about it when he returned.

That thought finally brought her mind back around to the reason she was standing next to Matthew on the depot platform. The whistle sounded again. The train huffed toward them and Matthew nudged her. She stopped fidgeting with her sleeves, convinced she shouldn't have added the lace but it was too late now. The bride had arrived.

The train puffed up to the side of the platform, sending everyone into a flurry. Friends and family waiting to greet the passengers crowded near the doors, cowboys from the ranches meandered closer to the depot entrance where the mail would be taken, and the young ladies twirled their parasols and stood on tiptoe to get a glimpse at the passengers not disembarking.

None were looking for Miss Viona Blake. Carter had made it clear he did not want anyone to know about his mail-order bride until she was comfortably settled. He didn't want to make a spectacle of her.

Ruth Ann and Matthew stood back from the ruckus as baggage was unloaded along with passengers. Then Ruth Ann spied her. But it couldn't be...

She tilted her head toward Matthew and whispered, "You don't suppose that's her, do you?" When he didn't reply, Ruth Ann glanced up to see the equally surprised look on his face. He recovered quicker than she did and cleared his throat. "Remember, a good first impression, little sister."

"Humph." Ruth Ann tugged on her skirt and moved forward with Matthew. They navigated through the bustling crowd toward Miss Viona Blake, who had turned her back to them, looking around expectantly.

Matthew cleared his throat again. "Miss Blake?"

She turned, and her dazzling green eyes lit up with hope. Flaming red hair was bound elegantly in a bun atop her head, glowing tendrils framing her fair face.

Her fair, very *young* face. Ruth Ann doubted Miss Viona Blake was much older than herself. Which wasn't a bad thing, but considering Mr. Carter was at least twice that age, Ruth Ann was having trouble maintaining her composure.

With undisguised excitement, Miss Blake breathed, "Mr. Carter?"

"Oh no…no ma'am," Matthew quickly corrected her. "My name is Matthew Teller, editor of a local newspaper and um, friend of Mr. Carter's. This is my sister, Ruth Ann. He asked us to welcome you to Dickens and show you around."

"Oh." Viona's countenance could not be brightened now, not even with the glowing tendrils. She'd obviously prepared herself to meet her future husband in this moment. What could help someone recover from that?

But Ruth Ann offered her hand with a smile. "It's a pleasure to meet you, Miss Blake. I hope your trip was pleasant."

"Yes…yes it was. Interesting countryside you have." Viona tried to smile as she glanced around the depot as if seeing it completely different. "Mr. Carter…is he not well?"

"Business trip. Didn't he tell you?" Matthew looked around as well as if looking for luggage so he could put himself to use in the awkward moment.

"No. Our last communication indicated he would be here. But I'm sure it was unavoidable. You must know him well…" Viona looked at Matthew hopefully. He smiled tightly but couldn't find anything to say.

Viona must have taken that as his answer and when she made no comment, Ruth Ann said, "Well, you must be ready for something to eat. We have a meal prepared at our home. Our mother is expecting us, and then we'll take you to the hotel. Mr. Carter already arranged for your bags to be taken there."

"Of course…" Viona kept her eyes on Matthew, who for once could not say or do anything helpful.

Ruth Ann motioned toward the steps. "This way, Miss

Blake."

"Please, call me Viona." The young woman moved to Matthew's side and he offered his arm in response. They led the way, leaving Ruth Ann to follow behind on the crowded platform. Heads turned to observe the new arrival and Ruth Ann groaned inwardly at the gossip she could already hear in her mind as Viona gazed up at the young man at her side.

One thing was certain...*someone* in the Teller family had made a good first impression on Miss Viona Blake.

♦♦♦

"Can I tell you a secret?"

This was the first thing Viona said to Ruth Ann as the two of them walked behind the house toward the barn. The young woman had asked to see their Choctaw ponies and Della shooed the young ladies out the door, assuring them she and Matthew would tend the cleanup.

Knowing her mother like she did, Ruth Ann knew Della would just as soon put distance between Viona and Matthew when she could. The young woman hadn't taken her eyes off Matthew during the entire meal—the most awkward meal Ruth Ann had the displeasure of stomaching.

But now that they were alone, Viona changed. She reached up and pulled the pins from her hair and shook out her unruly red curls. And she had asked to share a secret with Ruth Ann.

"Yes...I suppose so," Ruth Ann finally answered as she hauled the barn door open. The familiar smells of the horses and hay set her at ease. They stabled the horses mostly in winter, but it was an unusually warm day with the sunshine, so the animals had free roam in the small corral attached to the barn.

She opened a bag of sweet treats and handed one to Viona, who took it in her white hands willingly. At least the young woman wasn't afraid to get dirty, an important characteristic in Indian Territory.

THE EXECUTIONS

Ruth Ann didn't push the conversation as she opened the gate that blocked the corral off from the barn. The horses were already gathered there. Ruth Ann shooed them gently then let her own pony, Skyline, nuzzle against her while the mare took the treat. "This is Skyline and that's Little Chief."

"Lovely." Viona stroked Little Chief's forehead while letting him lip the treat in her other hand. She sighed and laid her cheek against his until he pulled away and stepped to Ruth Ann, dropping his muzzle to her apron pocket. Ruth Ann chuckled and shooed both horses away. They frisked against each other and trotted to the other side of the corral.

"This ain't me."

Ruth Ann turned to face Viona, cocking her head at the strange statement. "What?"

"This." Viona motioned up and down her elegant dress, even grasping the skirt and showing off her lace-up boots by sticking one in the air. "These ain't even mine. Sure and I got to mail them back tomorrow. The dress too. Friend o' mine let me borrow them, then."

"Oh." Ruth Ann didn't know how to respond to Viona's sad tone, nor the startling Irish accent that had suddenly burst forth.

Then Viona laughed and shook her curls out again. She fingered them. "Friend o' mine in St. Louis, she fixed me up, hair and all. Said I'd best make a fine impression on the man if I didn't care to get turned away. Ah, 'tis a double deception, seems. Mr. Carter's not what he wrote in the letters, is he, then?" Viona's sharp green eyes penetrated to the truth in Ruth Ann's own eyes.

Ruth Ann stammered a response. "Viona, I honestly don't know Mr. Carter well. I know he's shown unkindness and yet kindness to us, he goes to our church, he does own one of the largest businesses in Dickens—"

"But would he be the kind o' man my da raised me to marry up with and all?" Viona sighed and folded her arms. "I may be a roughneck who can barely hold to society for a few minutes and can only act refined with a lot o' help, and I may not be rich, but my da told me I was worth something and any man who looked twice at me had best understand it. But sure and then, my da wasn't supposed to die in the mines last year and leave me beggin' for scraps and having to travel west to marry a man—sight unseen."

Ruth Ann couldn't put herself in Viona Blake's borrowed boots. She didn't know what it was like to suddenly have no one to look after her, no family and the only thing a friend could do to help was loan a dress to make an impression on a man she'd promised to marry. But one thing she did understand and said softly, "I'm sorry about your father. Mine and my oldest brother were killed in a robbery four years ago."

Viona's green eyes sparkled with tears as she watched the horses. "Sure and whatever kind o' man Mr. Carter is, I'm glad he sent yourself to meet me at the station then. Yer good folks."

Ruth Ann swallowed and took Viona's hand with a squeeze. "I hope you'll be happy here in Dickens, Viona. It has more good folks. You'll see."

Viona sighed and straightened from the wood boards of the corral fence she'd been leaning against. A sharp tearing sound sickened Ruth Ann and Viona gasped.

Ruth Ann assessed the damage. "Don't worry, my mother is an expert seamstress. I'm sure she can fix this."

Twisting to see for herself, Viona surprised Ruth Ann by laughing. "No matter, love! Time for me to get shed o' this dress and wear something that fits me."

♦♦♦

At the hotel where her single carpetbag had been delivered, Viona hummed a tune in the Gaelic tongue like her da had sung every night on the way home from the mines. She would hear it off in the distance.

Sometimes she'd be busy wringing out the last of his red flannel drawers and hanging them to dry in the late summer evening. Sometimes she'd be spooning the last of the watered down potato soup into the cracked China serving bowl to set out on their plank board table. Sometimes she'd be on the arm of a young beau who was foolishly trying to woo her with promises of a better life away from the mines...someday.

It never mattered what her hands were doing—wringing flannels, dipping soup, holding a suitor's arm—when she heard the singing, the voice that bellowed above all the rest, she'd drop those hands and dash away without a thought to the consequences. She'd skip and frolic down the road the way her da liked to see her—happy, young, carefree.

She'd meet his singing with her own. Whether the winter sun had already nestled itself away or whether the late summer sun was still trying to smile at them, Viona would use whatever light there was to see her da's eyes. Her skipping turned into a run and she launched herself into his arms.

No matter how tired, no matter how long the day, no matter how old he got, her da would catch her in the air, swing her around and smack her cheek with a kiss. "That's me little Irish flame. Set fire to me heart and burn away the dross of the day."

So it had been every evening of her life since she was old enough to run. She'd never known her mother, only a handful of miners' wives and widows who had taken their turn tending her. But all her world needed was her da, and her evening run to meet him. She never grew too old for it—neither would he. He was a strong man, built like a bull. Nothing could knock him down. Except twenty tons of rock.

Viona fingered the dress in her hands. This worn-out green dress. It had been the last thing her da had caught her in. Viona wiggled into it quickly and spied herself in the mirror, the only one she'd ever looked in that wasn't cracked.

It wasn't an unpleasant sight and much more like herself with her red flames of hair draped over her shoulders. But her da warned her not to let them flames touch a man's eyes until the time was right, until she met the one who would call her his Irish princess. So she took a moment to plait those flames into a loose braid. She closed her eyes and imagined leaping into her da's arms once more.

Would Josiah Carter let her leap into his arms in that way?

Or would maybe, just maybe, another let her do it first? Viona opened her eyes. With one last grin at the mirror, she grabbed the box with the vexatious dress as she twirled her way out of the hotel room.

♦♦♦

Ruth Ann waited in the hotel lobby for Viona to emerge. This was an uncomfortable place and she fervently prayed the hotel owner—Sheriff Banny—wouldn't pop in. He was the last person Ruth Ann wanted to be caught having to introduce Viona to.

But thankfully, her new friend wasn't long and soon bounded down the stairs in a worn gingham dress of a lovely shade of green that complemented her red hair, now pulled back in a relaxed braid. In her hands was a brown box she held out away from her like a batch of rotten turnips. "We'll give this to yer ma later. First, I want ye to take me to that place I heard ye speak o'. The place where ye print words and make a newspaper out of them."

"Of course." Her words were willing, but inside, Ruth Ann hesitated. Matthew had gone on over to the print shop with the quiet request that she be Miss Blake's escort for the day. He had business to tend, and didn't want to leave Peter alone with the telegraph all day. Ruth Ann was sure taking Viona to him wasn't what he had in mind.

But the mail-order bride was already bouncing out the door. She halted on the porch and glanced back at Ruth Ann. "Are all Choctaws so slow as yourself, love?" She winked and Ruth Ann moved forward with a sigh.

Matthew had better turn off his charm today. Viona had enough to go around for all of them.

CHAPTER THIRTY-SIX

WHEN THE YOUNG WOMEN ARRIVED at the print shop, it was as quiet and reserved as Ruth Ann had come to love. Mr. Levitt sat at his back workbench, bent over a clock he was repairing. Sounds of a violin came from the back room where Beulah was giving a lesson. The newspaper side of the shop, though, was missing the one Ruth Ann had expected to see working on the next edition. Papers were scattered over the table Matthew used as a desk. It appeared he'd left in a hurry.

Mr. Levitt looked up with a smile as he said, "Good afternoon, ladies." Outside the Teller family, only the Levitts knew the reason Viona had come to Dickens.

Ruth Ann led the way across the length of the large, open building and introduced him. Viona cocked her head. "What of that heavenly music?" she breathed, eyes closed as the strains of rhythm surrounded them.

Mr. Levitt smiled, looking over his glasses at her. If he was surprised by the youth of the bride, he didn't indicate it as he welcomed her as warmly as anyone could. "My daughter, Beulah. You will meet her soon. She is finishing with one of her students."

A squeaky voice interrupted from behind them. "Hey, when are you loafers going to give me a break? I don't take to this much sitting. I'm a growing boy."

Ruth Ann rolled her eyes at Mr. Levitt. "I hope he hasn't been this difficult all morning."

Mr. Levitt bent his head back over his work, a quiet smile on his lips. Ruth Ann turned and put her hands on her hips. "Peter, you best mind your manners if you ever hope to be invited to dinner. Mama is making grape dumplings tonight."

Peter was hanging out the doorway of the telegraph office. He fell to one knee. "You wouldn't...couldn't...please show mercy on a wretched heathen."

Without hesitating, Viona dropped the box in her hands and rushed forward, falling dramatically on her face in front of him. "Please, mistress, don't be so cruel! To deny a boy, a mere child nourishment! Who of this world can have hope?"

A clap sounded from the doorway of the back room. Ruth Ann glanced back to see Beulah, eyebrows raised, applauding. Mr. Levitt joined her as Viona and Peter stood and took a bow as if they had rehearsed for weeks.

"Well done." Beulah smiled but it didn't quite reach her eyes. "From the stage play *Dungeons,* correct? The ending was quite tragic in that one."

"Sure and that's the smart thing about life...with enough fight, ye can change the ending."

Ruth Ann motioned to Beulah, who was bidding her student goodbye. The young girl was more than happy to scurry away through the back door. "Viona, this is Beulah. Beulah, Miss Viona Blake from Pennsylvania."

Beulah clasped her hands together and gave a slight nod. "A pleasure. If you will excuse me, I must prepare for my next student." She disappeared into the back room once again.

Peter had no trouble filling the silence. "Well, Annie, are you going to help me or not? Hear that clatter?" He cocked his head back toward the little room, listened a moment then winked at her. "I think it's for you. From your special friend up the line who's been asking about you."

Ruth Ann felt the burn of her cheeks when Viona grinned at her and Mr. Levitt raised his head. Before she could move, Peter and Viona disappeared into the telegraph office.

Oh no.

Ruth Ann hurried after them and halted at the doorway, suddenly breathless. Peter sat at the desk with Viona hovering over where he was taking down the message. She read aloud, "She is back, you say? Please tell my dear R.A. to say hello. Your loving description of her makes me want to chat all the more—"

Ruth Ann rushed forward and snatched the paper right from under Peter's pencil. "You shouldn't be taking such messages!"

Peter looked up at her with wide-eyed innocence. "You told me to take every message meant for this station. That's all I'm doing."

Viona had snagged some of the messages and was reading them. Ruth Ann grabbed them from her, tearing half of them in the process. "Confidential…this is supposed to be confidential. The telegraph is not a toy."

Peter was pecking out a message on the sounder. Ruth Ann caught a bit of it. *You should see her red face right now…*

Ruth Ann grabbed Peter's arm and hauled him from the chair. He may have grown half a foot taller than her in the past two months, but his skinny frame didn't outweigh hers yet and she used that to her advantage as she dislodged him from his post. Viona laughed as Ruth Ann dropped into the chair, gathered her composure and signaled to station *Rn*. *My apologies. My rascal of a cousin will behave from now on.*

Oh! I would like to see the scolding you'll give him. But don't be serious in it. He's bright and pleasant. As you are, my dear R.A..

Ruth Ann cleared her throat. *Chatting over the wire seems an abuse of privilege in my estimate. Please maintain only official communications.*

Oh! I had hoped you wouldn't be so stiff and formal as the man Carter was. He was positively a bore and I—

Ruth Ann realized Peter was using the shelf in the window to write down their messages. Viona leaned over his shoulder, reading them. Ruth Ann "broke" D's message by holding her key up and looking at Peter. "Out. Now."

The last thing Viona needed was an unseen operator saying bad things about her unseen fiancée. Ruth Ann sighed. When did relationships become so complicated?

Peter continued to lounge against the window. "Aw, come on, Annie. I'm just—"

"Out."

Viona lost her look of jesting as she took the message from Peter before he left. She stood quietly next to the window and leaned her head against the frame. "Tell me, love, what's he like, then? Really?"

Ruth Ann didn't know what to say. Where to start. So she asked, "What do you know of him? You said he wrote letters…"

Viona's laugh was hollow. "Three whole letters. One telling a bit o' his business and the town, one asking me to come be his wife, the other with money to come. Sure and the three added up wouldn't make a page."

Rn to Tn. Tell me about your new friend. Young P was about to introduce us when you came in.

Ruth Ann puffed an irritated breath and responded, *I cannot chat right now.*

Without knowing what was sent, Viona pushed away from the window. "It's alright, love. We can talk another time."

"No! No," Ruth Ann brought her too loud voice back into range as she stood and put a hand on Viona's arm. "I told him I was busy."

The sounder clattered behind her but Ruth Ann ignored the dots and dashes. Viona patted her hand. "Really, love. I'd like to be alone a spell. I'll be alright."

When Viona disappeared, Ruth Ann plopped back in the

chair. With nothing else to do, she took the next message from D.

Oh! D here. I hope I haven't caused trouble there at Tn. Is all well? R.A. please respond.

R.A. here. No trouble from you. Just a bit of romantic difficulties. Ruth Ann winced and wished she hadn't been so candid. But she truly wanted someone to talk to. Someone not directly related to the situation and who didn't know them all anyway. Not really.

Sounds tragic. Not a rogue beau of yours, is it?
No romance for me, thank you. It is a friend.
The lovely young Jewish lady P mentioned?
No. Another lady just arrived in town.
The mail-order bride then?

Oh, if she could strangle Peter without Uncle Preston knowing, she would! How dare he share confidential information over the wire? But then, Ruth Ann had slipped across that line a time or two. It wasn't difficult when one wasn't looking into the face of another.

I cannot speak of it. But tell me, what would you do if someone wasn't who or what you expected them to be?

I have feared that prospect since meeting you, R.A. I fervently hope you are as I picture you, but I am certain my fears are unwarranted.

I know nothing nor have any expectations of you.

Oh! That is good to hear. We can go on chatting safely now. Will you be in the office all day today?

I should be showing our guest around, but she wants some time alone.

Understand. A heart on the verge of breaking is not a pleasant thing to have happen before your friends.

I did not say she was in that state, but it is a concern. We have two days before we will know.

Well, it is a fine thing she has you by her side. Do tell her to come in sometime and say hello. Perhaps I can help brighten her spirits.

Ruth Ann cocked her head. It wasn't a bad idea. But not now. Viona wanted time alone. So Ruth Ann continued the conversation with D as they moved on to their favorite books, plays and life in Indian Territory. She was surprised by his wide range of interests and pleased to know they shared some in common, giving them pleasant things to discuss.

It wasn't long though, when Ruth Ann felt a presence in the door. She sneaked a glance behind her to see the innocent look of Peter. "I won't beat around the bush. Mr. Levitt asked me to come man the telegraph. He thinks you should go find Viona. He didn't say why, but I'm old enough to know."

Ruth Ann signed off with D as she stood, warning him P was about to take over. Absently, she asked, "Why is that?"

"She's out walking with Matthew."

The words from the play Viona had uttered earlier came back to Ruth Ann: *With enough fight, you can change the ending.*

Ruth Ann almost flattened Peter as she rushed through the door.

◆◆◆

They weren't out back. They weren't at the general store, but Mr. Bates, the owner, directed her to the path leading to the church in the field outside of town. Ruth Ann hurried down the dirt path, gazing at the quaint white building where they worshiped God with every race in town.

There was always peace and harmony within the walls. Ruth Ann felt neither as she approached the empty lot where buggies and wagons would crowd on Sunday morning. There was no sign of anyone outside, but as Ruth Ann mounted the steps of the unlocked building, she heard voices coming from the direction of the cemetery. She retraced her steps and rounded the building.

The cemetery, surrounded by a low fence, was mostly open grass with a few oaks giving shade to those who came to pay respects. That was not what Ruth Ann suspected Matthew and Viona were doing as they stood near one of the graves. Ruth Ann knew whose it was.

They were engaged in an interesting enough conversation that made them unaware of her approach until Ruth Ann had passed through the open gate. Matthew turned to her first, face flushed.

Viona turned partially around and smiled softly. "Yer brother was telling me about this man. Silas Sloan and how he turned himself in to be shot by his Choctaw brothers. That's some code of honor system ye have, then."

Ruth Ann nodded as she came up to them, looking pointedly between the two. "I could have showed you and told you the story if you'd wanted. I was there."

Viona shrugged and looked at Matthew. "I wanted to talk some things over with yer brother about Mr. Carter." She eyed him a long moment. When he stared back, she sighed, looked at them both and asked, "Mr. Carter worth having friends like ye two, is he, then?" Without lingering for a reply, Viona headed down the path toward the church and disappeared around the corner.

Ruth Ann frowned, a deep sadness in her own heart. "She really seems like a nice girl."

"I suppose so."

CHAPTER THIRTY-SEVEN

THE LONGEST TWO DAYS PASSED pleasantly for Ruth Ann as she volunteered to spend more than her share of hours in the telegraph office. She and D talked about the customers they had, politics, and the weather. They never seemed to run out of things to say, much to Peter's irritation. He hung around the print shop, wanting to take a turn at the sounder.

But Ruth Ann barred her cousin from being near her conversations for the time being, warning him he was on spring-thin ice with her. And speaking of spring, he should be spending a heap more time at his father's farm, helping with early planting. In truth, she loved having Peter around, but he needed to learn a lesson about not crossing lines with her.

Viona had chosen to take her meals at the hotel instead of the Teller home and Ruth Ann respected that. So she was surprised when the bell rang over the door and Viona appeared in the telegraph office moments later. Ruth Ann rose from the sounder, which was going off from one station to the other with an official message.

She greeted Viona warmly and held out both hands to her. "I'm glad you came by." She noticed the green gingham dress had been washed and freshly pressed. Though her hair wasn't in a fancy bun, Viona had pinned it nicely at the base of her neck and allowed a few tendrils to frame her face.

Viona smiled, though not gaily. "Will ye pleasure me by going to the train station with me?"

"Oh!" How could Ruth Ann have forgotten Mr. Carter's return today? It seemed every time she chatted with D over the wire, everything else left her mind. "Yes, of course. Peter is at our house now, helping Mama with chores. I'll see if Beulah can go fetch him, then I'll go with you."

"Ye really hadn't ought to bother her."

"Why?" Ruth Ann could think of no reason Beulah would mind. Beulah was her friend, and was probably in the back room preparing for her next student or...

Ruth Ann frowned. She really didn't know what Beulah was doing. She hadn't come into the telegraph office in days. She hadn't been to the Teller home in days. She hadn't said much of anything to Ruth Ann in days.

Or perhaps it was the other way around.

The sounder went silent a moment and then, *Rn to Tn, R.A. are you there still?*

"Just a moment." Ruth Ann released Viona's hands and signaled, *Going on break. Will return later.*

Oh! Do hurry.

"I'll be right back. Holler if you hear it going off." Ruth Ann hurried through the doorway and past Mr. Levitt on his workbench to go through the door to the back room. She found Beulah sitting in her corner where she taught lessons, softly dragging her bow across the violin strings in a mournful tone.

Beulah glanced up and lowered the instrument. "Do you need something?"

"Yes." Ruth Ann hesitated, then closed the door behind her before approaching Beulah, who remained seated. Ruth Ann plopped into the chair across from her. "I need to apologize."

Beulah raised her eyebrows. "For what?"

"I've not been the friend I should be, especially the past few days. I've ignored you and not at all included you since Viona arrived. Well, since that telegraph arrived, I've been engrossed with learning it and...and chatting with another operator."

Beulah nodded matter-of-factly, laying her violin in its case next to her chair. "You have been quite rude. But I have been known to be rude a time or two and found forgiveness. I can give it."

Ruth Ann breathed a sigh of relief and grasped Beulah's hand. "You're one of the best friends I've ever had."

Beulah laughed. "Then you must tell me all about the man on the wire. D. I have been dying to ask since Peter told me a bit of his interest in you. It must be an exciting prospect, to be courted by someone unseen."

"Oh! He's not courting me." Ruth Ann blushed and Beulah grinned but before she could continue her teasing, the sound of the front door banging open interrupted.

Mr. Levitt tapped on the door to the back room. "Young Peter is here and I believe Viona is waiting for you." As if to emphasize the point, the train whistle sounded in the distance.

Ruth Ann pulled Beulah up by the hand. "Come with us. Please."

Beulah shook her head. "Poor Mr. Carter will feel overwhelmed if three women are waiting to pounce on him. You will do well."

Ruth Ann shook her head. "I hope so." She hurried out the door to find Viona and Matthew standing by the front entrance, waiting for her.

The moment of truth had arrived.

♦♦♦

While the train puffed closer to the depot, Ruth Ann stayed at Viona's side. Matthew engaged in a conversation with G.W., their old cowboy friend from one of the ranches. They stood near the end of the platform, far enough away from all the young ladies to be intentional.

Viona dipped her head and said, "I asked around town about Mr. Carter. I know things he's done, and that he's no young man. Sure and I don't know whether I can go through with it." She reached for Ruth Ann's hand and squeezed it. "Tell me what's right, Annie, love."

Ruth Ann squeezed Viona's hand back as the train pulled alongside the depot, hissing steam and setting the usual excitement in motion. "As much as I wish I knew, I can't know, and I can't tell you what you need to do. Only God knows."

Viona nodded as if accepting that as her answer. Passengers disembarked and a few boarded. Mr. Carter was last to appear on the edge of the passenger car steps and he paused, looking around the depot. Ruth Ann hardly recognized him in his brown suit, Derby hat and the soft expression on his face. She didn't need to point him out to Viona. The young woman gasped when Mr. Carter's eyes met hers for the first time.

He hesitated, then came down the steps at a near run. He halted in front of Viona and removed his hat, clearing his throat. "You're more beautiful than I expected. I mean, more than I could have hoped for." He fumbled for words and looked to Ruth Ann for help. She smiled calmly. "It's good to see you, Mr. Carter. We've done our best to make Viona at home, and it's been wonderful getting to know her."

Carter nodded and held out a steady hand to shake Viona's pale one. "Sorry I couldn't meet you here myself. I really felt I should take care of that business and besides…" Carter gripped the brim of his hat with both hands and turned it round. "I feared I couldn't give you the best impression of Dickens and its folks and…me. You see, through them letters, I came to…to love you something fierce and I was afraid you'd turn tail and get right back on that train before I could say hello. The Tellers are good folks and I knew they'd take right good care of you."

Viona finally took her eyes off him to glance at Ruth Ann

THE EXECUTIONS

and Matthew, who had approached them and now offered a greeting to Mr. Carter. The man pumped his hand with a grin. "Thank you, son. I knew I could trust you to take care of things."

"Indeed," Viona murmured, drawing Mr. Carter's attention back to her.

He cleared his throat again. "Miss Viona, now that you've been here and met me and all, I want to say something. You don't have to marry me if you don't want to. I won't hold you to some promise made on a piece of paper, sight unseen. But if you're willing, I want you to know you will be my princess. And we won't stay in Dickens. I went up to St. Louis and made a deal to sell the whole kit and caboodle here and move up there. Got friends and a brother lives up that way and I always figured to go back after…" He halted and licked his lips.

Viona finished for him. "After ye Choctaw wife and young'un died?" There was a moment of respectful silence and Viona glanced at Ruth Ann, then at Matthew. Finally, she looked at Mr. Carter with a grin. "A bargain is a bargain, and I won't back out if you won't. St. Louis sounds fine to me; sure and I always wanted to be a city girl."

Carter's face flushed and he seemed to take his first breath since disembarking. He held out his arm to Viona and she took it with a smile. He said, "What's the sense in waiting? I'll tell my freight boys to ship everything later. No reason we can't catch the next train north and get hitched in St. Louis."

Viona nodded firmly. "Take me on back to that hotel and I'll get my things then. Got something special for the wedding. Something my ma left me."

"I'd like to see it." The sincerity in Mr. Carter's voice warmed Ruth Ann's heart and she smiled with equal genuineness when they looked her way. "See us off, love?" Viona asked.

"I think we should say our goodbyes now so I don't cry." Ruth Ann held her arms open and Viona tackled her in a hug. Viona squeezed tight and whispered in her ear, "Yer right, love. Sure and God knows."

Ruth Ann nodded and stepped back. She shook Mr. Carter's hand while Viona did the same with Matthew. Ruth Ann said, "Congratulations to you both, sir. And don't worry; we'll keep taking good care of the wire."

"Oh, that reminds me. There's a certain gentleman who likes to chat over the wire when there's no official messages going through. Watch out for him, he's a rascal." Carter shook his head with a little smile, and for a reason Ruth Ann couldn't explain, her heart did a flip.

Matthew shifted his attention to Ruth Ann. "I believe my sister has made his acquaintance."

"I see." Carter winked at her and Viona turned to face him, her eyes filled with mischief and perhaps—tears? Whichever or both it was, she sang out and took a step before launching herself at Mr. Carter. He looked shocked, but quickly reacted and caught Viona in his arms. He cradled her and swung around with a laugh.

Viona tossed her head and batted her eyelashes at Ruth Ann. "Careful, darlin'. Ye know what happens when love is in the air. It gets on everyone."

She glanced back at Matthew, but quickly turned her face to Mr. Carter and smiled. He smiled back. "Indeed."

The two left the platform with Mr. Carter carrying Viona while final goodbyes were called. Heads turned to watch the couple, the locals looking surprised as Mr. Carter tipped his hat awkwardly to various ones and grinned. Then they were gone. Ruth Ann exhaled. "Whew. That was a close one." She glanced at Matthew by her side, awaiting his response. He was looking toward the last place they'd seen the couple.

"I suppose so."

In that moment, Ruth Ann questioned how well she knew her brother.

CHAPTER THIRTY-EIGHT

BACK AT THE TELEGRAPH OFFICE, Ruth Ann and Peter were in an argument about who should run the wire until closing time when Matthew stepped in. "Ruth Ann, I need to speak with you. Privately."

She looked up at him, surprised. Matthew had called her by her full name. Peter grinned as he slyly slipped into the seat in front of the sounder. "You go right ahead, cousins. I'll take care of things here." Ruth Ann scowled at him but followed Matthew through the shop and out the back door.

This was a peaceful place, quiet mostly. Behind the false fronts of the stores that lined this side of the street, the backs of the buildings showed neatly kept disposal areas in the bit of grass that grew gradually into pastureland on this side of town. To the left and down was the back of the Levitt's quaint house the Tellers had helped build.

Right outside the door where they stood was a small army of crates Matthew used as a makeshift writing station when he wanted to get outside and work on stories for the newspaper.

The *Choctaw Tribune* had opened wonderful doors for them. If not for it, Mr. Carter would have never let them have the telegraph. And Ruth Ann was sure it would lead to the best things for the newspaper.

Looking at Matthew's grave face now, Ruth Ann knew that wasn't what he wanted to discuss with her. He motioned to the crates and they sat. He didn't say anything for awhile as he looked off toward the pastureland. Ruth Ann wiggled with impatience, wondering if D was on the wire chatting away with Peter.

Matthew was acting like Uncle Preston or even the Grandmother as he continued the contemplation period of silence they used to communicate. Finally, Ruth Ann broke in. "Okay, Matthew, I take it I've done something awful. I've already apologized to Beulah for how I've treated her and I'm willing to make any other apologies needed, so can we get on with it?"

Matthew snagged a blade of grass and stared at it while shredding slowly. "You sure are in a hurry to get back to the wire."

"Of course I am," Ruth Ann sputtered, suddenly looking for excuses. "I can't leave Peter to it all the time. He's still inexperienced…"

"So are you."

"But it's my responsibility."

"Ours."

"Are you feeling left out or something?"

"Let me ask you this: When you're on the wire, do you behave the same as you would with someone face to face?"

"What do you mean?"

Matthew snagged another blade of grass. "You're a modest girl, Annie. Sweet. Kind, even to people who don't deserve it. That's Christ's way. But how are you over the wire? What kind of things do you send that you wouldn't say to a man if he were standing in front of you, saying the things D says? How do you know he's so different from Banny? The sheriff can be polite when he wants to, even charming. It's easy when you can't see someone's eyes, hear their voice. It's—"

"You're comparing D to Sheriff Banny?" Ruth Ann nearly shrieked at the question. "Why, D is nothing like him!"

"How do you know?"

"Because...because...oh Matthew! You know what I mean. D and I have talked a great deal and he's very kind."

"You're different when you're on the wire than in person. How do you know it's not the same with D?"

Ruth Ann opened her mouth to protest, but realized she had no defense. Matthew was partly right. She really didn't know D at all, yet felt she could say and share things with him she wouldn't with others. Even if it meant the other operators listening in. For instance, the main reason she and Peter had been arguing over who would man the wire was because she wanted to tell D the details of what had happened at the depot. She'd even run ideas through her mind of how they might set up a private wire to chat on while working.

What an odd thought for Ruth Ann. Realizing how far she'd strayed from her normal behavior, Ruth Ann blushed and said nothing.

Matthew was right, and he'd been able to tell her so without scolding or fully explaining his meaning. He was a man in his own right.

When Ruth Ann remained silent, Matthew asked, "How would you like to meet D?"

Ruth Ann rocked back on the crate and gasped. "Oh no...no, not at all. I mean...what...what if..."

"He turns out different than you imagined or that maybe, just maybe, you are a disappointment to him in real life?" Matthew reached over and took Ruth Ann's hand, something he did more so since Daddy had died, but still not often. His hand was softer than it used to be when working on Uncle Preston's farm, but she could feel the hard spots on his finger from gripping a pencil and using it like a sword to form powerful words. Now he was speaking them and Ruth Ann listened, knowing God was giving her brother wisdom in this situation.

Feeling terrified, Ruth Ann jerked her head in a nod. "All

right. Only if you'll go with me."

"I wouldn't have it any other way."

That afternoon, Ruth Ann and Matthew boarded the second northbound train, intending to finally come face to face with D.

♦♦♦

Ruth Ann hadn't been so nervous in all her life. Scared plenty of times, yes, but never so apprehensive. What would D think of her if she wasn't even able to speak? What would he think of her at all? And what was he like?

She was all too happy to let Matthew lead the way when the train stopped at Sopperville, or more familiar to Ruth Ann now, station *Rn*. She'd been to the farming community before but not in some time, a place just large enough to justify a telegraph office, a small store, and an eatery in the back of the depot. Matthew asked if she was hungry and Ruth Ann shook her head, lips pinned tight. Her stomach protested at the mere thought of food. She wanted to meet D.

Ruth Ann took Matthew's arm and together they stepped off the depot platform and rounded the building where Matthew halted. He cocked his head toward the back and Ruth Ann followed his gaze as he said quietly, "That's the telegraph office."

From where they stood, Ruth Ann could see the wooden shelf not unlike their own back in Dickens. It only took one step forward to see the sounder and the man seated by it, transmitting a message.

His hair—what was left of it—was a dark brown with white flecks heavy through it and he wore a green visor as if to shade his eyes from the late afternoon sun. Pudgy and the crinkles around his eyes showed a jolly type of fellow like Ruth Ann had come to know. She took a deep breath and glanced at Matthew. He led the way.

At the shelf, Matthew cleared his throat and the man held up one finger without looking up as he signed off. Ruth Ann deciphered his message: *Be right back. Customers you know.* On the left hand he held up, a gold band sparkled in the evening light.

She held her breath again as he stood and turned fully to them. His face lit up with recognition. "Well, hello there, Matthew Teller. Covering a story up this way, are you? Got some official reporting to send through?"

"Not this time, Daniel. I brought a surprise for you. This is my sister, Ruth Ann."

"A pleasure." Daniel held his hand out to her with a grin as wide as the railroad track. Ruth Ann shook his hand, and suddenly breathed an immense sigh of relief. "Likewise, Daniel. It's good to finally meet you in person."

"Wait a second..." Daniel pushed his visor further up his shiny forehead. "Ruth Ann...You're not little R.A. from station *Tn*, are you?"

She smiled and Daniel slapped his leg with a laugh as he pushed open the side door of the telegraph office and waved them in. "How about that? Matthew, you never told me your sister ran the telegraph. Well, then again, guess I haven't seen you for a month's time and ol' Josiah just gave it up not long ago I reckon. Ruth Ann, you're just as sweet looking as your rascally cousin said. Won't my little woman take a shine to this story tonight? You should have both introduced yourselves when you got on the wire. As it was, I had to grind information out of little Ruth Ann bit by bit."

In the cramped office slightly larger than their own, Ruth Ann felt quite comfortable as she glanced around the sparsely furnished room. Daniel offered her the chair by the sounder with a chuckle. "Send your feisty cousin a message from us; tell him he's missing all the fun."

For the next hour, the three chatted over the wire with Peter and with one another. Ruth Ann discovered that, though significantly older than her, the married Daniel was every bit as pleasant in person as on the wire. But thoughts of anything more left her mind for good.

With the glowing sunset, they bid Daniel goodbye, promising to stop by again sometime. They had barely cleared sight of his office when Ruth Ann balled up her fist, turned and slammed it into Matthew's stomach. She hadn't given him a chance to tighten his muscles and he gasped for air as he bent over and sputtered in Choctaw, "What are you doing, crazy woman?"

"You...You!" Ruth Ann put her hands on her hips. "You knew Daniel all along and didn't say anything. How long were you going to keep it a secret? And why not just tell me back in Dickens instead of bringing me up here?"

Matthew inhaled and exhaled as if testing his now tender stomach. "Would you have rather I did that?"

Realizing once again she had no defense and that Matthew had handled the situation perfectly, she folded her arms and scowled at him but it dissolved into a shy smile. "I'm sorry. For everything. Can we get something to eat before the train gets here?"

Matthew rubbed his stomach. "I'm a pretty tough Choctaw. I guess I can take a crazy sister and stomach a little food."

As they strolled away from the telegraph office, Ruth Ann listened to the clatter of the sounder going off and was in awe at the pleasant sound it made.

♦♦♦

The breeze offered a cool touch to Matthew's face as he sat hunched on a wooden crate behind the print shop. All the articles for the next edition of the *Choctaw Tribune* were written and ready to go, save this one. Ruth Ann had offered to write it, but he shooed her off to work the telegraph, assuring her he had all under control.

How close to a lie that was.

Under normal circumstances, it would be easy to write this story. A mail-order bride come into town to marry one of the prominent men and then them moving off to St. Louis with all business affairs settled. A story of happiness and well wishes for the new couple. There was only one problem. Matthew had his doubts about their happiness. Yes, Viona had seemed happy enough at the train station as Mr. Carter carried her off. But could she truly be happy with a man old enough to be her father, a man who was little more than a stranger at that?

But what business was it of his? Just because there had been an interest in him from the young Irish lady...

And that was the crux of it. As a reporter, he was not required to feel any kind of happiness. As a guardian, he was not meant to experience emotions. As a man...that was the part he struggled with now as he tried to form the story in his head. But he was too close to the story. He should have let Annie write it.

But no. This story was for him to write. He would not be able to live in peace with himself if he did not.

Bowing his head with closed eyes, he sat quietly. Maybe a few minutes, maybe more. He didn't keep track. He let his heart calm, his thoughts settle.

In time, he felt oneness in his spirit again, and he felt oneness with the Spirit. Someday, there would be that special one for his heart. But it was not to be Viona. She would find her own happiness; he his. That was his peace.

God knows.

With a final sigh, Matthew scratched out the title for the article: *A Happy Ending*

CHAPTER THIRTY-NINE

"ANNIE, ANNIE! COME QUICK!"

Ruth Ann sighed as patiently as she could while ignoring her cousin's shout from the telegraph office. She sat at the makeshift newspaper desk, choosing words to summarize the pastor's sermon the day before. The piece wasn't due until Wednesday but she wanted to get ahead on her work for once. Especially with Matthew gone for two days to cover the latest shooting scrape over the past tribal elections, and the Levitts home for the morning, decorating their relatively new living space. The newness of the telegraph had worn off and things settled down. At least, as much as they ever did for the *Choctaw Tribune*.

But Peter couldn't be ignored. He charged through the doorway between the newspaper office and the telegraph office and kept shouting. "Annie, you've got to read this!" He waved a slip of paper in the air as he halted himself by shoving his other hand into her table. It jolted her arm, sending a pencil scratch across her Sunday sermon column.

"Peter Abraham Frazier! Stop this instant." She held up her hand, palm out, and shook her head. "You have broken three rules: one, never leave the sounder unattended for no good reason. Two, never interrupt me when I'm writing unless the building is on fire again. Three, no, listen! Three, never show a telegraph meant for someone else to anyone but that person. Now, I will stay with the sounder while you deliver the wire, but make it quick. I want to finish this article before noon."

Finally caught up on his breath, Peter sputtered, "Annie, listen. There's a lynching going on outside of Paris. Right now. A great big public one. There's nothing secretive about it! The wire is meant for Dr. Anderson. A friend of his wires him all the important news in Paris. And you're an operator. You'd have known if you'd been at the sounder."

Ruth Ann was on her feet before she realized it. She blinked, frozen. Peter shook her arm. "Let me go on down there. I'll get whatever I can from it and you can write the article. I'll call Beulah to come help watch the shop."

His words finally made sense to Ruth Ann and she halted him with a calm hand on his arm. "I'll go." Her voice was a quiet but determined whisper.

Peter's eyes bulged. "You can't. Matthew would skin me alive if I let you go off into the middle of a riot. You just stay here—"

The train whistle sounded in the distance. The southbound train. The one headed for Paris.

Ruth Ann gathered her tablet, pencils and reticule with enough coins in it for train fare. Peter watched her with wide eyes. "Annie—"

"The train will be here in a minute. I'll be on it. I'll ask Beulah to come over." As if in a dream—or maybe a nightmare—Ruth Ann didn't move fast as she collected herself and strode out the back door toward the Levitt house. She wouldn't tell them why she was leaving. She wouldn't be afraid. She wouldn't beg for Mr. Levitt to go with her.

Ruth Ann was a reporter for the *Choctaw Tribune*. They reported on all the important happenings as soon as they happened or fairly close to it. If they broke a story like this in a special edition before the *Dickens Herald*, they were one step closer to pulling even with the powerful newspaper.

That was worth putting her fear aside for.

♦♦♦

While Ruth Ann sat fidgeting in the passenger car, she gazed out the window at the Dickens depot. What was taking so long? Few passengers had boarded along with her and they were already seated in the relatively empty car. The train stopped for anywhere from four to ten minutes, but it felt well past that now. It was as if the train were waiting on someone. Or maybe it felt so long because Ruth Ann had to fight the urge to run out of the car before the train jerked her away from the depot and the familiarity of Dickens to take her on an unknown journey down in the big city. A city she'd never entered alone. She swallowed hard.

Then she saw the reason for the delay. It had to be. Ruth Ann's stomach somersaulted, then a knot formed in it.

The derby hat was held in place by the jogging man wearing his gray suit. In the other hand, he clutched a satchel. With sickening dread, Ruth Ann recalled how the doctor who had received the telegram was a personal friend of this leading citizen.

The editor of the *Dickens Herald* leaped up the platform steps and to the same train car Ruth Ann sat in. She tried to keep her eyes out the window, but from one corner, she noted the man striding toward her.

"Is this seat open?"

Though there were dozens available, Mr. Maxwell gestured toward the empty bench across from Ruth Ann. With nothing quick to say, she gave a stiff nod, eyes everywhere but his way as he sat across from her.

"Seems we're traveling the same direction. For the same reason, no doubt."

Ruth Ann tried to relax her pinned lips but she had no intention of saying anything unless she had to. The train whistle blew and the ride began.

Maxwell adjusted his coat and removed his hat, using it to fan himself. "Whew, just barely made it. Glad I was able to send one of my boys to hold the train while I gathered what I needed. One of the perks of having the prime newspaper in town, I suppose."

Ignoring the jab was harder than ignoring Peter. Still, Ruth Ann watched the countryside flash by as she tried to find comfort in the swaying motion of the car.

"I suppose your brother is up Tuskahoma way, covering some little something with the tribe? That must be exciting for him." Maxwell's dry tone edged Ruth Ann closer to saying something but she held her peace as she noted the thick clump of pine trees they passed. She wouldn't be pulled into chitchat about newspaper business, and that a shooting was no little affair. One thing they didn't need was to give the *Dickens Herald* any kind of edge.

Maxwell seemed to understand she wouldn't be drawn out so he settled his satchel on the empty seat beside him, opened it and set about shuffling through scribbled notes and newspapers. A familiar piece caught her eye and she realized it was the latest edition of the *Choctaw Tribune* with red marks on it. Alarmed more than flattered, she swallowed and kept her eyes out the window. A long ride lay ahead.

♦♦♦

The train rumbled into Paris, Texas, before the noon meal. The depot was nearly vacant much to Ruth Ann's surprise. It always bustled with activity more so than Dickens, three times in fact. Now it looked like it belonged in a ghost town.

Mr. Maxwell buckled his satchel as the train came to a stop, the action making Ruth Ann jump in her seat. Maxwell leaned forward, preparing to stand, but he was unnecessarily close when he said quietly, "It's a man's world out there, Ruth Ann. Take care to remember that."

Her palms sweated from the heat of the unusually warm

early spring day as she gripped her reticule and tablet. "Thank you, sir, I will, if you will so kindly be a gentleman and address me as Miss Teller." She stood on shaky legs, awkwardly sidestepping him as she tried to exit her seat gracefully. He chuckled softly and tipped his derby hat before allowing her to leave the train car first.

When her laced-up boot touched the wood platform, Ruth Ann had no idea what to do. Where was the riot? Should she rush right into the middle of it? What would Matthew do? Knowing Maxwell was right behind her, Ruth Ann strode toward the depot's open door and entered as though that had been her intention all along. Thankfully, it wasn't Maxwell's plan. She sighed when she watched through the windows to see him leave the platform from the other side.

She stood awkwardly inside the nearly empty depot, looking around and trying to gather her thoughts. She hadn't had a cohesive one since Mr. Maxwell had boarded the train.

A shrill whistle sounded across the room. "Say there, are you R.A.? I mean, Ruth Ann Teller?"

Ruth Ann spun at the sound of her nickname on the wire and noted a young man behind a cage window near the ticket counter. He held something up. "I have a telegram for you from P. You operate on the wire too, don't you?"

Relieved at something familiar, Ruth Ann moved over to his counter. "Yes. P is my cousin Peter. Is he behaving?"

Before the young man could answer, the sounder clattered and he sighed as he took the message while still speaking. "This thing hasn't stopped all day. Every reporter from all over is wiring for news, and every reporter is pouring in here and sending it out. Quite the doings we've had going on."

"May I see my telegram please?" Ruth Ann held out a hand to receive the slip of paper the young operator absently handed her while taking the incoming message. She unfolded it and read the scribbles.

Return immediately. Matthew's orders. Situation dangerous. Bad reports coming through.

So Peter had managed to contact Matthew during her ride. And Matthew, of course, didn't want her in danger. But surely she had faced worse since they'd started the newspaper—she could face this. Although the difference this time was she was completely alone.

With a deep breath, she wrote out a crisp response. *Understand danger. Will be careful, in contact soon. R.A.*

She handed it to the operator and tried to pay him but he waved it off. "No worries, R.A. I've got this one for you." The sounder clattered once again and Ruth Ann took the opportunity to exit the depot into the humid air of Paris.

The brick streets by the depot ended quickly into dusty roads and Ruth Ann didn't know which to take. She slowly went down the steps and glanced as far up the streets as she could. So much emptiness. Where was everyone in this big city?

Hooves clacking on the brick sounded behind her, but she paid them no mind until she heard someone call, "Can I offer you a lift, ma'am?"

Ruth Ann turned and squinted in the bright sunlight to see the outline of a man sitting high atop a carriage pulled by matched grays who bobbed their heads in unison as they came to a halt beside her. The man seemed to recognize her at the same time she did him. He lifted his hat off his short auburn curls and bowed his head to her. "If it isn't the young lady without her crutches. Where's your fine brother this day?"

Ruth Ann smiled up at the man, Aaron Greiner—more well-known as Cabby—and answered, "Off covering another story. I'm here to see about a lynching of some kind. Do you—" She hesitated at the shadow that came across Cabby's face as he looked off over the empty streets.

He said to the streets, "Was hoping not to take anyone else out there today. Was hoping you wanted to go to the new ice cream parlor or maybe the Merrick Hotel. But I reckon a lady who visits jails might apt to want to go anywhere."

Ruth Ann blushed, not certain how to respond. She finally said, "I'm a reporter for the *Choctaw Tribune*. I have to

THE EXECUTIONS

report from firsthand experience, not hearsay. I'd be grateful if you would take me to whatever is happening."

"You really don't wanna go, miss. Ain't a pretty affair," Cabby grumbled while hopping down from his high spring seat to open the hack door for her. "But I'll take ya there. 'Bout four miles out of town."

The ride through the dry streets was different from the last time she rode in this hack while it hauled her through ankle deep mud. Much different. Then, she'd had Matthew leading, taking care of everything, making the way. She had to make her own way now.

The hack left the abandoned streets and turned toward open country, following a well-traveled road out of the city. It was a fairly long ride, and felt like a few lifetimes had passed before the noise level rose. Trying to see what she could through the side windows, Ruth Ann noted they were in a field.

The sound of cheering sent chills through Ruth Ann despite the ever warming temperatures. Her father's saying that was tucked in the corner of her heart whispered to her now.

God knows.

The hack halted. Moments later, Cabby opened the door and offered her a hand. "Close as I can get, miss. You might want to stay back yourself."

When she stepped from the hack, Ruth Ann immediately was assaulted by the smell of horse flesh mixed with the dust and sweat of hundreds of people. Something was burning, adding a rancid, wicked smell to the air.

Most of the town was there. Rows and rows of people stacked and crowded together, all pressing forward in human mass before Ruth Ann. Some were dressed as if for Sunday service, others more casual in overalls like factory workers. Had they all left their jobs and their senses?

Ruth Ann took a step forward before realizing Cabby still held her hand. She glanced up at him, surprised by his height. She'd always attributed it to the high seat he sat on, but he truly was a tall man. He held her hand and her eyes a moment. His words were almost lost in the din about them. "Folks might have come from all over the country for this kind of entertainment, but you really don't want to be here, miss."

Ruth Ann took a shaky breath. "You are correct. I don't. But I must. It's my job."

He released her hand with a shake of his head and muttered, "Women ought to be in the kitchen."

Ruth Ann allowed herself to be amused as she opened her reticule and withdrew coins. But Cabby shook his head. "No, ma'am, I'd…I'd feel like it was blood money. I'll be around if you need me. And you will." Before Ruth Ann could protest, Cabby hauled himself back aboard his hack and clucked to his horses. "Get on, Tom, get on, Jerry."

Alone in the turmoil of people, Ruth Ann drew a fortifying breath, said a hasty prayer and pressed herself into the crowd, trying to see the reason for the thrill charging the air like lightning bolts. She felt eyes on her and glanced back, wondering how close Cabby would stay, but was surprised instead to see Mr. Maxwell coming across the beaten grass toward the crowd. He must have rented a horse or buggy from the livery stable, putting him on the scene after Ruth Ann.

Determination to do the story as well as the *Dickens Herald* ignited enough fire in Ruth Ann to turn her eyes forward again and worm her way through the cheering and gasping crowd. She took a different strategy than most who simply tried to jostle their way to the front. Staying low and arms tucked close to her sides, Ruth Ann's head ducked under elbows while she took in the various kinds of boots and shoes the people wore. It told a good deal about the crowd gathered. They were both rich and poor. Shiny buckles showed the little boys and girls there. Some feet were bare, rubbed on top of one another to satisfy an itch they couldn't bend down to scratch for fear of missing something. These bare feet were white. And black. And brown. Large and small.

The pins in Ruth Ann's bun loosened. Strands of hair fell

over her shoulders as she stayed bent, pressing forward. It was all she could do to cling to her tablet and reticule, where she'd stuffed her pencils.

The thickly packed bodies and their odors were so heavy Ruth Ann could scarcely breathe. The dust choked her and stabbed her eyes with grit. Needing relief, Ruth Ann stood and was drawn into the swaying and jostling of the dozen or so within arm's reach. It felt like coming up for air after having her head held beneath the water as one bully from school had done several summers ago. Philip had taken that boy into the bushes and beaten him, but the terror never left Ruth Ann when she entered water. She felt that terror now. She could not escape the crowd. She could not see anything ahead. Rocks flew over her, toward the direction Ruth Ann was going.

Gasping and with sweat pouring down and tangling in her ruined hair, she glanced around once more and saw Mr. Maxwell still following her. What an advantage to be a man. He could elbow his way right through the crowd as if they were merely resistant stalks of corn.

Determination renewed, Ruth Ann pressed on low through the mass of bodies, determined to see something worth reporting. Hopefully something the *Dickens Herald* would not.

It was soon to come. Too soon.

The stench grew stronger and with disturbing clarity Ruth Ann knew what it was—scorched flesh. A scream ripped through the air, louder than the loudest heckler, louder than the loudest shrieking child. It was unearthly, nonhuman. It brought Ruth Ann straight up and straight into the face of horror.

CHAPTER FORTY

WARMTH FLOWED AROUND RUTH ANN'S body that slowly gave way to a tingling sensation in her fingertips and toes. Gradually, the darkness receded, followed by a sense of feeling throughout her body. She lay flat on her back on something soft and airy. It firmed more as the rest of her senses came to her. Two tiny spots of light formed in the center of her eyes and pushed the black away until Ruth Ann stared at the high ceiling with ornate wood trim and honey color wallpaper.

Her eyes were able to focus and her ears picked up a soft humming sound coming from somewhere in the room. She turned her head and winced when sharp needles stabbed her forehead. The hum turned to tongue clicking and a melon-sweet voice, thick with a Dixie accent. "I wouldn't if I were you, missy. You took a mighty good gash to the head."

Closing her eyes, Ruth Ann reopened them and was able to make out a woman sitting a ways from her in a plush velvet rocker. She looked odd and out of place, yet perfectly comfortable as her dark, crooked fingers worked a needle and thread through worn gingham fabric. She didn't lift her head as she continued speaking. "Some folks got no sense, others let theirs take a trip now and again. Mighty hard on them and them around them."

Ruth Ann shook her head and managed to prop herself on her elbow even though it made the room spin and the darkness covered her vision. She blinked. "What happened?" Her voice was a pitiful croak and she coughed on the remnants of dust in her throat. "How did I get here?"

Instead of answering, the woman stood and laid aside her sewing to pour a glass of water from the nightstand pitcher. She offered it from a distance it seemed to Ruth Ann who stretched out to clasp it in shaky fingers. "Yakoke," she murmured as she took a sip. That cleared her mind enough to repeat in English, "Thank you."

The woman settled back into the rocker. It protested the heavy weight with a loud creak as she picked up the cloth again. Seeing clearer, Ruth Ann noted how aged the woman was. Perhaps around the age of the Grandmother, maybe not quite so old, but worn looking. Dark spots on her face stood out even on her dark skin, and her cheeks sagged, having long ago lost any shine. A kerchief held her hair out of sight, but Ruth Ann imagined the white streaks in it.

Ruth Ann spoke again, thankful her throat didn't still feel as though a bullfrog had taken up residence. "What is your name, ma'am?"

The woman chuckled. "Not ma'am, certain. Folks here about call me Mama Tippy."

Smiling at the homey name, Ruth Ann set the glass on the table and swung her legs off the bed. She winced and held her head. That was when she felt the bandage on the burning spot of her forehead. She closed her eyes and breathed deeply as she tried to conjure up what had happened. She must be in Paris. In a hotel. On a bed, fully dressed and with a gash in her head. The sun-streaks she'd noted coming through the partially drawn drapes told her it was early evening.

What had brought her here? "The riot."

The creak of the rocking chair stopped and Mama Tippy spoke from somewhere more distant than the room. "If that's what you call it, missy."

Ruth Ann opened her eyes and studied the woman, who had grown still and sat staring at the gingham in her lap. "What would you call it, Mama Tippy?"

"Evil for evil. It be what it be. No changing it."

Before Ruth Ann could make sense of the words, an anxious knock sounded on the door. She moaned at the needles the noise stirred in her head.

Mama Tippy set aside her work and waddled to the door. She called out, "Who be there?"

Ruth Ann didn't understand the reply, but she did recognize the voice. "Oh, Beulah! Please let her in."

Mama Tippy barely got the door open a crack before it was pushed wide by Beulah, who dashed to Ruth Ann's side. Beulah grasped her hands in a squeeze before stepping aside and letting Ruth Ann see a beautiful sight—her mother.

"Oh," Ruth Ann murmured as she allowed Della to engulf her. She burrowed her face into the sweet smell of her mama's cotton dress, soaked with scents from home. The place Ruth Ann most wanted to be.

Della pulled back first, clicking with her tongue as she peeked under the bandage on Ruth Ann's forehead. It all flashed back to Ruth Ann and bubbled out. "I was in the crowd. I tried to run away and one of the rocks hit me. I fell into someone's arms..." Here she drifted off as her consciousness had.

Mama Tippy went back to her rocker. Beulah plopped beside Ruth Ann, shaking the bed frame. "Dear, dear Ruth, why on earth did you run off down here like that? Alone! I love your adventurous spirit, but really, there has to be bounds. This was one of those times."

Her senses returning fully, Ruth Ann noted the shrill pitch in Beulah's tone. It unnerved her and she wasn't able to look at her friend. She turned her attention to Della, who took a seat on the other side of Ruth Ann, still examining every inch of her head. "I'm sorry, Mama. I didn't mean to put myself in harm's way. There were so many people there—

including women. I thought as a reporter, I certainly belonged in the middle of things. But perhaps...I got a little too close."

Without warning, a flood of tears burst from her eyes even before the images were clear in her mind. She was shaking, sobbing, and only partially aware she was truly safe in her mother's arms. None of that relieved the horror of what she'd seen.

In a voice still too shrill, Beulah asked, "How did you get here? In the Merrick Hotel?"

Ruth Ann inhaled deeply and pulled back from her mother's arms. "I really don't know. When I woke up, here I was with Mama Tippy..." She trailed off, looking toward the old black woman who continued her sewing.

Not looking up, Mama Tippy said, "That fancy white man from your town, he brung you in Cabby's cart and paid up for you to stay the night here. Reckon he wired your folks, too."

Della took her eyes off Ruth Ann long enough at nod to Mama Tippy. "Thank you for caring for my daughter."

But Beulah stiffened and Ruth Ann finally glanced at her, noted her pressed lips as Beulah stared at the woman in the rocker. "You may go now. We will take care of Miss Teller."

Mama Tippy shrugged and hoisted herself out of the rocker, gingham dress in hand. "Shore thing, miss. That man, he paid me to stay with her long's she needed me. Reckon it's been long enough."

"Indeed."

Ruth Ann glanced at Beulah again before struggling to her feet despite Della's tongue clicking against it. She reached out and grasped Mama Tippy's knuckles on her left hand that clutched the cloth. They were sharp and tough, like the smile the old woman gave her. No words passed between them. None were needed.

CHAPTER FORTY-ONE

STATIONED AT THE WIRE BY sunrise the next morning, Ruth Ann scribbled away on her article. She felt only one thing—rage. Pure, unchecked, raw anger at what she'd witnessed in Paris. There was no desire to tame it; instead she used it to fuel the spark of each word she penned for the front page article of the special edition newspaper she planned to put out that afternoon. How she would do it alone, she didn't know. The only thing in her vision were the words written in ink that may as well have been blood. The words would not be erased, they would not be silenced or burned. The time had come.

Behind her, a presence filled the doorway. Ruth Ann had been alone this day in the telegraph office, earlier than anyone in town might consider milling about to do business. Who the presence was mattered not to Ruth Ann. It was someone with a key, but whether it was Beulah or Mr. Levitt or even her mother, it mattered not. Only one thing mattered when she had disembarked from the newly scheduled early train that morning with her mother and Beulah in tow. That one thing was not a bath or a fresh change of clothes. She wanted the dust and blood on her dress to fill the pages of her article, the one thing that mattered that morning. The only thing, not the presence that moved closer behind her. Even if it was Sheriff Banny himself, it mattered not. She felt called to conquer evil this day. No matter what form.

A hand settled on her shoulder and Ruth Ann relaxed at the familiar touch. With Matthew's help, she had no doubt of the success of getting the special edition out. And the urgency to accomplish that had nothing to do with besting the *Dickens Herald*. Nothing so trivial as that would drive Ruth Ann to continue her scribbling even as Matthew's hand covered hers in an attempt to still her writing. She brushed it aside and kept writing, angrily refusing the tears that threatened to come.

"No, Matthew. I must do this. I have to. For him. For them. For us all."

The scrape of a chair sounded and Matthew sat by her, settling his hat on the corner of her desk. "I came home a day early to see about you, Annie. Not talk to the back of your pen."

Slowly, slowly, Ruth Ann brought her pen to a stop and the ink dried on the tip. She didn't re-dip it. She stared at the words strewn across the page. None of them made sense. Nothing in the past day made sense. She shoved the paper toward Matthew and dropped her pen, defeated.

The paper's movement sounded loud in the respectful silence of the room as Matthew lifted the page and scanned it. He read parts aloud. "What drives man to take joy in the destruction of another's life? Literal destruction of burning flesh, seared before a mass of cheering folk…where is the justice of our land? Who stands on the side of right?"

He laid the article back near her hand and waited in silence. Matthew was far too good at the silent ways, ways Ruth Ann fought against at times like these. This wasn't the time for pondering, it was time for action. She looked Matthew in the eyes. "Will you print it?"

"It's fine writing, Annie. But where's the story?"

Ruth Ann shot to her feet and pounded the paper, crinkling the words and smearing them. "You can't see it?"

Remaining seated, Matthew looked up at her. "You can't go on emotions. You have to have the facts."

"Should you not have both?"

Matthew leaned forward, using one finger to slide the paper closer to her. "Yes. And that's the key. Both."

Ruth Ann flailed her arms before folding them tight against her chest and turning away. "I was there. I *saw* it."

"There's always more to a story. You have to find out more than anybody else."

"I don't want to know more." Ruth Ann closed her eyes and rubbed the skin around the cut on her forehead. She knew enough. She'd experienced enough. She had to...had to...

Her body swayed and Matthew's arms were around her before she realized he'd moved or that she'd almost stumbled. His voice was close. "I understand we owe a hearty yakoke to Mr. Maxwell."

Ruth Ann sagged in her brother's arms. She'd forgotten all about the man, how they'd tried to beat each other to the story, how he'd saved her in the crowd and now she owed him. It was not the kind of debt she relished repaying. Her knees weakened at the thought.

Matthew squeezed her shoulders. "I'm taking you home. You rest. I'll take care of the special edition."

"But...but it isn't finished..."

"Your part is, Annie. You did your part."

♦♦♦

The sun was straight up in the sky when Ruth Ann woke in her own bed where she'd been carefully attended to that morning. She was in her own nightgown, snuggled under the handmade quilt given to her as a birthday gift a few years ago. She ran her fingers over the lovely design, so carefully wrought by the women in their Choctaw community. They loved her. She belonged among them. A sudden, intense desire filled Ruth Ann. She wanted to be out on the farm with

Uncle Preston and the Grandmother. Just seeing them would set her mind at ease from whatever was troubling it so.

Throwing aside the quilt, Ruth Ann swung her feet off the bed and tried to sit up. She moaned and held her head, the quick movements making her dizzy again. She sighed and listened in resignation as she heard soft steps ascending the stairs to the attic bedroom. Della would scold her and pin her under the quilt again, like all good mothers do. But Ruth Ann had crossed a threshold. She was no longer a child, but a young woman with full knowledge of the desperate evil that lay in the world beyond her mother's love.

Della appeared at the top of the steps carrying a tray with a steaming bowl and small coffee cup settled in the middle. She looked at Ruth Ann and shook her head as she approached. "Stubborn, stubborn Choctaw. Like your daddy. Like your brothers."

Ruth Ann pulled her feet back onto the bed in a cross-legged position as she accepted the tray. "Like you, Mama."

She saw the folded paper on the tray. It was a familiar kind of paper with printing on both sides. With a soft gasp, Ruth Ann unfolded the special edition of the *Choctaw Tribune*. She scanned the front page article. It was hers, most of it kept intact as her first draft had read that morning, with a few additions such as the location and date. Nothing more. A raw, unapologetic verdict on the events of the previous day. No cluttering of facts or unattached opinion. Pure emotion.

Ruth Ann fingered the paper and scanned the other articles with dull eyes. It contained a piece about the shooting Matthew had gone to cover, and a meat sale at Bates' General Store. Nothing that compared to her spewed words on the front page. She lowered the paper to the quilt and stirred the now lukewarm soup. "It doesn't feel right. Nothing does."

As if understanding the time to talk had come, Della pulled a side chair with its woven cane bottom close to the bed as Ruth Ann continued. "I thought if I showed the world—at least the world of Dickens—how awful and evil things were, and how I could handle the story myself—I thought it would mean more. But it means nothing. I don't even know his name or what he'd been accused of doing, only that he was being burned alive."

Hand trembling, Ruth Ann spooned the soup between her lips. Tasteless. "I'm a horrible reporter. A horrible Christian. A horrible…everything!"

She sighed and plopped the tray over the article, sloshing soup over the headline. Hands on her knees, she bowed her head and waited. She knew it would be awhile, so she bit her tongue and thought of how patient the Grandmother was. How patient Matthew was. How impatient she was.

A hand rubbed her shoulders, and Ruth Ann relaxed them, drifting into the comfort of her mother's touch and away to a distant place on her words. "Love and hate. God made us to be able to do them both. But what should we do? What do the words of the preacher say every week? We have those words in our own language too. They say love. Forgive. Or we won't be forgiven."

Fingers dug deep into the muscles of Ruth Ann's sore shoulders and she winced but made no reply. The sharp pain felt good. Della continued. "Raw pain and hate made them do that to that man. Made many a man do more bad than good in this world. Too much hating in the world. That's why we must love so."

Ruth Ann leaned her head over and her mother's shoulder was there. "Is that the other side of the story, Mama? The side I missed? But there was no love in fifty miles. No sanity, either. But I sure missed plenty of simple facts. Facts I have to go back for. I have to finish the story in the right way before the next edition."

The way her mother stiffened told her she didn't care for the idea, but neither did she object. Della had a keen sense and wisdom about her children and she knew this was one of the times to allow them a lesson on their own. She offered only two words. "God knows."

♦♦♦

Stubborn Choctaws. What was a businessman to do with them? He'd tried to shove them aside, woo them, crush them. But the young, stubborn Matthew Teller and his lovely sister couldn't be bought out, driven out, or talked out.

Christopher Maxwell leaned back in his quiet office in the *Dickens Herald* print shop. Quiet except the pleasant background of the press clacking and workers pulling together the special edition that would push him further into dominance and prestige in the booming town of Dickens. He'd staked everything he owned and the very reputation he'd cultivated from boyhood on the success of this town and his place in it. Plenty threatened the fragile existence of a new town in the unpredictable follies in Indian Territory. But little risk, little reward, his father had drilled into him, and now was the time to see epic rewards—or epic failure that would reach his prestigious family and friends in his place of rearing, Washington, D.C.

As a boy, his father had given him two choices in life—politics or influencer. He'd chosen the latter, seeing an opportunity to shape an ever-growing country, even his own. Dickens was his own.

Another wagon rolled through his street view. Choosing this room for his office had been easy. He could see the entire main street of Dickens from the window angled such that few passersby noticed it. He liked the advantage of watching all while none noticed. His view once included the *Choctaw Tribune* shack next to the freight office. When it burned to the ground—with some help from Banny—he figured to have taken care of the final thorn in his side, leaving him free to shape his little country in the way that pleased him.

But the thorn grew back. After all his strategies and allies had failed, there was only one thing left for a well-bred, intelligent man to do. Listen to the ancient wisdom of his father.

Kill them with kindness.

Young Matthew Teller now owed him a great debt, one

to count on when the next crisis arose or was created.

Christopher Maxwell propped his feet up on his desk and interlaced his fingers behind his neck. News of epic failure would never blossom and reach home.

CHAPTER FORTY-TWO

THE JOURNEY WAS NOT TO be made alone this time. That was Matthew's condition when Ruth Ann arrived at the newspaper office the next morning, later than usual. She'd had a dreaded errand to attend to first, but mercifully, Mr. Maxwell had not been in the *Dickens Herald* office. She'd been able to deposit a note and basket of cookies with his secretary without having the humiliation of facing the man. She would have to face him someday, but not today. She had enough ahead of her.

Matthew was manning the wire that morning, partly because Peter wouldn't come until noon, partly to keep an ear on the latest news from Paris. Ruth Ann sat next to him, ready to receive his instructions and conditions on her proposed trip back to Paris for more firsthand accounts of what had happened. And to get the facts, although many of them were flying over the wire still that morning. But the *Choctaw Tribune* didn't want to rely on secondhand stories when they could seek out their own.

Matthew finished jotting down the latest wire before leaning back in his seat and looking at Ruth Ann. "I'm going to ask Mr. Levitt to go with you. No—no buts, Annie." He shook his head and she folded her hands in her lap, secretly relieved as Matthew continued. "He is a busy man, yes, but I will not have you going off alone again, and I have to get the next edition articles sorted and prepared. I'm counting on you to bring me another front-page story." He didn't smile, but Ruth Ann sensed his forgiving spirit at her blunders and his willingness to allow her to try again. She nodded.

Voices drifted in to them, announcing Mr. Levitt and Beulah were at the back of their half of the shop, chattering away. Matthew raised his eyebrows toward the telegraph doorway and rose to follow Ruth Ann out and to the back of the larger shop that held the printing press and makeshift office area for the *Choctaw Tribune*.

Beulah immediately spotted them and met Ruth Ann with hands outstretched. She squeezed them with a sympathetic smile. "I hope you rested well, dear Ruth. Such a trying experience, to be sure."

Ruth Ann tried to smile, but unable to, she turned her attention to Mr. Levitt. "Sir, I have an enormous favor to ask. I'm leaving on the noon train for Paris and wondered if you could accompany me. Beulah, maybe you'd care to go too and do some shopping…" The trail of words was lost in the stormy expression suddenly on her friend's face.

Beulah released her hands and crossed her arms. "Why are you going there? The deed is done, Ruth. You have written your story and it is time to move on now. The incident of one Negro man is hardly worth more risk."

The man had been black? It had been impossible for Ruth Ann to tell the man's skin color for the scorched flesh.

She took a step back, confused at Beulah's cold tone. She searched Beulah's chilly blue eyes, so unlike the character of her Jewish friend. "The life of a Negro? What if he were a white man, a Choctaw or a Jew? Would that justify the cost of more words on a piece of paper?"

Beulah seemed to make an effort to relax her stance but remained stiff. "I did not mean to infer it was an issue of race. It just seems when one story is finished, it is finished. You were endangered and as I recall, I am the one who received the telegraph and alerted your mother. I was the one who slept upon the floor of the hotel while you recovered enough to return home. Do you have no gratitude, or do your feelings for a stranger outweigh loyalty toward a friend?"

Ruth Ann tried to calm herself enough to speak without a tremor in her voice. Knowing that wouldn't be possible, she spoke slowly and chose her words with great care. "Beulah, you are one of my dearest friends. When you first arrived, it didn't matter to me that you were Jew no more than it mattered to you that I was Choctaw. We had a common bond—we both knew the sting of prejudice but also the pride in our race. Shouldn't that bond extend to any race?"

Beulah dropped her arms and looked off through the windows at the front of the shop as if her next words were too weighty to speak to Ruth Ann alone. She spoke to the world. "I believe Indians—particularly Choctaws—were gifted by God with a civilized intelligence. They are able to rise above their circumstances and make a better life for themselves and society. I have never seen that sort in the black man who allowed himself to be enslaved in a country where freedom is abundant. His intelligence is lower than other races."

Stunned, Ruth Ann stared at Beulah. This wasn't something Beulah had come up with in this moment. More than a little thought had been given to her words and beliefs. They were not at all what Ruth Ann could have imagined. "You can't mean that."

Beulah leveled her eyes on Ruth Ann again. "You are a small town girl, Ruth. You do not know of the changing world out there. If our races are to survive—yes, even thrive—we must align ourselves with the ones who are rising. That requires a distinguishing of ourselves from lower classes of civilization, lest we be taken down with them."

Unable to absorb all the words and the meanings behind them, Ruth Ann yielded to the step forward she had seen Mr. Levitt take. All eyes turned to him as he stepped to Ruth

Ann's side and faced his daughter. His voice was kind and gentle and small as the man himself. "Dear daughter. Were not our own people slaves in a land where they were once free and even honored?"

Beulah crossed her arms. "Papa, you know that is back in the ancient history of our ancestors."

"Is it not their blood that flows in our veins? And according to our belief in God, are we not all one race?" This time, he didn't wait for her reply as he spoke to Matthew and Ruth Ann. "I will go with you, child, and see about this thing that happened."

A harsh sigh was the only thing Beulah added as she spun away and went through the storeroom door. It closed with finality.

◆◆◆

The train ride to Paris was peaceful. Mr. Levitt sat across from Ruth Ann, reading a newspaper that had migrated down from Fort Smith. She didn't care to see a newspaper at all and turned her attention to the flashing countryside out the window, gathering her thoughts for the coming work. She braced her heart, admonishing herself to be professional, a reporter like Matthew. One who dug out the emotions but also the facts. And always both sides of the story.

After arriving at the depot, Ruth Ann led the way down several blocks to the Lamar County Jail. She could have tried to hail Cabby if she waited at the depot, but she knew the way. And a brisk walk would help fortify her for the task, though she found she had to slow her pace to accommodate Mr. Levitt. His short stride and relaxed stroll at which he took in his surroundings made Ruth Ann antsy. This was not the time for sightseeing. But in the same accord, she knew a path was better when traveled slow enough to remember the way home. So the Grandmother often said.

In shorter time than Ruth Ann expected, they were in front of the sheriff's office and ascending the steps. A deep breath later, she entered through the door Mr. Levitt held open. She was struck with the strong smell of coal black coffee and sweat. She was glad to have already taken a deep breath.

As her eyes adjusted to the dim light, she approached the nearest desk where a man sat leaned back in his chair, feet on the desk. His face was half-buried in a large tin cup. Judging from the dribbling in his beard, Ruth Ann guessed it was a meal of cornbread and milk. She cleared her throat to gain his attention while smoothing her skirt self-consciously. She'd prepared for the occasion in her most business-like dress, a muted gray with a trim skirt and jacket. "Excuse me, sir. My name is Ruth Ann Teller, a reporter for the *Choctaw Tribune*, out of Dickens. I—"

"The who outta where?" The man with a deputy badge slurped his spoon clean and dropped his feet to the floor, riffling his free hand around the shamble of papers on his desk until he found a broken pencil. He tore a strip of weathered paper from an old wanted poster and scribbled something.

Ruth Ann tried again. "The *Choctaw Tribune* in Dickens, Indian Territory. I would like to ask a few questions about the...the event the other day south of Paris. Would you—"

The man let out a low whistle as he flopped back in his chair. "Some doings, wasn't it? And imagine, a woman reporter from an Indian newspaper here to cover it. What will they think of next?" He chuckled and dug into his cup again.

After swallowing the contents of the spoon whole, he continued. "Yeah, I was there. Deputy Jameson, ma'am. We caught that filthy killer, tracked him all the way to Arkansas to bring him back. Brought in a crowd, yes sir. Paraded him right through town with a noose already around his neck. Longest ride he ever had, I 'spect. Did you see it, ma'am? Was a sight, all right. Glad ol' Vince and his young'un had their right on the scaffold when they got out to the farm. Yes sir, burned him all over with hot irons 'fore we poured on the oil for burning and finished him off with snapping his neck at the end of a rope."

Deputy Jameson reached into his shirt pocket and held up a photograph. "Got plenty of these. Makes nice mementos and reminder that we serve out the right kind of justice. Yes sir, that's what the mayor had us paint on a board and nail to the scaffold—*justice*."

Ruth Ann couldn't find her voice. She tried to remain strong, but she was a puddle. She wasn't ready for this, this real world beyond her little, little town. But even in this moment, God had used those around her to give the help she needed.

Mr. Levitt, hat in hand, spoke up. "Deputy Jameson, what was this man's crime again?"

The deputy pocketed the photograph and flopped back in his chair, wide-eyed as he stared at the small man. "Why, you don't know? Everyone in the country knows!"

In truth, Ruth Ann knew that Mr. Levitt did possess some knowledge, but the question was for her benefit. She'd intentionally shielded herself from the facts as they came over the wire and through the *Dickens Herald*. She had to gather the facts for herself, firsthand. And Mr. Levitt was her aid in doing so. *Bless you, sir.*

The deputy tipped up the end of his cup and gulped the rest of his cornbread and milk. Wiping his beard with the back of his sleeve, he hurried on with his flood of words. "Well, everyone except you knows, but that dirty dog, we've hauled him in drunk more than once. Deputy Vince Shelton, he had to give him a good clubbing that last time. Well, that done it. That dog went to cussing and swearing revenge. Sure enough, a few weeks later, he busted into Vince's farmhouse and got his wife—beat and strangled her dead. Thought he could get away with something like that! Hot irons and burning was too good for that monster, but at least the family can have some peace about it."

Ruth Ann noted Mr. Levitt rubbing his chest as he asked, "What evidence was brought forward for his guilt?"

Deputy Jameson halted before answering, eyeing Mr.

Levitt like he was crazier than he'd first suspected. Hostility edged into his next words. "Plenty more than I need to say. Folks who saw him near the farm that day, and he even confessed, though it did take a little to convince him. But if you want details, get a copy of the Paris paper. Or Arkansas. Tennessee. New York. They got all the facts you want."

Ruth Ann wanted to vomit. Wanted her mother to wrap the bandage of love around her bleeding heart. She thought of Reverend Anoletubbee shooting dead the woman he believed had killed his wife and child. How could someone keep a sane thought at such a time? Deputy...what was his name again? Vince Shelton. What had he felt when cradling the lifeless body of his brutalized wife? What ends of the earth and insane reasoning would he not reach for to exact justice and a sense of rightness in his soul?

But what had it really cost his soul and the soul of every human being that day? Did it at all bring rightness? The kind of civilization this country stood for?

Ruth Ann managed to focus her eyes on the inflamed ones of the deputy. "In your...in your opinion, did he receive no trial and was tortured to death because he was a Negro?"

The deputy blinked. Then he smirked. "Yeah, I heard there was that misinformation going around, and his skin being all burned black added to it. But Homer Gentry was a young white cuss. Lowest of mankind. Weren't a soul not glad to see him dead."

So he hadn't been a black man like they'd heard. Matthew was right about getting the facts. Doing that first would have preserved Ruth Ann and Beulah's friendship for a time.

The door behind them slammed open and a young boy hollered, "Vince got him! They're bringing his buddy in now! Won't be long before they string him up, no show this time. Better hurry if you want to see!"

Deputy Jameson started from his seat, snagging a greasy hat from the corner of his desk and waving it at Mr. Levitt. "You come on and see for yourself what kind of justice we serve out here!" He disappeared through the door after the young boy and three other deputies who'd been lounging around in the back rooms.

Ruth Ann froze. It was Mr. Levitt who stepped close to the open door where a crowd could be seen gathering near the lone tree on the lawn between the sheriff's office and courthouse. He turned back to her, hand on his chest, waiting for her decision.

With a job to do, Ruth Ann took a step forward, then another and another and soon she was standing on the porch, seeing the gathering mob much like before, only smaller this time and more urgent. A rope sailed over a level branch of the tree.

Justice?

Ruth Ann realized she was hurrying down the steps and straight toward the mob. A horse whinnied in protest. An unearthly scream, a begging yelp. Mr. Levitt's harsh pant behind her.

Someone grabbed her arm. "Not too close, missy!" Deputy Jameson held her fast, just within sight of the wild-eyed horse that pranced to one side as a middle-aged black man was thrown up on it, hands tied behind his back, noose around his neck. The deputy hollered in her ear, "Since you want all the facts, this here fella was a drinking buddy of the woman killer. He hid the monster out fer days, wouldn't tell us where he'd gone off too. He took off too, but they got him. Yes sir, we got him."

Another scream and a slap against tight horseflesh. A snap. Silence.

A moan. Ruth Ann and the deputy turned in time to catch Mr. Levitt as he pitched toward them, right hand balled against his heart.

CHAPTER FORTY-THREE

THE SUN SET. THE SUN rose. The sun set. The sun rose. At least some things were unchanged in Dickens.

Ruth Ann had delivered a great many regular editions of the newspaper today. The edition that featured her article front page, with all the details, all the facts, all the emotions. Both sides of the story. The heinous crime. The heinous punishments. No side for justice.

Ruth Ann left the post office in no hurry, but the sight of a letter with postage from New York halted her on the platform. It was addressed to the *Choctaw Tribune*. She slipped her thumb under one corner of the seal and opened it. A single white sheet of paper with crisp writing made a simple request:

To the Editor of the Choctaw Tribune:

I wish to subscribe to your newspaper as a means of staying current on events in Indian Territory. I need a reliable source. Address below.

Sincerely,
Angus Rice

Editor, The New York Times

Ruth Ann didn't know what to make of the New Yorker's letter. She should be thrilled with this honor after all the *Choctaw Tribune* went through its first year. But the numbness in her heart blocked any response. It all felt meaningless, hollow. Like visiting the Levitt home.

Beulah welcomed her stiffly with a nod toward the bedroom door off the front room. It was cracked open. "The doctor said Papa is well enough for visitors, but please do not excite him." Her eyes went to the basket Ruth Ann held on her arm as if inspecting it for inciting material, such as a copy of the *Choctaw Tribune*.

Ruth Ann kept her head low as she crossed the threshold, taking in the herbal aromas always present in the Jewish home. She loved this place she'd so often been welcomed into, but today the only pleasant prospect was seeing Mr. Levitt for the first time since his heart had failed him at the lynching of Otis Wright. After seeing a doctor, Mr. Levitt had insisted on coming to his own home to recover or die, and everyone had experienced the small man's strength of will even in illness.

That strength still emanated from the man and filled the room Ruth Ann stepped into with a sense of reverence. Though his eyes were closed, a smile was on the sagging face of the man laid out on his bed, covered by a thin white sheet. It seemed to Ruth Ann that he looked far too ready for the undertaker, but when he opened his eyes and directed the smile toward her, she relaxed and moved to his side. "I should ask how you are feeling, but that seems rather silly. But I know you are too strong to slip away from us so easily."

Mr. Levitt nodded, his sparse hair brushing his pillow and flattening in funny shapes. "There are too many good ways to die here in your country than to simply let my heart stop beating." His eyes went to the partially closed door where he no doubt knew Beulah waited on the other side, giving them a sense of privacy but still hovering over him.

He looked straight into Ruth Ann's eyes, straighter than most people ever dared to, so straight his soul showed and touched hers. "Give her patience and grace, child. Our people are not a simple people, nor are our challenges and fears. Ah, fear. Do not let it take hold in your heart, no matter the circumstances that arise. It will choke you, enslave you, cause you to damage even your most valued relationships." Another glance toward the door, and Ruth Ann followed his line of sight. A soft sob came from the other side.

Mr. Levitt lifted his hand slightly above the sheet and touched Ruth Ann's fingertips. "Do not fear. God is always with us." His eyes closed and his breathing settled into a peaceful sound, like he'd said something he had needed to say for a very long time. Ruth Ann brushed the back of his rough carpenter's hand with her fingertips and took a quiet step back and back until she was slowly closing the door to his room from the other side.

Beulah stood by her, eyes swelled with unshed tears. They fell into each other's arms, clinging tight in desperate hope that all could be forgiven. Healed. For grace to cover them. For love to wash away hate.

♦♦♦

I do not hate them, I do not hate them, I do not hate them.

As Beulah sat by her sleeping father's side, she repeated the words over and over to herself but they still did not ring true. She did hate. She hated the social divides of race, the structure of a society that forced them to align themselves with the successful or be cast into the pits of the lowly. Her people had faced their share of hate over the centuries. It would happen again, in this great land, if they did not distinguish themselves appropriately. Yet at what costs? Had she truly wanted to protect Ruth Ann or would her response have been different if she'd known the riot hadn't been one of race after all? She'd been a fool.

When they first landed in Indian Territory, Beulah felt

safe. Free to proudly proclaim who she was and who her people were, to show the world their equality and place in society. Surely among those who had risen above racial divides, having shown their competence in white society, they could find friends and allies, shared dreams and futures. Beulah had found that within the Teller family. But even here, with them, the Levitts were very, very much alone.

Beulah bowed her head, the familiar burn in her heart for her people, her kinsmen. Rarely had she not been among her people, sharing their strength and ways no one outside could understand. At first, she thought to enjoy such release, a chance to prove a Jew alone could still stand proud and make good on the breeding of her ancestors. But now that was shattered.

She'd chosen the way of modern thinkers—to continue the cliques and distinctions of her people, yet blend carefully in with the whites of her contemporaries. One thing was clear on that road—the darks did not belong with them and had to be shunned as the whites shunned them. This was an unconscious decision for Beulah, for she had never befriended a Negro and felt no special connection with them or their plights. They did not feel the fears nor understand the fragile existence of someone like herself—a young Jewess isolated and terrified for the future of her people, her race, her distinction.

Choctaws much better understood this, could understand her. They had proven their intelligence, resourcefulness, and remarkable endurance and faith. Whether others accepted it or not, the Choctaws deserved an equal place on the platform with the whites, just as her own people did. But they would all be dragged off by mixing sympathies with blacks.

Her father sighed in his sleep and a tiny bead of sweat formed a dot above his eyebrow. Beulah lifted a clean cloth from the side table and gently dabbed it away. Why had he shown sympathy? And dear Ruth? Did she believe Beulah hated the blacks? Why could those she loved most not understand her feelings and the importance of distinction if they were to survive and thrive in this land?

Do not fear...do not be afraid...fear will destroy...
I do not hate...I do hate...I do hate fear...

Beulah clutched the cloth in both hands, settling it in her lap, refusing the tears. If hate was the only thing that could overcome the fear, perhaps it was the only way to live. But what kind of living would it be?

CHAPTER FORTY-FOUR

AFTER HAVING REFRESHED HERSELF IN Beulah's washroom, Ruth Ann made her way down the wood boardwalk on the main street of Dickens. People were in a special hurry, the kind they always were when the sky threatened rain as it did now. But Ruth Ann didn't hurry. She would walk along the boardwalk, pass Bates General Store, pass the freight office and near the depot before crossing the road to home.

Ruth Ann had walked much this day. Walked to deliver newspapers. Walked to the post office. Walked to deliver a basket of goods and goodwill to the Levitts. Walked now through the streets of her town. Yes, her little, little town far from the comforts of the Choctaw family farm she'd been raised on. Far from the life she knew with her father and brother Philip.

What would they think of her now? Was she the kind of young woman her father would point his chin at and say to friends and strangers alike, "That's my daughter, there. That's Miss Ruth Ann Teller, one good Choctaw girl" and smile?

God knows.

Pain was pain. Evil was evil. Good was good. And above

all, God was still God. In Dickens, Indian Territory. Paris, Texas. Springstown. With Silas Sloan, New York reporters, Mr. Barnes, G.W., Uncle Preston, Beulah, Reverend Anoletubbee, Deputy Shelton. The Grandmother. Mama Tippy. Black. Jew. White. Indian. Mixed.

It was so clear now Ruth Ann felt it had always been a part of her, awaiting a chance to shine bright on every thought in her mind. These places, these people, these injustices and tragedies. It wasn't a condition of race. It was a condition of the heart. The human heart that beat differently in every individual, including her. And the heart of every story.

God knows.

Thunder rumbled in the distance but it didn't drown the harsh scrape of a set of boots that plunked themselves hard on the boardwalk in front of her and turned sharply, blocking her path and forcing her eyes up. Up into the eyes of Dickens mayor, Thaddeus Warren. He didn't smile, didn't nod in greeting, didn't feign politeness. He was grim and terrifying, not at all the ample-waisted blowhard they knew him to be.

His frown was fierce as he stared down at her. "Miss Teller, I received my latest copy of the *Choctaw Tribune*, and it disgusted me. I have tolerated your brother's insolence and deceits, his bullheaded charges into matters that don't concern him. And a fine thing he did in partnering with a newcomer behind my back to land his print shop right in my building. But he has far crossed the line of decency this time. My wife was humiliated as every woman in town was when we discovered he is now allowing a female—simple-minded creatures that should know their place—to report on matters only a man is capable of commenting on. Women have no place in politics or any such matters of society."

Ruth Ann stared at him with no response. And no tremors. She'd faced worse.

The mayor yanked his signature white handkerchief from his overcoat and dabbed over his lips. "You are a disgrace, Ruth Ann Teller, and I mean to see you never do such a thing again. A woman's place is in the kitchen and if you know what's best for your brother, that's exactly where you will stay from now on!"

As if trying to give finality to his victorious words, Mayor Warren snorted and brushed past her, causing Ruth Ann to lose her balance. The wind increased, threatening to blow her to the ground as well. But she held fast to her place on the boardwalk, her place in the society and social structure in Dickens and the world.

Thunder rumbled closer and lightning jagged its way across the sky in the distance. A drizzle began. Ruth Ann whispered, "There's nothing more powerful than the press." She looked to the sky and let the healing rains fall on her face. "Except You."

Glossary

Chahta sia hoke: I am Choctaw!

Chihowa: God

Chi hullo li: I love you

Chi pisa la chike: I will be seeing you, or I will see you later

Chukka: Old winter-style dwelling

Halito: A friendly greeting

Luksi: Turtle

Ohoyo: Wife or woman

Pokni: Grandmother

Yakoke: Thank you

Author's Note

While these stories were presented in fiction form, they drew a good deal on actual happenings from the times, including the real execution of a man named Silon Lewis. This event is generally accepted as the last Choctaw execution performed by the Lighthorsemen. The witch hunt and mansion shoot-out were based on actual events.

The description of Beulah Levitt as a blonde, fair-skinned Jew may seem odd to some. However, this description, as well as the Jewish names, came from actual Russian Jewish immigrants who settled in Kansas and Missouri. Many migrated to Indian Territory.

Dickens was inspired by the history of two early towns in the Choctaw Nation, Hugo and Antlers, Oklahoma. The laws and politics follow closely the actual conflicts in Indian Territory before statehood.

Yakoke

Thank you to the following people who helped to ensure the accuracy, detail, and heart of these stories:

My mama, Lynda Kay Sawyer, for guiding me along the trails of our ancestors. I love her dearly, and without her, this book would have never realized the level of accuracy and emotion it has. My brother, Doug, is a part of this family team. He's my check and balance when it comes to writing historical fiction based on true events. *Chi hullo li* to you both.

Francine Locke Bray of Antlers, Oklahoma, for reviewing early drafts of the manuscript and offering input. *Yakoke*! Also to her husband, Michael, for hosting my mama and me in their home. They took us on a grand tour up the muddy roads on Black Jack Mountain and to Medicine Springs to see that Choctaw horses exist today. They introduced us to a special man, Bryant Rickman, who has undergone unimaginable difficulties to save these horses. Thank you all for your work in preserving the Spirit of Black Jack Mountain.

Kay Black at the Pushmataha County Historical Society provided wonderful details about the town of Antlers, Oklahoma, an inspiration for Dickens.

Mark Barbour, Director and Curator at the International

Printing Museum, gave me excellent input and resources on printing in the 1890s.

Yakoke to Choctaw author Curtis Pugh for digging up facts to make the setting and scenes accurate to the time period.

Friend and fellow Choctaw Jennifer Wingard provided critique and insights as well as personal encouragement. Thank you!

Jos Erdkamp (www.kodaksefke.nl) provided an abundance of information on camera types, operations, and uses in the 1890s.

Betsy Mills with the Lamar County Genealogical Society sent me neat information for 1890s Paris, Texas, including "Cabby," a real man I may never have known about.

Adam Burns with American-Rails.com was super helpful in finding information such as time tables and shipping information with the real Frisco Railroad that ran from St. Louis to Paris.

There were some special people who provided early feedback on this story, and their words mean so much to me. Thank you to fellow authors Julie Cantrell and Rilla Askew. Your literary prowess gives me something to strive for. And yakoke Dr. Ian Thompson, (Director Historic Preservation Dept.) and Chief Gary Batton, both of the Choctaw Nation of Oklahoma. Your endorsements of this story helped confirm the path I am on with sharing the history of our tribe.

On that note, thank you to the many others within my tribe, the Choctaw Nation of Oklahoma, for your support of my literary work. Honoring our culture and our ancestors has been and will be a priority in all my Chahta stories.

Thanks to Kathi Macias who did initial editing on the stories. Thank you for being such a sweet soul to work with!

And yakoke to fellow author and tribal member, James Masters, who provided an excellent final edit, putting a shine to this book.

I'd like to extend a big thanks to graphic designer and friend, Josh McBride, for patiently developing the cover design 5,000 miles south in Chile. Thank the Lord for Skype. (See more of Josh's work at josh360.com)

Special appreciation to First Peoples Fund for their support of my work and this book through the Artist in Business Leadership Fellowship.

Finally, my inspiration, motivation, and drive come from far above myself. Far, far above. To God be all glory.

About the Author

SARAH ELISABETH SAWYER is an award-winning Christian author and Choctaw storyteller of traditional and fictional tales based on the lives of her people. The Smithsonian's National Museum of the American Indian has honored her as a literary artist through its Artist Leadership Program for her work in preserving Trail of Tears stories. In 2015, First Peoples Fund awarded her an Artist in Business Leadership Fellowship. She writes from her hometown in East Texas, partnering with her mama, Lynda Kay Sawyer, in continued research for future novels. Learn more about their work in preserving Choctaw history at ChoctawSpirit.com.

TRAITORS
CHOCTAW TRIBUNE SERIES, BOOK 2

"Someone's going to be king in this territory. No reason it can't be me. It sure won't be you."

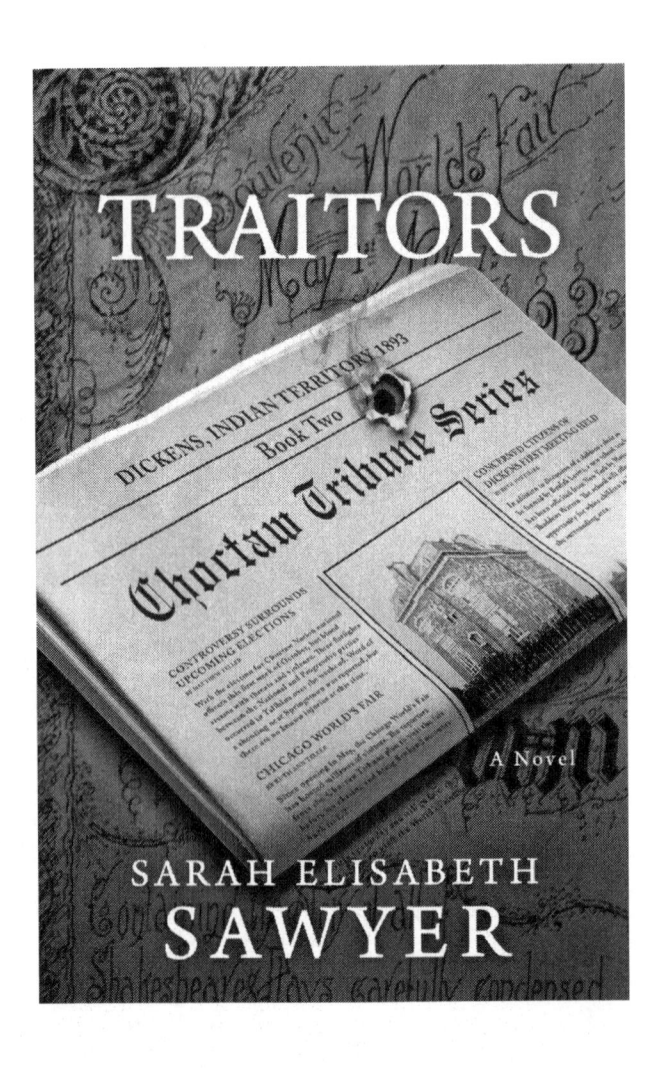

Betrayed.

Someone is tearing at the fabric of the Choctaw Nation while political turmoil, assassinations, and feuds threaten the sovereignty of the tribe, which stands under the U.S. government's scrutiny.

When heated words turn to hot lead, Ruth Ann Teller—a mixed-blood Choctaw—fears losing her brother, who won't settle for anything but the truth. Matthew is determined to use his newspaper, the *Choctaw Tribune*, to uncover the scheme behind Mayor Thaddeus Warren's claim to the townsite of Dickens. Matthew is willing to risk his newspaper—and his life—to uncover a traitor among their people.

But when Ruth Ann tries to help, she causes more harm than good—especially after the mayor brings in Lance Fuller, a schoolteacher from New York, to provide a rare educational opportunity for white children. How does this charming yet aloof young man fit into the mayor's scheme?

When attacks against the newspaper strike and bullets fly, a trip to the Chicago World's Fair of 1893 is the key to saving the *Choctaw Tribune* and Matthew's investigation. But Ruth Ann must find the courage to face a journey to the White City—without her brother.

***Traitors* is available on Amazon.com**

For this collection of short stories, Choctaw authors from five U.S. states came together to present a part of their ancestors' journeys, a way to honor those who walked the trail for their future. These stories not only capture a history and a culture, but the spirit, faith, and resilience of the Choctaw people.

Tears of sadness. Tears of joy. Touch and experience them.

Touch My Tears **is available on Amazon.com**

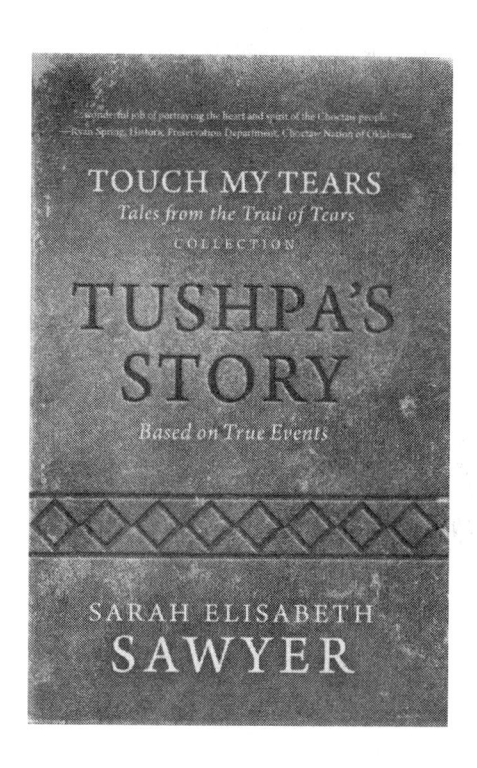

> "Protect the book as you do our seed corn.
> We must have both to survive."

The Treaty of Dancing Rabbit Creek changed everything. The Choctaw Nation could no longer remain in their ancient homelands.

Young Tushpa, his family, and their small band embark on a trail of life and death. More death than life lay ahead.

***Tushpa's Story (Touch My Tears Collection)* is available on Amazon.com**

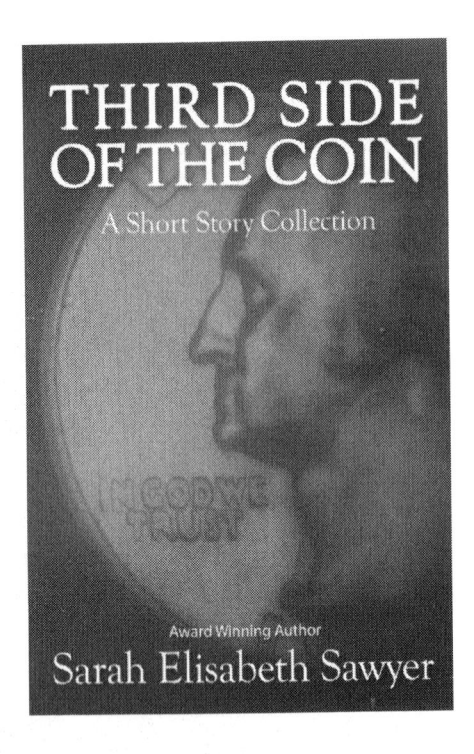

With the gift to find real meaning in a story, author Sarah Elisabeth Sawyer creates tales to stir the heart and evoke deep, often buried emotions. Not one to shy away from tragedy or crisis of faith, she explores human conditions through engaging short stories.

Third Side of the Coin **is available on Amazon.com**

Made in the USA
Lexington, KY
24 July 2018